**The Parkrı**

**By Simon P**

CW00427960

**Special thanks to Mylene Cayer for the amazing cover**
**design.**

The Parkrunner.

Chapter 1

It was quite small and insignificant really, the thing that started it all off. In fact, if Martin hadn't been prompted by his daughter he probably wouldn't have realised that it was in there at all. "Come on Dad it's your turn to open one". Abi stated, matter of factly as the family sat taking it in turns. "I haven't got any left". Martin protested, "So it's over to you Max". "There's one left in the bag Dad if you look carefully". Abi continued, knowing that her dad hadn't yet opened the gift she had bought him. Martin put his hand in to the bottom of the bag and felt around. It was indeed as his daughter had stated and he pulled out a thin envelope elegantly wrapped in red and gold paper tied with a yellow bow. He took it out and felt the small package, running his fingers over it, feeling for clues as to what it may contain. There weren't any; it felt exactly as it looked, like an envelope containing perhaps a letter or a piece of thin card. Martin looked at his daughter somewhat bemused.

It was Christmas day; Tuesday 25th December 2018 in the Price family household. The ubiquitous 'Fairytale of New York' sounded out from the radio as Martin and his two adult children were sat in the lounge opening their presents, not unlike many other families up and down the country. The ritual they had adopted in recent years was to take it in turns opening their presents, making a prior guess as to what each package contained. This was an endeavour to prolong and actively enhance the otherwise meagre amount of excitement that existed between three adults at Christmas when opening yet another pair of socks! At least the speculation of guessing gave a brief glimmer of hope that there may be something of value or intrigue within.  What used to be a five-minute frenzy of frantic present opening when the kids were younger was now a more sedate affair with Max and his sister Abi now in their twenty third and twenty first years respectively. Max grasped a rectangular shaped package wrapped in red and white paper; "Lynx shower gel and body spray!". He stated emphatically, as he shook the package in his hand before knowingly removing the paper. "Dad, you shouldn't have!". He stated ironically, in a reference to a magazine article the two of them had read some weeks previously, outlining what not to say when opening a Christmas gift that was somewhat underwhelming. Martin retorted by stating; "It's just what I've always wanted!", upon opening a pair of somewhat bland grey slippers before Max put the icing on the cake by exclaiming; "I've been saving up for one of these for ages!". Upon guessing correctly and subsequently unwrapping a Terrys chocolate orange.

It was however now Martin's turn, and upon kneading the small package between his thumb and forefinger for what seemed to the others like an eternity he was unable to come up with a plausible guess as to its contents. "Come on Dad, just open it will you! None of us are getting any younger you know and I'm rapidly losing the will to live here!". Max chipped in. Martin cast him a glance before eventually sliding his thumb into the envelope and pulling out a folded piece of paper. "What is it then Dad?". His son enquired, as Martin opened it and scanned it attentively. "Well it looks like it's an entry form for a race?". Martin stated, his voice rising in intonation as he looked towards his daughter to question if that was indeed correct. She smiled back and nodded before Martin read its contents aloud; "Bridgetown 10k official entry. Congratulations on entering Bridgetown Amateur Athletic Clubs annual 10k race on Sunday 6th May 2019. Your race number is 498. We will forward you your official race package and further details approximately two weeks prior to the race date". Martin looked at his daughter and smiled at her. It was a bit of a puzzled smile; a cross really between a smile and a chuckle and he thought for a moment about what an appropriate response would be to such a random gift. He looked longingly at his son for inspiration, but none was forthcoming, and Max merely sat there looking as baffled as his dad was, wearing a stupid grin across his face. "Thanks Abi, I think!". In as enthusiastic a tone as he could muster, was all that Martin could offer after a few moments' deliberation. His daughter could sense the bemusement in his face and offered up an explanation; "Well Dad we don't actually do a lot together do we? You and Max have your football, but we don't really spend a lot of time together do we. OK, we're at home together at the same time occasionally but that's not doing anything specific is it? We could both do with a bit more exercise, so I thought this would be a good way of combining the both. We can do a bit of training together in the run up to the event, spend some quality time together and get fitter in the process, what's not to like?".

Martin noted the look of enthusiasm on his daughter's face and could sense it in her voice. She had entered them both into the race and produced a similar entry slip with her own details on for the others perusal. There was no doubt that her words did indeed ring true; being fitter never hurt anyone and she had obviously put a lot of thought into the gift and it was encouraging that at her age she still wanted to spend some time with her dad. Martin ran the details around in his head and quickly warmed to the idea; in fact, to both the ideas of getting fitter and spending some time with his beloved daughter. "OK Abi. Sounds like a plan". Martin eventually concluded, nodding his head in approval; "Let's give it a go".

At 51 years old, Martin Price cut a tall lean figure. At 6',1" in height and weighing in at just over eleven and a half stones, he had always been relatively fit. He had played football regularly all his life and indeed still enjoyed playing five a side football a couple of times a week to this day with a mixture of friends and work colleagues. He had plied his trade in the various local leagues around the South West in his younger days and even had a brief spell playing professionally for Exeter City in their 1989/90 promotion winning season, which he always described to anyone who would listen as the pinnacle of his career. This was despite having made only sixteen first team appearances, with five of those coming off the bench as a substitute! He had to cut short his playing career however when his wife became ill, sadly passing away at the age of thirty five after struggling with a long illness. Martin never made a lot of money out of playing in the lower leagues and even his earnings at Exeter City were relatively modest, particularly in comparison to today's standards. When his wife's condition was diagnosed his priority was to care for her and his footballing career was put on the back burner. Unfortunately, he never did return to it and he never had the opportunity to know what his full potential may have been. At eight and six years old, the children were relatively young at the time and Martin did the best he could for them and raised them as a single parent. It wasn't the easiest of times, but he did what he could to support and provide for them, eventually returning to the profession he initially studied for whilst at university. He now somewhat reluctantly earned his living as a Civil Engineer working for the Local Railway Authority specialising in works at bridges and level crossings. His heart however always remained in football and he still harboured desires to one day return to the profession he loved in some format or another; the prospect though was looking increasingly unlikely as the years progressed and Martin was becoming more resigned to the fact that it was unlikely ever to happen. His current career choice wasn't one he particularly relished by any stretch of the imagination, but it paid the bills and put a roof over the families' head. Whilst they certainly weren't what you would class as rich, they weren't poor either and Martin had worked hard over the years so that the family could at least enjoy a relatively comfortable lifestyle.

Martin had always been extremely fit throughout his playing career and in his younger days always had energy to burn with a blistering turn of speed on the pitch as well as the stamina and ability to go the duration. In his preferred position of right back there were very few attacking players that could match his speed and one of his attributes was the ability to outpace the opposing forwards to make a last-ditch tackle before they had a shooting opportunity, even if they had a yard or two head start. He still kept in touch with the club and followed the fortunes of his beloved Exeter City through thick and thin having also introduced his son to the often-dubious viewing pleasures of the beautiful game some years earlier. As season ticket holders the two of them now attended all the home games they were able.

In relation to his personal life, Martin had never remarried or indeed even once contemplated the thought and along with his children missed his wife Jane terribly. She was certainly the only one for him and the two of them were soul mates that shared every aspect of their life together. In a world where it's said that there is someone for everyone, Martin was at least glad that they had found each other and spent the precious years they had together. He held those memories dear and always would. Being childhood sweethearts Jane was a constant in his life who had always been there to support and encourage him throughout his footballing career and provide sound advice when needed, as well as a shoulder to cry on. His spark and his zest for life had certainly diminished since her passing and without her the three had formed a close bond and were very supportive of each other. Whilst time may have had eased the pain, the memory was still strong and particularly so at times like Christmas.

He was proud of how his children had grown up though and knew that his wife would have been too. He would have given anything for her to be back by his side, if only for a moment, to see how they had turned out and to meet the adult versions of the young children she once knew. His daughter however was a constant reminder and as each day passed she grew to resemble her mother more and more, not only in looks and stature but also in her caring attitude and outlook on life. Max and Abi, both still lived at home with their dad and Martin was dreading the day when they would ultimately fly the nest and leave him on his own. He knew though that it was an inevitability that was edging ever closer and closer and when the time came for them to spread their wings he certainly wouldn't stand in their way.

Although they were brother and sister the two were as different as chalk and cheese and from an outsiders' perspective it was difficult even to tell that the two were siblings. At 5',6" tall Abi was certainly pretty with her mums' slim physique, long dark hair and brown eyes. Max, the elder of the two, was a blonde; ruggedly handsome with piercing blue eyes and designer stubble that he meticulously cut regularly so it was neither too long or too short. At 6' tall he was a bit shorter than his dad but sported a far more muscular physique, honed through physical exercise and gym work. Despite his apparent strength, Martin however could still beat him in an arm wrestle, stating to his son that it's always mind over matter that counts, and mental strength is just as important as physical. He knew however that one day soon his son would beat him and that he would never hear the last of it!

Christmas day progressed, and once the presents had been opened and wrapping paper tidied up, the family attended to their obligatory duties; spending time with the in-laws, delivering presents, exchanging pleasantries and eating and drinking far more than is good for anyone in any given day. Later that night before retiring, Martin stifled a tear as he raised a glass in memory of his wife, recalling to himself fond memories of Christmases long since passed.

The New Year came and went, and it wasn't long before it was inevitably time for the three of them to return to their respective places of work.
"How was your first day back then Dad?". Abi enquired, as the three were sat around the table to their evening meal. "Shit!". Martin replied forlornly, as he looked up briefly from his plate towards his daughter and shrugged his shoulders. "Same shit different day, in fact!". Martin stated, holding up his phone to display a photo of a white van he had seen earlier that day with that exact message lovingly etched into the dirt on the back. "It may be a new year but there's certainly not much happiness in it at the moment! With the time off over Christmas I almost forgot how much I hated my job; I was however promptly reminded at nine o'clock this morning when I opened up my inbox!". He smiled wryly. "Never mind Dad". Replied his daughter, "You'll soon get back into the swing of it". 'Great!'. Martin thought to himself, 'That's just what I've always dreamed of; getting back into the swing of dealing with crap all day!'.

The family exchanged conversation and discussed their respective experiences of their first day back at work in the New Year, none of which were particularly complimentary, before Abi changed the tone of the conversation in a vain attempt to lighten the mood. "I've got something that will cheer you up Dad!". She announced. "Oh yes, what's that then?". Martin raised an eyebrow in his daughters' direction in anticipation. "Well we're going to start our training on Saturday morning, look at what I've done for us!". With that she pulled out two small pieces of paper from her pocket and handed one of them to her dad. "What's this then?". Martin enquired, examining it in more detail. "It's your parkrun barcode Dad. I've registered us both; we have to take these barcodes along on the day of the run and get them scanned at the end when we've finished. Once we've done that we get given our times". "What's parkrun then?". Martin enquired, somewhat confused.

"Dad, what planet are you on?  Where've you been all these years, everybody knows what parkrun is!". "Well I don't!". Martin stated. "Dad, wise up, even Uncle Andy used to do parkruns, I'm fairly sure I've even heard you speaking to him about them in the past!". Martin did indeed have a poor memory it was true, but he dug deeply into the annals of his mind and eventually vaguely recalled speaking to his brother previously about running around the park for some unknown reason on a Saturday morning. "Oh, now you say it I do seem to recall him saying something about it now". Martin declared, eventually managing to correlate the events in question.

He held the small piece of paper that his daughter had presented to him in his hand and studied it in more detail; "Vitality parkrun, A3260697, Martin Price". He read out aloud. "Hmm very impressive! OK Abi, no harm giving it a go I suppose, I'll leave the details up to you, just tell me where and when". "Well it aint rocket science Dad, its Bridgetown Park at 9 am on Saturday morning. We have to be there ten minutes early for the briefing, so we'll leave at about eight thirty or so if that's OK?". It was indeed only about a ten-minute drive from the Price household to the park and so with that, the provisional arrangements for the inaugural training session had been made. The family went their respective ways for the evening with Abi going out to meet her boyfriend, Max settling down in front of his computer and Martin retiring to the lounge to watch the inevitable repeats that were on the television, such was the excitement of his winter evenings!

# Chapter 2

"Chris, for God's sake, shut up will you! Keep quiet before somebody bloody hears us!". Chris looked behind him observing that the noise had come from a plant pot that he had knocked off its stand as he was crawling along the floor in the darkness. He had inadvertently caught it with his trailing foot as he was trying to shimmy along on his belly keeping below the height of the shop window that fronted onto the pavement. "Sorry". He whispered back, sheepishly. Thankfully the pot hadn't smashed but merely fell onto the ground spilling its earthy contents over Chris's Jeans and the surrounding floor. "It's those bloody great feet of yours Chris, try and keep them under control you clown!". The three young men pushed on regardless towards their target with Paul 'tutting' to himself at the front, Mike in the middle and Chris bringing up the rear.

Chris Clarke had just turned eighteen years old; a tall slim individual with youthful good looks, sharp features and jet black hair. His main distinguishing characteristics however were his size twelve feet, leading to the rather undistinguished nicknames he had acquired over the years of 'penguin' and 'flipper' along with the less subtle 'Bigfoot'! Chris preferred not to answer to any of them and hearing them again now used in anger grated with him.

Chris wondered how an earth he had got himself into this predicament. He wasn't a bad lad really, not by any stretch of the imagination and if truth be known he wasn't really what you could call friends with Paul and Mike anyway. Sure, they had befriended him during his time back in the days of the home, but it was more a question of what was in it for them rather than looking after his needs. They were all he had though and as close to a couple of friends as he was likely to get given his background of constantly moving from place to place during what he could remember of his somewhat impoverished life. Bouncing around from foster parents to children's home then back to foster parents again when a suitable couple could be found. The inevitable cycle continued with Chris never being able to lay down firm roots anywhere. The families in general were kind to him though and there were some he liked more than others; John and Jenny were a case in point and the years he spent with them between eleven and thirteen were probably amongst the happiest he could remember. Circumstances changed though and when they had their own son the dynamics of the household changed and it was soon obvious to Chris that there was a significant difference between the way they treated their own son and their foster son; he supposed it was only natural though, after all if his own parents had abandoned him as a child why would anyone else want to look after a kid that wasn't their own flesh and blood; would he have done anything different if in the same position himself; he supposed not. He inevitably drifted back into the system once again and climbed back onto the merry go round, doing the rounds between children's homes and foster parents. His current situation was comfortable enough though but inevitably he had come to regard any situation he found himself in as purely temporary and now he had entered adulthood his time being looked after in the system was drawing to a close and he had to face the fact that the time had come to make his own way in the world. Exactly what way that would be though, he currently had no idea!

"I think we're nearly there now, it's just up the end of this aisle". Mike turned and stated as they crawled on in the darkness. Chris's thoughts were broken from that of his childhood and the harsh reality of where he was again suddenly dawned on him; crawling along the floor of a Tesco's Express store on the outskirts of Exeter at two o'clock in the morning as part of some half-arsed plan that Paul and Mike had concocted to rob the place. Despite all the odds, Chris had managed to secure an apprenticeship at the store working as a sales assistant with a built in structured training plan which he hoped would lead on to a supervisory or managerial position. He was trying to turn his life around and make something of himself but had allowed the other two reprobates to talk him into assisting them with their plan and providing a means of entry through his workplace key and knowledge of the alarm system. With every second that passed however he was regretting his decision more and more and his heart was beating faster and faster as they approached the tills. By the time the three got there Chris was sweating profusely and as he rose to his feet at one of the tills the beads of sweat accumulating on his forehead were starting to run down into his eyes. He wiped them off with his sleeve, blinking as he did so to try and remove the excess liquid from his eyes.

The three stood around the till in the dimly lit room; a glimmer of light from the moon and the distant street light through the shop window, the only illumination. Paul pulled out a small blue torch from his pocket, clicked it on and pointed it at the till. "Right how do we get this thing open then Chris?". Chris looked up at Paul and shrugged his shoulders. "Look guys, I don't think this is a very good idea". He stated. "Why don't we just knock it on the head and get out of here?". "Chris stop being such a bloody wimp, you need to man up a bit, anyway it was your idea in the first place!". Said Mike. "It bloody well was not". Chris responded. "The bloody till's locked isn't it". Complained Paul, shining the torch at the keyhole on the side of the till after randomly pressing as many buttons on the till face as he could in a vain attempt to open it. "Well I don't know how to open it do I!". Chris protested somewhat apologetically. "I've had enough of this, come on let's get out of here whilst we still can". "You're not going anywhere Chris". Growled Mike. "Not until we get this till open anyway, shove over so I can have a look!". Mike pulled out an old rusty wooden handled chisel from beneath his jacket and proceeded to try and wedge it between the opening drawer of the till and the main body. After a couple of attempts he realised it wasn't going to go in. "I need something hard to hit it with!". He stated emphatically. "Try your head!". Chris muttered under his breath. "I heard that! Just find me something to hit this with will you!". Chris fumbled around in the darkness and located a shelf containing some cans, he picked one up and passed it to Mike. Mike located the chisel into the gap and struck the wooden end as hard as he could with the can. On the first blow nothing happened but on the second the can split and spewed its contents all over Mike, the till and the counter. Mike erupted; "Chris you bloody idiot, how am I supposed to break into a till with a sodding can of baked beans!". He prised the embedded can off the top of the chisel handle and threw it across the shop. It clattered against some shelves knocking two bottles of red wine onto the floor and smashing them. Mike snatched the torch from Paul's grasp and began to search around, fumbling in the dark to try and find something that resembled a hammer to try and gain access to the till. At the back of the shop he came across a small store cupboard and tried the handle. The door wasn't locked so Mike opened it up and shone the torch around. He could see the obligatory mops, buckets and cleaning utensils along with what appeared to be a small mountain of toilet rolls but nothing obvious that would assist him with his quest. Upon moving some black bin bags in a box on the floor however he came upon a small plastic ice cream container containing a few assorted screwdrivers, a tape measure, a junior hacksaw and most importantly a small claw hammer. Mike picked out the hammer and weighed it up in his hand before making his way back to the till. It wasn't quite the size or weight he was hoping for, but beggars couldn't be choosers and it was at least a hammer. The other two were still busy wiping the remainder of the contents of the bean can from the counter and till as he returned. "Out of my way you Muppets!". He exclaimed as he shoved them to one side to get access to the till. Chris noted the size of the hammer. "What the hell are you going to do with that one…crack some toffee!". "Well it's better than your bloody baked bean can isn't it, what was your next step, to hit it with a bag of bloody marshmallows? Stand back and watch and learn!". Chris and Paul moved back out of the way as Mike stepped forward once again and prised the chisel back into the small gap between the drawer of the till and the main body. When he was satisfied he had it firmly wedged in he drew back his right hand and gave it a swift blow with the hammer. The tapping sound it made however only went to confirm the wholly inadequate size of the hammer for the task in hand and after more blows than Mike cared to count he threw the hammer and chisel to the ground in frustration. Chris and Paul looked towards each other and smirked. 'Yes, I'm certainly learning a lot here!'. Chris thought to himself. Mike by now had had enough. "For God's sake!". He shouted, and with that grasped the weighty till in anger and threw it to the ground with all the effort he could muster thus making an almighty crash. "You'll wake the bloody dead in a minute". Paul cried. "What's the point of us sneaking in along the ground if you're going to make all that bloody racket. I don't know why we didn't just put an advert in the Local press; "To whom it may concern, on Friday night next week, three local dickheads will be breaking into the Tesco's Express store on Riverside Road and making a godforsaken racket as they do so. Any police or Tesco's staff wishing to catch them in the act please wait at the front entrance where they will be seen exiting at around two am covered in bloody baked bean juice!". "Right that's it, I've had enough, I'm out of here". Stated Chris, shaking his head in disdain. "This is a bloody disaster, I knew it was a bloody stupid idea, I don't know why the hell I agreed to go along with it!". Mike looked down at the somewhat battered till on the floor and before Chris had the opportunity to head towards the exit announced to the others that the blow had opened the till. Chris sighed despondently and turned back, joining the other two on the floor to assess the situation. Mike pulled open the somewhat battered drawer of the till and his expression slowly changed from excitement and anticipation to despair and anger upon discovering it was bereft of contents. For Chris it was the final straw and he turned and made his way towards the shop front. He didn't bother crawling along this time however as he supposed that all and sundry would have already heard the noise anyway so what was the point. As he reached the door and slipped out he turned to see Mike now stood upright kicking the till repeatedly whilst uttering various expletives. Eventually he and Paul followed suit and did likewise, grabbing some carrier bags and stuffing them with Silk Cut and Embassy cigarettes and as many bottles of assorted spirits as they could manage as a consolation, before slipping away out of the door and into the darkness of the night.

# Chapter 3

"Any idea where those trainers of mine are Abi? You know those grey ones with the air filled soles!". Martin hollered out of his bedroom doorway in frustration as he knelt on the floor pawing his way through the contents of the bottom shelf of his wardrobe. It was Friday night; Martin had just returned from his second game of five a side football that week and had dumped his sports bag down in the hallway before heading to the bedroom to seek out some running attire for the next morning. "What am I Dad, 'the Trainer Police!' Anyway, what do you want those old things for, they're knackered! I thought you were saving them for wearing around the garden. Wear your football trainers!". Abi's voice replied, as she approached the bedroom door and peered in. "I can't, they're not designed for running, they're more for indoor use". Martin protested, still searching in vain for the items in question. "Well you run when you're playing football don't you?". Abi retorted. Martin ignored the response and continued the search through his wardrobe for what he perceived to be the best pair of trainers he had for running in. He pulled out various shoeboxes from the bottom shelf, some of which hadn't seen the light of day for years. He made a mental note to himself that he must have a sort out sometime as it was unlikely that he would ever wear half of these shoes again; in particular a pair of black leather brogues reserved for weddings and funerals that he last wore to a colleague's committal five years ago which were now covered in flecks of mould. He thought twice about throwing them out there and then but upon further deliberation thought better of it and half-heartedly wiped some of the mould off before replacing them back in the box. 'The state some of my friends are in I may be needing these again soon!' He thought to himself as he lifted an orange 'Nike' shoebox and slid the somewhat tattered green box containing the brogues underneath. Logic would have dictated that the Nike shoebox would have contained a pair of Nike trainers or at least something along those lines. Martin's mind didn't work along those lines however and upon opening the box up it was found to contain two pairs of flip flops. 'That's strange as I don't even wear flip flops!' Martin thought to himself, before once again carefully replacing the contents of the box and sliding it back into its position between a green fire extinguisher that was three years out of date and an old brown leather effect briefcase; contents unknown and for now to remain that way.

Upon examining the plethora of various coloured shoe boxes in various states of repair and satisfying himself that they were as neatly restacked as he was able to manage, Martin scratched his head and refocused his search to under the bed, pulling out a couple of old footballs that had seen better days along with an old guitar amp that he had forgotten about, covered in dust. He carefully slid the contents back again and pondered as to where else the trainers could be. After searching various places around the house his search turned in vain to the garage whereupon the offending items were eventually found in the grass box of the lawn mower. Martin surmised that he must have last worn them in the summer when cutting the grass and their colour had now turned from what was grey with an orange swoosh to a mixture of brown and green where the mud and grass had stained them. He took them outside and banged off what loose mud and grass he could with a few sharp taps on the concrete step leading to the back door of the garage. He looked them over, prodding the various flaws and pieces of sole that were parting company from the rest of the shoes, which by now had gone almost solid due to being in a damp cold garage for the best part of the winter. He tried them on though and ran up and down on the back patio to try and soften them up a bit. They weren't nearly as comfortable as he remembered and although they were 'Nike Air' trainers, it was evident that whatever air may have been in them back in the day had long since disappeared. They did still fit though which was a bonus, so he took them off on the back doorstep, so as not to walk mud or grass onto the carpet and went back inside.

He returned to the bedroom to gather together some other running attire; a pair of long black football socks with copious quantities of holes in them and elasticated tops that were so loose that Martin's legs would have to have been twice the size they were to keep them up; an old pair of black Umbro football shorts, again with a hole in one side where they had lost an argument with the washing machine many moons ago and a black sports top purchased some years previously from a Marks and Spencer sale, which had been in the wardrobe for some years now and still had the price tag on. '£2.49' Martin observed as he pulled the tag off and discarded it into the bin. 'Not bad!' Well he did love a bargain! He pulled out a pair of elasticated briefs from his chest of drawers for a 'bit of support' and neatly folded up what was to be his running attire for the following morning and placed it on the bottom of his bed before retiring himself.

At seven o'clock the following morning Martin's alarm clock rang out in earnest. He reached out in the darkness and fumbled around, still half asleep, his right arm flailing fervently trying to silence the intrusive device situated on his bedside cabinet. Once he had successfully completed the operation he turned over, pulling the thick duvet back up over him to envelop his entire body and head in blissful warmth before drifting back to sleep again. It was an hour later at eight o'clock that Martin was awoken by the sound of his daughter's voice. He wearily raised his head and looked up to see Abi stood there ready and waiting for the morning's event. Even through half opened eyes stuck together with 'sleep' Martin could see that his daughter looked resplendent in her pink and black lycra running bottoms complete with matching pink T shirt all set off with a slightly darker pink pair of trainers. Her long brown hair was tied up in a ponytail and she was brimming with energy and the joys of the day. "Come on Dad, get your arse in gear!". She enthused as she jogged on the spot in the bedroom doorway, beaming from ear to ear. Martin acknowledged his daughter and eventually found the energy to push back the duvet and swing his legs out of bed. They were still aching from the previous night's game. He got up and had a good stretch to work out the kinks in his arms and legs and yawned widely before heading to the kitchen to make a cup of tea. He retrieved two chocolate digestives from the biscuit tin and retired back to the bedroom where he sat up in bed listening to the radio, trying hard to wake himself up.

Martin had always had a sweet tooth and had only recently managed to cut the sugar down from two teaspoons to one in his cup of tea; in coffee he had been known to take as many as four! He supposed today however that it may give him a bit of extra energy and after finishing the tea and biscuits he returned to the kitchen for more sustenance. He placed two Weetabix into a bowl, added the necessary milk and sugar and once again retired back to bed. Abi meanwhile was carrying out some stretching exercises in the hallway, concentrating on her calves and thighs in preparation for the run. Martin's warm up in contrast, when he did eventually get out of bed again, was to consist of rubbing copious quantities of deep heat onto his legs to invigorate his muscles, much to his daughter's distain; "Do you have to do that in here Dad, it stinks!". She stated emphatically. Martin merely smiled before picking up the garments he had so lovingly prepared the night before and heading to the bathroom. Around ten minutes later he emerged, having brushed his teeth, shaved and changed in to his chosen attire. "Bloody Hell, its Stig of the dump!". Max quipped as he emerged from his bedroom and observed his dad dressed in varying shades of 'off black'. "This parkrun isn't fancy dress is it?" he smiled, twisting the knife in a little more. Even his daughter had a small chuckle to herself as she gazed in awe at what her dad was wearing, noting the contrast between his gear and hers. Martin wished that he had tried the Marks and Spencer's T shirt on prior to purchasing it, as although a medium in size it was obviously far too big for him and probably looked better back on the hanger. "It's not about what you wear is it, it's the taking part that counts, and at least I'm giving it a go aren't I!" Martin protested. "Mind you don't get mugged by any tramps who've been sleeping on those park benches Dad; they'd love to get their hands on that top-quality gear!". Max shouted after them as they left.

Martin and Abi weren't the only ones making their way to the parkrun that morning and as well as a number of others who were walking, jogging or driving in that direction, Dave Macready was also winging his merry way towards the park. Dave, 'Speedy Macready' to his friends, was a resident of the nearby town of Summerfield and loved nothing more than running; in fact, if truth be known it was what he lived for. As a founding member of the Summerfield Roadrunners athletics club, there weren't many miles of tarmac in the local area that Dave hadn't pounded along at some stage or another. Age had slowed him down slightly but having just turned fifty he was still proud of the fact that he was one of the best athletes in his age category in the South West of England. Over the years he had competed both locally and nationally in races across all distances from five kilometres to the marathon and done well in them all. Although his once blonde hair was now greying at the sides, and the lines in his face were becoming more prominent, his lean but muscular physique still had the ability to propel his 5',10" tall frame around the track at a pace many a younger man would have been proud of. He shot a final glance into his car mirror to check his appearance, his piercing blue eyes staring back at him as he flicked his comb through his hair one last time before exiting the car and jogging the remaining distance to the park.

Martin noticed Dave leaving his car as he manoeuvred his own black Volkswagen Golf into a vacant space behind him on the road opposite the supermarket. As he brought the car to a halt he nudged his daughter and pointed to the thermometer on the dashboard. The weather outside was a balmy two degrees, a brisk wind blowing in from the east making it feel even colder than the already low temperature suggested. He turned to Abi and gave her a look; it was the kind of look that said, 'What the hell are we doing here!' She smiled back at him and the two of them rubbed their cold hands in the blast of warm air that was being omitted from the vent in the centre of the dashboard before Martin turned off the engine and the heater fan died to a halt. "Come on then Abi, let's do it!".

The two jogged along the footpath and crossed the road to the park entrance past the plaque on the ornate entrance gates commemorating its opening in 1912 to celebrate Queen Victoria's reign. Martin recalled the many happy hours he had spent there when the children were younger, playing on the swings and slide or swimming in the warm but shallow children's pool that was open in the summer months. Today it looked sad and neglected, devoid of water and its once blue walls were now predominantly green with algae.

Abi fondly noted the large fort that she and her brother had played in as children, its stone ramparts proudly displaying nine cannon that dated back to the time of the Spanish Armada, now shrouded in their brown and amber patina and last fired in anger over four centuries ago.

As father and daughter made their way past the dormant flower beds and now blossomless Magnolia and Cherry trees that lined the edges of the pathways, Martin evoked memories, not only of the times he had spent playing in the fort with his children but also the times he had spent there himself as a child, both with his parents and indeed even his grandparents. A lump came to his throat as he pictured the whole family playing there together one particular summer's day before his wife was so cruelly taken away from him. He afforded himself the opportunity of a warm smile as he remembered the time fondly and looked lovingly towards his daughter, proud of the fine and caring young woman she had now grown to become.

Chapter 4

It was the morning after the night before and it was Chris's turn to work that Saturday. His bedroom that morning resembled something of a war zone; with Chris tossing and turning all night and sweating profusely, the covers and pillows had been scattered all across his room. He hadn't slept a wink all night but had just managed to drift off when he was disturbed by a knock on his bedroom door. "Cup of tea for you Chris!". The shout came from the hallway. It was kate, his current foster mum; one half of a duo of retired teachers consisting of English teacher Kate and her husband Roger Masters, a recently retired philosophy lecturer at Exeter University. Upon asking him once what philosophy was actually all about, Roger told Chris; "I have no idea, it's all a load of bollocks if you ask me, all I know is that unless you want to teach it don't do a degree in it as it's no good to man nor beast and won't get you anywhere in life!". Sound advice indeed, Chris acknowledged.

Kate opened the door and popped her head around it to make sure Chris was decent before entering the room and placing the tea down on his bedside cabinet. Chris rubbed his bleary eyes, acknowledged her and thanked her for the tea. "Tough night Chris?". Kate asked, observing the state of his room. "Yes, I didn't sleep too good!". Chris replied. "You're telling me!". She exclaimed, raising her eyebrows as she further purveyed the situation. "I didn't hear you come in, so you must have been fairly late, I hope you haven't been out getting up to no good with those 'so called mates' of yours?". The words reverberated through Chris's head like it had been hit with a sledge hammer. He knew that he had indeed been out getting up to no good with his 'so called mates' but this time it was more than just the usual high jinks and it was inevitable that he would shortly have to face the consequences. He wasn't sure which he was most worried about though; letting down Kate and Roger; getting in trouble with the police or letting down his employer and facing the prospect of losing his job. He had been mulling it over through the night, trying to convince himself that everything would be OK, that no one would be able to link him to the break in and that in any case it was only a few fags and bottles of booze that were taken, so it was hardly the crime of the century. He then remembered the broken bottles, the baked beans, the mess all over the counter and the smashed till on the floor which in itself would probably cost a couple of thousand pounds to replace. He didn't want to go into work, he couldn't face it and wished the bed would open up and swallow him whole rather than have to face up to the consequences of his actions. He gathered his thoughts. "Yes, I didn't get in till late, I can't remember exactly what time it was though". He eventually responded. "Well come on then get yourself moving or you'll be late for work. You've got a good job there, so you want to make sure you hang on to it!". Just hearing the words made him feel physically sick as the chances of hanging on to his job in the current circumstances were somewhere between slim and non-existent. He picked up one of the pillows from the floor and placed it on the bed before lying back down and covering his face with his hands. Kate departed the room to leave him in isolation with his thoughts.

It was about half an hour later when Chris was awoken again by another knock on the door. He jumped up and stared at the now cold cup of tea on his cabinet. This time it was Roger's head that peeked around the door. "Come on Chris, you'll be late!". He stated in his deep silky tone. "Get yourself moving and I'll run you in if you like". Chris eventually dragged himself out of bed and quickly showered and dressed before heading downstairs for breakfast. Roger was sat at the table ready and waiting. Chris quickly consumed what he could stomach out of a bowlful of frosted flakes and headed out to the car with Roger. He sat in silence, eyes firmly fixed ahead of him as the two made the ten-minute trip from home to the shop.

All looked in order as Roger dropped Chris off at around 8.45 am. He sheepishly got out of the car and bade his thanks and goodbyes to Roger before he drove away, putting his hand up and giving a wave as he did so. Chris surveyed the shop front and peered in through the window, straining his eyes towards the back of the shop to see if anyone was in there. It was devoid of customers and he couldn't make out any of the staff members. As he made his way to the front door and was about to go in he noticed a piece of A4 paper sellotaped to the front of it upon which were written the words; 'Closed until further notice due to break in, apologies for any inconvenience caused'. Chris's heart started to beat a little bit faster and he felt decidedly faint as he gingerly pushed the door open.

Michael looked up from the back of the shop as the front door buzzer rang. He saw that it was Chris and shouted over. "Chris we're over here by the till... well what's left of it anyway!". He stated, upon once again surveying the wreckage in front of him and shaking his head. "Make sure you don't touch anything as the police are on their way over and want to do some forensic tests!".

Michael McGuilicutty, known to everyone as Mac, was one of the shop managers. Him and Charles; for he liked to be called Charles even though the staff insisted on calling him Charlie, much to his distain, were the two managers of the shop and worked on a rota basis. One of them was always on duty and of the two it was Mac who Chris liked the least. Mac was the elder of the two by some years and was an ex site agent for a pipe laying firm who had been made redundant some years earlier and had diversified into the retail trade. He was a hard man and a taskmaster and knowing of his past reputation Chris feared what Mac would have done to him should he ever find out what his part was in the burglary. It was Charles who had taken Chris on and with whom he had a much better rapport.

As Chris made his way down the shop he noticed the debris from the night before; the earth on the floor from the plant pot he had knocked over; the broken wine bottles, whose spilt contents had by now covered a significant area along one aisle, forming a large burgundy stain on the linoleum floor. Upon reaching the till he observed the carnage which he himself had attributed to less than eight hours previously and it seemed even worse in the daylight than it had the night before. He did however afford himself a small smile as he remembered the incident with the baked bean can but was quickly brought back down to earth. "Bastards!". Mac could be heard saying the word repeatedly as he paced up and down the shop shaking his head. "If I were you Chris I'd keep out of Mac's way for a bit, he aint happy!". Paul was the other shop assistant working that morning and had arrived around five minutes before Chris. "Reckons he's going to kill whoever did this with his bare hands if he ever gets hold of them!". "Bastards.... Bastards!". Mac was returning from the other end of the shop and stopped at the counter and stared hard at Chris. "Bastards!". He shouted out as he slammed his fist down on the counter in frustration. "Do you know what I'm going to do Chris if I ever find out who did this?". Mac stared directly at Chris, his icy blue eyes boring a hole straight into Chris's brain. Chris didn't answer and at this stage was unsure exactly what information Mac had at his disposal in relation to the previous night's events. "I'm going to string them up, that's what I'm going to do!". Mac made a gesture eluding to the fact that he was going to wring their neck with his bare hands, his face contorted in anger, and his eyes bulging. "Do you know what actually happened then?". Chris enquired quietly. "No not yet!". Mac snapped. "We're waiting for the police to arrive and have a look over the shop. They want to see if there's any finger prints or anything that will help them, so make sure you don't touch anything or disturb anything!". "Did they get away with anything?". Chris enquired. "Mainly booze and cigarettes I think, but they were obviously going for the till thinking there would be cash in there. Good job we empty them every night, but the trouble is they've wrecked this one and they cost a couple thousand pounds to replace". "I suppose we're insured though?". Paul enquired. "Yes, we're insured". Mac sighed. "Bloody typical though isn't it, couldn't happen when old bloody Charlie was on could it, had to be me that sorts the mess out, didn't it?". Chris thought Mac was finally calming down a bit, but it wasn't long before he was pacing back up and down the shop again, shaking his head and muttering various expletives under his breath!

Chapter 5

"Welcome to Bridgetown Parkrun everyone". Michelle announced, reading from the clipboard held aloft in front of her; the cold easterly wind tugging at the paper pages trying to free them from the bulldog clip that was holding them precariously to the piece of thin plywood. Michelle was today's race director and as such proudly sported the regulatory blue and white 'Race director' tabard as she stood aloft on a solitary park bench next to the hedge that separated the bowling green from the rest of the park. In addition to Michelle there were several other volunteers gathered immediately adjacent to the bench wearing their yellow fluorescent tops proudly bearing the wording of 'Marshal' on the back. "I bet they're the Marshals!". Martin winked in his daughters' direction, tapping his nose knowingly. "Dad you're an idiot!". His daughter responded. The two stood attentively with the gathered hoards on the somewhat muddy grass in front of her as Michelle read out the introduction and instructions for the mornings run, brushing her long blonde hair repeatedly out of her eyes to little avail as she did so, only for the next gust of wind to blow it straight back down again. Eventually she gave up and resigned herself to it whipping around her face untamed before continuing.

As he looked around observing the other runners, Martin surmised that there must have been around a hundred and fifty or so participants that particular morning. There were males and females of all ages and shapes and sizes, some had their dogs with them and he could see at least two with young children in pushchairs. Never had he seen such an ensemble of brightly coloured lycra all in one place before. He looked down at his own T shirt, shorts, socks and trainers and suddenly started to feel very self-conscious, folding his arms as he wondered if indeed he should have put in a bit more effort! He refocussed his attentions on the announcement as the race director went through her standard spiel explaining that the course was a multi surface event (although it wasn't today as it was all on tarmac due to it being the winter course!) and that it consisted of completing three and a half laps of the park. "Is there anyone here visiting from another parkrun?". Michelle enquired, looking around at the crowd in expectation. A few hands went up and each was duly asked where they had come from; each response being meet with an enthusiastic round of applause from the remaining runners. "Any first timers?". Michelle continued. Martin and Abi looked at each other sheepishly in a sort of, should we or shouldn't we, kind of way and the last thing that Martin wanted was to draw any more attention to himself than his attire already had. Abi however had already instinctively put her hand up, so Martin reluctantly did likewise after noting that they weren't alone and that a few other first timers had also raised their hands in the air. They were greeted with a similarly enthusiastic applause from the crowd. 'Friendly bunch!'. Martin thought to himself, feeling a little more comfortable now as he nodded around the crowd generally in a gesture of thanks. "Anyone doing a milestone run?". The director enquired; "10, 50, 100?". She looked around for raised hands, but none were forthcoming, so she moved on. Abi turned to look around the park to see that not all the runners were listening to the announcements. Some were carrying out various stretches or stood chatting in small groups and some were running up and down on the part of the track that went past the adjacent rugby ground. These were the regulars; the hardened parkrun fraternity that ran on a weekly basis and knew the course and the instructions inside out; all on first name terms with each other and who knew their competitors' performance and personal best times down to the last second. Martin and Abi would find out more about this in time but for now the two of them were the newbies, as were the other first timers there that day.

'Hmm I wonder who the best is?' Martin thought to himself, reminiscent of a scene from the Top Gun briefing room, as he scanned the other athletes. His daughter nudged him in the side knowingly; "Dad in case you're wondering who the best is. It's him over there in the blue and white track suit; Rob Williams, he wins it virtually every time he enters". Abi pointed to the young man in question who was engaged in carrying out some stretches on the tarmac path underneath the large Oak tree. The same tree whose branches had weathered many a storm and given grateful summer shade to numerous runners and park goers alike over the years. Martin looked over at Rob and then at the tree and noted how small and insignificant he seemed in comparison to its majesty. It now stood bereft of its foliage but still strong, tall and proud and a testament to its creation. Martin admired the size and shape of the tree and its gnarled branches stretching out in all directions. He gazed up through its branches, upwards again to those at the very top and then beyond the tree to the sky above. As they often did, his thoughts once again turned to his wife for a moment, and he wondered whether she was somewhere up there looking down on him too. Just knowing that there was a slim chance she may have been gave him some comfort in times of uncertainty and the will to carry on. His eyes ran back down the tree and then re focused back on Rob, now without his track suit and sporting the black and white striped vest and shorts of his club; he certainly looked young and fit, but then perhaps no more so than Martin himself would have done in his youth. Eventually Martin turned to acknowledge his daughter and nodded. "So, he's 'Iceman' then!".

Abi brought him back down to earth with a bump; "Anyway, never mind who the best is Dad, how about who's the coldest; I think it must be me because I'm bloody freezing my arse off here! If he's 'Iceman', I must be the bloody 'Ice woman'". Abi stated, rubbing her hands together briskly and blowing into them in a vain attempt to keep them warm. Martin too was feeling the cold but was trying his best to ignore it. He noted that many of the other runners still had their coats or track suits on, generally of a high visibility bright yellow or pink colour, which they no doubt took off just before the run to expose their equally brightly coloured and patterned running tops and shorts. He also noted that tight multi-coloured lycra leggings appeared to be 'de rigueur' not only for the women but for the men as well! As he stood there getting rapidly colder he was wishing that he and his daughter had the foresight to have donned some similarly warm attire. "Never mind Abi, I'm sure we'll warm up a bit when we get going!". he replied somewhat half-heartedly.

Although Dave Macready turned up in time for the briefing and religiously gathered there with the other park runners, he wasn't in the habit anymore of actually listening to them. Akin to a frequent flyer on an aeroplane who saw the safety announcements as mere background noise, he didn't need to. As a veteran parkrunner with over a hundred runs to his name, the briefing was more of an inconvenience and he had long forgotten how many laps of the park he had run previously. He was stood at the back of the crowd and was oblivious to the instructions being bellowed out from the race director as he compared notes with Steve, Colin, Wayne and keith; other members of the parkrun fraternity who regularly gathered for their Saturday morning fix. "You trying for a personal best today then Keith?". Dave asked his fellow runner. Keith was always striving for a personal best but made a few excuses about how he was unlikely to get one today as his hamstring was playing up a bit and that he had also had a bit of a heavy night last night. It was always good to get a few potential excuses to the fore prior to the run just in case things didn't go quite as well as expected and as the age of the group of runners wasn't getting any younger it was often the range of injuries they were suffering from that was the main topic of conversation!

Martin too also suffered from his fair share of injuries, mainly received from playing football due to the twisting and turning and sudden changes of pace associated with the game. Up until a few years ago though he had managed to remain virtually injury free but in the past couple of years he had noticed that the aches and pains weren't so easy to overcome as they had been in his youth and like others of a more mature nature he was an inevitable victim of the aging process, much as he hated to admit it. He had always been fiercely competitive however in all he did and his grit and determination to do well in his chosen pursuits and to prove that he still had what it takes certainly hadn't diminished as the years rolled by.

"And remember this is a run not a race". The race director concluded as the pack dispersed to make their way to the start of the race. Rob Williams smiled to himself as he turned with the other runners to make his way towards the start line. Like Dave, he had also heard the line numerous times before but to him this was very much a race. Indeed, every time he lined up on a starting grid, whether it was for a parkrun or a marathon there was only one thing on his mind and that was to cross that finishing line in first place come hell or high water. Rob was in his early thirties and belonged to the local Athletics club, the Road Warriors. He was renowned as being one of the best runners in the area, if not the country, and regularly completed five-kilometre races in under fifteen minutes. He had also represented England successfully in a range of distances and was a regular in the top 100 of the 'Run Britain' rankings. The accolades just kept on coming and he was admired by his compatriots for his running ability and achievements even if not all were as pleased as they may have been when left trailing in his wake with the familiar sight of his black and white striped vest disappearing off into the distance.

The success hadn't necessarily come easy to Rob though, yes, he had the natural ability and had been running since a young age, but he still had to put in the hard work to maintain his fitness and keep on top of his game. There was rarely a day go by when he wouldn't be engaged in some sort of training, be it speed work, tempo runs, long runs or just exercising generally in the gym. He was a creature of habit when it came to races though and for the park runs it was no exception. Every Saturday morning, he would run the twenty minutes or so from his home to the park before carrying out some stretches to his calves and thighs underneath the Oak tree on arrival. He would then carry out a series of quicker sprints along the rugby ground straight before returning to the tree and taking off his track suit. Some final stretches would ensue before ultimately lining up for the race. Once he had completed the race he would put his tracksuit back on before running home.

Martin and Abi made their way to the start line with the other athletes. Rob was already there and waiting and lined up at the front of the pack on the inside line as father and daughter made their way through the crowd towards the back. The timekeeper got into position ready to start the run. 'Speedy' Macready, Steve, Colin, Wayne and keith were also lining up on the front of the grid. The remaining runners lined up in position behind them with the faster ones slotting in towards the front, eying up their fellow runners as they did so, trying to judge how fast they may be in comparison to them and fitting in to a starting position accordingly. The slower ones headed to the back as did Martin and Abi who eventually stopped when there was nowhere further back to go. They lined up on the back row in between a female runner with a black and white border collie and a young male in his late twenties with a pushchair. Martin glanced to his left at the occupant of the buggy in question and a young child of no more than two years old beamed back at him. Martin turned to his daughter. "Abi whatever we do, please don't let us get beaten by someone with a pushchair!". He whispered. "Dad, remember it's a run, not a race!". She smiled.

# Chapter 6

It wasn't long before a police car pulled up outside the Tesco's Express and two officers stepped out. Chris looked at his watch and noted that the time was 8:55 am. He started to feel nervous and swallowed deeply as a tall male officer alighted the car from the driver's side and fixed his cap onto his head, adjusting it slightly by looking at his reflection in the car window to ensure it was on straight. His female colleague got out of the passenger door and the two exchanged a few words before heading towards the shop front. They initially stopped there, looking around the entrance for some considerable time before eventually pushing open the door and stepping in to the shop. Mac walked over to greet them and the three of them made their way back to the till area where Chris and Paul were waiting.

The officers introduced themselves as police constables 'May' and 'Taylor' with PC May being the tall male officer who seemed to be taking the lead in the conversations. Chris eyed him up and was sure that he had seen him around before, possibly even having some involvement with him in his younger days. Mac explained to the officers what little he was aware of in relation to the incident and how he had entered the shop that morning to be greeted with the scene that the officers were now observing. PC May seemed most interested however with the means of entrance that the perpetrators had used, noting that there was little sign of any forced entry. Once again Chris's heart sank, knowing that the finger would inevitably be pointed at one of the employees and the question he was dreading soon arose. "How many people have actually got keys to the shop then?". PC May enquired of Mac. "I'm going to need all of their names and addresses so that we can question them". Mac reeled off the names of the three present at the time and gave the officers their contact details. He also furnished them with details of Charles, the other manager and the other employees of the store. "We're going to have to get the forensic team here to look things over in a bit more detail, see if they can find any fingerprints or other clues that may point us in the right direction as to who did this". PC May explained. "What I would say however, and don't quote me on this, is that where there's no sign of a forced entry there's usually some inside involvement so the team will probably be around to question the employees within the next few days. I'll make a couple of phone calls in a minute to see how quickly forensics can get here as obviously you'll want to be open and up and running again as soon as possible. Whilst I do that P.C Taylor will take an initial statement from each of you and ascertain your movements last night just to rule you out of our enquiries. Don't worry unduly though it's just a formality". Chris knew that for him however it was anything but a formality, having been in similar situations numerous times in the past. He was hoping though that he wouldn't be the first to be questioned whereby he would at least have time to get his story straight and work out how he was going to play things. "I'll start with you first Mr McGuilicutty if that's OK?". PC Taylor enquired of Mac. "Is there anywhere private that we can sit down so that I can take some notes?". Mac nodded and led the officer to the staff rest room at the back of the shop. It was a small room furnished with a random selection of chairs of all shapes, colours and sizes that had been acquired from various employees who had donated them from home when they were no longer required. There was no table to write on so PC Taylor sat back and recorded Mac's answers with the note book alighted on her lap. When she had finished her questioning and made the necessary recordings she closed her notebook and leaned forward. "One final question Mr McGuilicutty, and this is strictly off the record; do you think it's possible that one of your employees could have done this?". Mac thought for a moment before answering. He hadn't even considered the possibility before as he had been so wound up over the break in that it hadn't crossed his mind. He now however started to think about it in a bit more detail and put two and two together. "It couldn't be Chris could it?". He stated out loud, looking somewhat puzzled "I don't know...could it?". PC Taylor enquired, raising her eyebrows and tilting her head slightly to one side as she did so, enticing Mac to provide a bit more information. She clasped her hands together and leaned in a little closer. "What makes you think that?". Mac paused for a moment and looked around the bare walls of the room then up to the ceiling pondering the possibility as he did so. "Well, nothing specific really." He stated, rubbing the fingers of his right hand through the stubble on his chin. "It's just that he's had a bit of a chequered past that's all. He's been in and out of children's homes all his life and has had a bit of a tough upbringing. I know he got in with a bad crowd back along and he's been in a few scrapes in the past, but I did think all that was behind him now and that he was back on the straight and narrow. I can't imagine that he would have done this, well not off his own back anyway as he's been a bit of a model employee since he got here and really turned himself around". "And this 'bad crowd' he's got in with, do you know anything about them?" PC Taylor asked. "No not really". Mac replied. "Look I'm probably barking up the wrong tree completely, I don't think it would have been Chris, he's got too much to lose really for the sake of a few packets of cigarettes and some booze and besides I'm sure he would have known that the till was emptied every night". "OK thanks for that Mr McGuilicutty, that's been really helpful. Can you do me a favour please and don't mention any of this to Chris; as you say we may be barking up the wrong tree entirely, so I'll see what he has to say when I interview him". With that the two got up and shook hands before proceeding to leave the room. "Oh, one quick thing I forgot to mention". stated P.C Taylor "And that is, do you have CCTV here and if so can we have access to it please?". "Yes, that's no problem". Replied Mac. "I will say though that it's not the most reliable system in the world and the quality isn't that good in the dark. We use it more really for identifying shoplifters during working hours when the shop is lit, you're welcome to have a look at it though. I can save it onto a memory stick if you like?". "OK, that would be excellent. If you are able to do that before we leave it would be a great help". With that the two left the room and entered back into the main shop.

Chris and Paul had been chatting to themselves whilst Mac was being questioned by PC Taylor. Paul had been speculating on what might have happened during the night, proffering up all kinds of theories from gangs of marauding dwarves to aliens having robbed the shop, with each offering being slightly more implausible than the last. Chris however knew exactly what the chain of events were that had unfolded the previous night and was the next to be called in by PC Taylor for his interview. As she was leading him into the room PC May had just finished his phone conversation. "Jan!". He shouted over to PC Taylor. "Before you go back in, I've just come off the phone to the desk; the forensic team can come over this afternoon". He strode purposefully back towards the tills. "Mr McGuilicutty, in light of that we've got two options we can explore really; we can either leave the shop closed until they've finished, or we can try and cordon off the bits they will need to investigate, it's your call?". Mac thought about it for a while before reluctantly deciding to leave the shop closed until the investigations had taken place, surmising that it would be virtually impossible anyway for customers to access the shop adequately with the aisles in question closed off. Arrangements were made in that respect and PC Taylor and Chris made their way through to the staffroom with Officer May taking a statement from Paul.

Whilst Paul's statement was both information and guilt free, the same couldn't be said of Chris's and as the two sat down in the rest room Chris had already got his story worked out in his head; He was out with his friends last night for a drink in the Turks Head and then headed home about midnight and went to bed shortly after. Well the first part of it was true anyway but as he sat looking at the female PC he doubted that he had the ability to see it through. She must have been about 25 years old and Chris noted how attractive she was with her big brown eyes, black hair and olive skin. He also noted that she had what he could only describe as a kind looking face. How could he look her in the eye and blatantly lie to her? He was trying to move away from the sins of his past and here he was again in exactly the same situation. He didn't know how much Mac knew and what he had told her. He didn't know if he would be identified on CCTV. He also didn't know if his story would stand up; they only had to ask his foster parents what time he had come in, or the barman what time they had left the pub, or ultimately his 'mates' who he knew would have no hesitation in passing the buck and putting the blame on him. He was in a right quandary.

"Ok then Chris." said the PC as the two of them sat in the rest room and had finished the introductory small talk. "Perhaps you could explain to me exactly what you know about last night's events?".

# Chapter 7

Silence fell upon the start line in anticipation. It was broken by the race directors voice; "Everyone ready? Three, two, one, go!". Michelle shouted, as she started the race. Those at the front sped eagerly away with those behind filtering along and starting to jog and then break into a run as and when the space in front of them allowed. Martin and Abi set off at a steady pace and almost immediately passed a few of the obviously slower runners before they had even reached the starting line. Abi felt a sense of relief as they passed a few more along the opening straight, realising that at least they weren't going to be the last over the line on their inaugural run. The pack soon started to thin out and as the two of them ran side by side along the straight behind the bowling club, the quicker runners could already be seen disappearing around the corner, beyond the café and heading past the ornate double wrought iron entrance gates towards the toilets.

Martin had no idea how fast he and his daughter were running but to him it seemed fairly quick and he felt relatively comfortable during the initial stages. Any illusions of speed that he may have had however were firmly extinguished when the runner with the pushchair quickly whipped past him and Abi as they crossed the starting line again having completed the first lap of the park. Martin turned to his daughter and laughed. As they turned right towards the rugby club the faster runners were already heading back towards them on the opposite side of the path, keeping to the right of a line of cones down the middle to segregate the runners going in opposite directions. It was soon evident that the Status Quo was being preserved and Rob Williams had already opened up a clear distance between himself and the next group of four tightly packed runners and as he passed Martin and Abi he was veritably flying in the opposite direction.

A couple of laps in to the run and Rob was coasting, he had by now really opened up the legs and was easing further and further away from the chasing pack. Although he was used to running on his own it was inevitably harder to achieve a quick time in this fashion. He had his watch of course to tell him how quick he was going but in Rob's eyes there was nothing like the sound of another runner breathing down your neck to give that real injection of pace and to get the adrenaline going. With Rob way out on his own though there was little chance of that happening this morning and he ploughed on safe in the knowledge that no one would catch him today. A very real contest was materialising behind him though and that was the battle for second place being played out by 'Speedy' Macready and Keith Collins. Although some way behind Rob, the two had broken away from the rest of the pack and opened up a distance of around twenty metres or so from the next closest runner. The two were matching each other stride for stride as they made their way around the park, sharing the lead in the duel between them and both digging deep to ensure they stuck with their competitor before trying to kick on again themselves.

Keith was in his prime; he had just reached his thirty fifth year and was an avid runner being a member of the Toddington Trotters athletics club. Theoretically he should have easily had the better of Dave due to the age difference, but age wasn't always necessarily a barrier when it came to running and Dave wasn't one to let theory get in the way of practice when showing the rest what he was capable of. He knew that to be successful you had to put in the miles, do the training, do the leg work, the hill work, the speed work, the long runs, and get out there and train come wind, rain or shine, hell or highwater whether you felt like it or not. As such trained hard, ate well and led a healthy lifestyle to sustain his level of fitness and he hadn't earned the nickname of 'Speedy' for nothing. Many years ago, a competitor had the audacity to tell Dave that he wasn't a 'proper runner.' It was down to the fact that when he started out, although enthusiastic, he had piled on the pounds a bit and certainly wasn't the quickest runner in the world by any stretch of the imagination. If he could run though, as far as Dave was concerned, he was a proper runner and the recollection of those words in his head over the years, and even now during a race, only spurred him on to do better. With age came determination and mental strength and Dave was soundly of the opinion that the mind was as powerful as any leg muscles when it came to competing. His results in numerous races certainly bore the theory out as there had been many a time when his body had all but given up due to exhaustion only for his mental strength to give him the will to push through the pain barrier and see it through to the end whatever the consequences may have been. He also took great comfort in the fact that he was now a much quicker runner than the person in question and although the two rarely spoke, Dave always had time for a wry smile in his direction on the occasions the two lined up for a race together.

Martin and Abi's mental strength however wasn't at the same level as Dave's quite yet! "My bloody shins are killing me Abi!". Martin grimaced, as they passed the toilet block for the second time out of four. "How are you feeling?". "Well I'm not aching but I'm struggling a bit with my breathing". His daughter wheezed. "And by the way, the reason your shins are aching Dad is because your trainers are so bloody old they haven't got any give in them have they! You'd be better of running in a pair of clogs than those things!". Martin looked down as his feet as they slapped loudly on the ground in front of him alternately. As the race progressed he could feel every step now giving him a sharp pain in each shin and he was wishing that he had indeed acquired some more appropriate footwear. They struggled on however and as they were nearing the end of their third lap the veritable whirlwind that was Rob Williams sped past them, sprinting for the finish line and coming home in a time of 16 minutes 3 seconds; a literal stroll in the park by his standards. He routinely accepted his finish token, proudly displaying the number '1' on it, from the Marshal and handed it in along with his barcode to the volunteer scanner before donning his tracksuit and heading for home, unperturbed by the morning's events.

The battle for second place was eventually won by Dave Macready, who, having managed to pull away from Keith Collins on the last lap came in at a time of just over 18 minutes. Keith duly collected his third-place token but not before holding off a last-minute challenge from two of the younger club runners who had picked up the pace and gradually reeled him in as the race drew to a close. Keith stopped his watch as he crossed the finish line and was pleased with the time considering the conditions of the day. Indeed a 5k time of between 18 and 19 minutes was a very respectable one in anybody's book and for runners of a more mature age anything under 20 minutes was considered to be something of an achievement.

Not everyone's run was over though and whilst some of the faster ones had finished and were heading for home, the vast majority, including Martin and Abi were still going. The two of them struggled on and somehow resisted the burning urge to stop running and walk the final lap. They ultimately jogged past the finish line to receive their own tokens. There was a steady stream of runners finishing around the same time as them and Martin looked across to see that the baby in the pushchair had long since finished and was grinning from ear to ear having been bounced around the track in his very own three wheeled custom chariot. "I'll get you next time!". Martin thought to himself, as he gave him a little wave. Once father and daughter had taken the opportunity to catch their breath they handed in their barcodes to the young lady scanning them in. After clapping some of the other runners across the finishing line and thanking some of the Marshals that were milling around at the finish they headed out the back gates of the park towards the car. Martin was hobbling a bit due to his shins and despite the brief respite since finishing the race his daughter was still a bit short of breath. "Well we know we came 75th and 76th". Martin stated, referring to the numbers on their finish tokens, as they strolled along the path, "But how do we know what time we did it in?". "You'll get an e mail later

Dad". Replied Abi. "I've set it all up for you and once they've processed all the results they'll send them out".

It was about 11am that same morning, Martin was sat at home in the lounge having a well-earned cup of tea and biscuit whilst reading the paper, when his daughter came bursting through the door. "Dad they've arrived!". "What's arrived?". Martin enquired, looking up from an article he was reading on how Chelsea football club had purchased a promising youth academy player from Exeter City. "Our times, they've come through on an e mail; here have a look". Abi sat down next to her dad on the sofa and held her phone out to show him the results. "Here you go; I came 75$^{th}$, and you came 76$^{th,}$ both in a time of 24 minutes and 33 seconds. That's not bad for our first run and out of one hundred and sixty-five runners we've at least come in the top half!". "Yes, that's not bad I suppose". Martin responded, as he put down the newspaper to study the figures in more detail. As Martin was a bit of a technophobe when it came to anything IT related his daughter showed him how to look at the full set of results and filter them into the various different categories. "Those times are our Personal Bests now". She explained, pointing to the end column, where 'PB' was proudly displayed adjacent to their times; "We'll have to try and beat them next week!". 'Yes, I'm sure we will!' Martin thought to himself, as he put his feet up on the sofa and lay back and closed his eyes for a well-earned rest.

# Chapter 8

Abi awoke the next morning feeling refreshed and ready to face the day and after a light breakfast she breezed out the front door to head over to the gym. Martin, on the other hand, awoke that morning suddenly realising how unfit he was, with both his thighs and shins aching considerably. He pulled back the bed covers, placed his knees together and rolled out of bed before ambling gingerly around the house trying to walk off the pain and stretch his legs out a bit. He quickly concluded that this wasn't working however so he gave in, took two paracetamols and retired back to bed. He was awoken sometime later by a knock on his door. "Dad are you in there... are you OK?". It was his son, enquiring as to his dad's whereabouts and wellbeing, as it was unusual for him not to be up and about at this late hour. "Yes, fine Max, I Think!". Martin responded, still half asleep. It was by now nearly lunch time and Martin came around this time feeling somewhat better than during his previous attempt to get up, the tablets at least having taken the edge off the pain.

"Looks like that run yesterday did you the world of good then Dad!". Max remarked sarcastically, as the two of them sat down to some bacon sandwiches. "I'm just not used to it at the moment am I, it's a bit different than playing football as you're running constantly instead of in short bursts of speed! I'm sure I'll get into the swing of it. Why don't you come along with us next time, I'm sure you'd enjoy it?". Max looked his dad up and down and puffed out his cheeks. "Well looking at the state of you Dad, you're not exactly selling it very well are you; perhaps you could be the face of their advertising campaign; come to Bridgetown parkrun and end up looking like this!" Max laughed. "Anyway, it's not really my thing is it, running, I'm not designed for it am I!". Max continued. "I suppose your body is more designed for lying in bed relaxing then?". Martin responded with a smile. "Well if God had wanted us to run we would have been born with trainers on wouldn't we!". Max quipped. "Anyway, I'm off back to bed for a bit, oh and by the way I'm out tonight so I'll need a lift into town if that's OK?". Martin nodded in agreement as his son headed off back to his room with Martin inevitably left to do the tidying up. He decided there and then though that the next thing he would do would be to invest in some better running shoes!

True to form however Martin didn't replace his shoes there and then or unfortunately for him anytime soon and the next Saturday found him running again in the same pair. Two more Saturdays followed before he and his shins had finally decided that enough was enough and he headed off to buy something more appropriate. Accompanied by his offspring for moral support and guidance the three of them headed to the local Nike store to see what was available.

"Can I help you at all?". Jack Dixon was one of the young assistants on duty that morning and had noticed Martin, Abi and Max wandering around aimlessly in the shoe section. "Oh Hi, yes please". Martin responded, putting down a pair of luminous green football boots that had caught his eye, but which he had no intention of buying or indeed any need for. "Pair of football boots you're after is it?". Jack enquired, looking Martin up and down and surmising that he was far too old to be playing football, and particularly in a pair of bright green boots. "Ah no, I was just looking at those out of curiosity, my eleven a side playing days are over I'm afraid". "Walking football for you these days Dad isn't it!". His son smirked. "I'm after a pair of running shoes really". Martin continued, doing his best to ignore his sons jibe. "Any idea what it is you are looking for and how much you're thinking of spending?". Jack asked, leading the three over to an aisle at the side of the shop which displayed several different types of running shoe. "All the men's running shoes are in this aisle here; I can recommend these". Advised Jack, picking up a pair of 'Nike Air Vapormax' and handing them to Martin. "Yes, they feel really light". Martin enthused, examining the pair of shoes in question in more detail, thinking how much he liked the look of them. "How much are they then?". "They're £130". Jack informed him. Martin suddenly liked the look of them slightly less than he had done previously! "Hmm that's a bit more than I was looking to spend really!". Martin confessed, quickly putting them back down on the shelf again. Jack showed him a few more pairs that were available, explaining the various merits of each and the type of material they were constructed from along with the differences in the type of 'sole technology', all of which was going way over Martin's head. All he was seeing was the price tag and after Martin had dismissed everything in the more expensive price bracket, Jack led the three to the back of the shop where there was some end of line half price offers. 'Now you're talking my language!'. Martin smiled to himself. "Have a look through these if you like, there's all sorts there but you may have to sift through them a bit". With that Jack left them to it and moved on to another customer who he hoped wouldn't be quite so 'careful' with their money. Upon looking through the various boxes Martin's luck was in and he managed to bag a pair of 'entry level', as Jack would later describe them, 'Nike Downshifter' running shoes in a resplendent but conservative black and white, for a bargain basement price of only £20. 'Sorted!'. Martin thought to himself after trying on a pair of size tens that fitted. He didn't get away that lightly though as whilst there, and at his daughters request to save her the embarrassment of being seen with him looking like a tramp, he pushed the boat out and purchased a new pair of shorts, a black running top and a pair of long compression running socks. He emerged from the changing room to a nod of approval from his son and daughter. "Well at least you look the part now, even if you can't run!". Max stated emphatically.

The following Saturday brought about the first serious trial of the new equipment. Martin and Abi's times had been getting progressively quicker as the weeks passed and some light midweek jogging for the pair had also upped their levels of fitness. That Saturday they lined up a bit closer to the front of the pack and after the first lap it was apparent that they were running a lot faster than they had previously, pushing each other on as they ran. Martin's new trainers had made a significant difference and the shin pain he had experienced previously was nowhere to be felt on that morning. Whilst Abi was reaching her limit in terms of speed, Martin was veritably cruising around and starting to really embrace being out in the open air and enjoying the experience of competitive sport once again. He certainly had a lot more in the tank to give and that week they both broke the 22-minute mark and came in a respectable 20th and 21st place.

After a few more weeks of improving fitness and as such their race times, it was fast becoming apparent to Abi that the two athlete's physical capabilities were somewhat different, and Abi was aware that her dad had more to give in terms of running ability and pace. "Dad, perhaps it's time for us to run on our own now as I think you could go a lot quicker and I'm holding you back a bit". "Well it's not all about how quick you can do it is Abi, it's about doing something together". "Go on Dad, see how fast you can go; you know you want to!". Martin was indeed itching to see how fast he could run, however for today he resisted the urge to do so and ran the race in its entirety with his daughter, spurring each other on as they did so. As they headed down the finishing straight they held hands and sprinted for the line, coming in at just over 21 minutes. "Well done Abi, that was quick!". Martin praised his daughter as she was bent over double with her hands on her knees, panting hard and sweating profusely. She looked at her watch. "My heartbeat is over 180 beats per minute!". She spluttered "No wonder I can hardly breathe!". They ran together for a couple more weeks with Martin heading off at his own pace for the final lap, passing several of the other runners as he did so and upping both his time and position. It felt good to be running at full capacity and reeling some of the other runners in before eventually passing them. He knew though that he still had more to give and to be able to achieve his best he would have to be given a free reign right from the start.

That day came on a grey and overcast Saturday in April and Martin and Abi had agreed that today they would both run at their own pace. For Martin it was the first real opportunity for him to see what he could do; to compete with the other athletes on his own terms and indeed for him, today was the first time it was a race rather than a run. The two arrived at the park in good time, Martin's body primed on a breakfast of Weetabix and bananas washed down with a strong black coffee, and raring to go. Today as Abi lined up in their usual position near the middle of the pack, Martin lined up a bit closer to the start of the grid, noting as he did so some of the other athletes alongside him. He wasn't part of the running clique yet and as such wasn't familiar with all the other faces. He had exchanged pleasantries and passed the time of day with some of them and tried to work out who they were from the names on previous weeks results. In his own inimitable way however, he had given some of the quicker ones their own nicknames. There was obviously "Iceman" of course but there was also 'The Running Rev', a vicar who regularly participated and generally came in the top ten; 'Tango Man' who always wore a bright orange T shirt and shorts; 'The old guy' who inevitably was probably younger than Martin but didn't necessarily look it due to his thinning grey hair and straggly beard, the 'Bouncy Guy' for reasons that were apparent to anyone who had seen him run and 'Nitro' who always wore a black T Shirt with the words 'Nitro Circus' on the front and 'Happy to be Nitro' on the back. As this was the usual view Martin had of him he was happy to have named him accordingly. All however were good runners in their own right and Martin could only ponder what nickname they may have come up with for him! He looked around for Rob however today he was conspicuous by his absence and his distinctive black and white vest couldn't be seen anywhere. He supposed that he was either late or merely had an alternative engagement and as he stood on the starting grid Martin surmised that at least there would be a new name claiming first place today even though the chances of it being his were slim.

The athletes didn't have to wait long before the start and they were soon off and winging their way down the first straight towards the left turn at the bowling club. A few runners had gone off quickly, but Martin sat back with the main pack and headed off at a steady pace. By the time he had reached the Café however he was in 6th place and counted off five other athletes stretched out in front of him in the distance, some of whom he recognised and some that he didn't. He overtook one of them; a young slim male around 6 feet tall clad in sky blue T shirt and shorts, whilst on the small incline heading towards the toilet block before accelerating down the gentle slope beyond that lead back to the start line. By the time he had run the long straight past the rugby ground and headed onto the grass section his watch he felt his watch vibrated, indicating that he had completed the first kilometre. Martin glanced down at his wrist to see that his time for the first kilometre was a relatively quick, 3 minutes 45 seconds. If he was able to keep this up he would have been well on his way towards a finish in under 19 minutes which to him would have been some achievement. He knew however that there was a significant difference between running a fast kilometre and a fast five kilometres and that the coming four wouldn't necessarily be as easy as the first. It gave him some encouragement though and at least he now had something to aim for; a sub 19-minute 5k which for someone of his years would have been very respectable. He pushed on around the grass of the rugby pitch.

Martin wasn't particularly keen on running on grass and today it seemed particularly wet and stodgy, sapping his energy and slowing him down. The uneven ground wasn't the kindest on his ankles, which were susceptible to injury even at the best of times. Martin looked down and tried to pick out safe positions where his feet could plant on firm ground rather than focusing ahead and his stride started to become somewhat erratic as he did so. He could physically feel that he wasn't running anywhere near as fast as he was back on the tarmac and this was borne out when he could hear the loud rhythmic breathing of another athlete rapidly encroaching on him from behind.

Aron Amberry was a parkrun tourist that Saturday morning. A tall slight male, 25 years old and already a veteran of 100 parkruns, he usually spent his Saturday mornings lacing up his trainers at the Cannon Hill Parkrun in Birmingham. For the past three years he had been a member of the Bournville Harriers running club in the West Midlands; situated in Rowheath in the leafy suburb of Bournville; the place best known to others as the home of Cadburys chocolate. It just so happened that this Saturday morning he was in Bridgetown with his girlfriend visiting relatives and was doing what the majority of parkrunners like to do when they're on holiday; running other parkrun courses. Aron ran regularly both at parkruns and club events and had a sub 18-minute personal best over a 5k distance. He wasn't particularly looking for a PB today though and was just out to enjoy the morning. He approached Martin and passed him to his left and it wasn't long before he had put some distance between the two of them. Although running with someone of a similar speed often spurred Martin on to do greater things he didn't appear this morning to have the energy to respond and try as he might to dig in and go with him, his legs simply weren't having any of it. Martin eventually was resigned to letting him go and watched helplessly as the distance between them inevitably increased. He continued at his own pace and was relieved to feel his feet once again bite into the firm tarmac surface as he exited the grass of the rugby pitch back onto the tarmac path that circumnavigated the park. It felt good on his legs not to be bogged down and he took a couple of deep breaths and gritted his teeth in determination as he headed past the bowling club and into the cool light headwind that greeted him. He shook his arms out and refocused his mind before upping his pace and accelerating as hard as he could down the back straight until he was once again on the shoulder of the Bournville Harriers runner.

Martin preferred any runner he was aside to be on his right. He wasn't sure why this was but if they were on his left and they were running together it just didn't feel right for some reason and he simply couldn't concentrate on the task in hand. He manoeuvred himself alongside, so he was positioned to the left of his competitor and could feel the young man glance over at him and start to put in a response.

Whilst Aron wasn't necessarily on course for a PB today, the 'old guy' who had the audacity to appear back on his shoulder after he had so easily breezed past him earlier was both starting to intrigue and mildly annoy him. Martin dug in but could feel the young athlete next to him put on a spurt to try and shake him off and once again put some distance between them. This time however Martin wasn't having any of it and responded with every ounce of juice in his body to stick with him. Martin's breathing became faster and more erratic than his usual rhythmic pattern and he was well aware that their pace had quickened significantly. He wasn't sure if it was one that he would be able to maintain for any significant length of time. After a further half a lap of the park Martin had his breathing back under control and it was soon to pass that the two athletes breathing, and stride had become synchronised. Breath in, take four strides, breath out, take four strides, breath in; the pattern was repeated over and over again with the two matching each other stride for stride and for pace. Martin's watch vibrated again; it was now starting to hurt, and he glanced down at his wrist to see that the second kilometre had been completed in a time of 3 minutes 42 seconds. Martin was surprised at the rapidness of the pace given his slower speed over the grass section but was pleased he was still on target for a good time and that two fifths of the race were at least behind him. It was now all about what he had left for the final 3k.

Up ahead Dave Macready was running on his own in fourth place. Martin and Aron were by now rapidly closing in on him as they approached the grass section for the second time and it wasn't long before they systematically passed a somewhat surprised Dave either side of him just as they exited the tarmac. Once again, the grass was Martin's downfall as he struggled to keep up with his competitor on the uneven wet surface. A ten-yard gap had opened up by the time they came off the energy sapping grass for the second time and Aron was satisfied that this time he had done enough to put an insurmountable distance between them. He didn't suppose for one moment that someone who looked old enough to be his father would have the stamina to come back at him again. Unfortunately for Aron though Martin had other ideas and ten yards to him was far from insurmountable. Once again, he accelerated as fast as he could down the back straight of the park and onto the left shoulder of the young park runner once again. "Well done mate!". Aron looked to his left and this time acknowledged Martin as he once again ran along beside him. "I thought I'd lost you!". Martin wondered how Aron actually had the energy to speak as all his own was being expended simply trying to suck in as much oxygen as possible and convert it into the precious energy required to propel his body around the track. As he didn't have the power both to run and speak he simply acknowledged his competitor with a somewhat tired nod and a thumbs up. The third kilometre was completed in a time of 3 minutes 41 seconds and however exhausted he may have been, Martin knew that if he was able to keep this up he was in line for a personal best. He knew though that his time would ultimately be dependent on whether he was somehow able to find the inner strength to keep up with his competitor rather than running on his own and simply against the clock.

On passing the start line again the two pressed on and Martin could see up ahead that they were closing in on the third placed athlete. Although Martin's eyesight wasn't the best, he could see by the silhouette and shape of the body and the colour of the vest that it was "Nitro"; a very decent local runner. As they hit the grass for the final time the two were now only around ten feet behind Nitro and pressing him hard. Martin this time though wasn't going to make the mistake of dropping back again and increased his breathing and quickened his stride to keep up with Aron. 'Bleep'; his watch sounded again and vibrated, and Martin wearily rose his arm to view it. The digits it showed were almost a shock to him as he noted the time; 3.33 on the dial. This was unprecedented, but he now had renewed inspiration to spur himself on. 'Only one kilometre to go' he told himself, 'it's now or never, come on you can do it!' Aron and Martin came up on Nitro just as they were rounding the tree stump on the corner. It was an awkward place to pass and Martin's foot caught a divot and he could feel his ankle start to go over. Quick as a flash however he tried to right himself, stumbling for a few paces as he did so but managing not to go over. He cursed himself under his breath for being so stupid and for being too eager to pass at an inappropriate place. He now found himself a few yards behind both Aron and Nitro with less than a kilometre to go. The last of the grass section was approaching and the pain was etched on Martin's face as he started to grimace with the anguish that was running through his body. He began to doubt whether his aging body was designed for this as he looked up to see the other two starting to pull away. 'Not far to go now though' he thought, 'I'm never going to get a better opportunity'. Only the back straight and then past the café and the toilets before the sprint to the finish. He dug deep once again as he rounded the corner past the bowling club and again into the light headwind that was blowing into his face. He felt its cooling effect with appreciation and held his head aloft to embrace it. Up ahead Aron and Nitro were having their own personal battle totally oblivious to the fact that Martin was giving it everything he had down the back straight. The distance between them was slowly but surely diminishing; six yards, five, four, as they headed past the toilet block for the last time. Three yards and then two, Martin wasn't holding anything back as they headed down the tarmac path before turning onto the home straight; a 100 metre section along the grass to the finish line. The three hit the turn simultaneously, Martin though was in the ascendancy and had the element of surprise with him with, the others being engrossed in their own battle. Fifty metres to go and Martin hit level with Aron's shoulder, pumping his legs and arms like a hydraulic machine. One final stomach wrenching, lung bursting surge and Martin looked across at the finish line to see that he had made it with just a matter of inches separating the three of them. He staggered down the finish funnel and collapsed at the end, not even having the energy to collect his finish token. He rolled over and lay on his back desperately trying to feed his lungs with the oxygen they were severely lacking, wheezing like an asthmatic bulldog prostrate on the floor. He closed his eyes and just lay there breathing as deeply and quickly as he could manage in an endeavour to recover.

A little while later he felt a shadow being cast across his body and opened his eyes to see Aron standing over him. "I think this one's yours". he stated, reaching down to hand Martin his finish token. "Third place; not too shabby!" He acknowledged nodding his head. "Thanks". Martin replied. He tried to stand up, but his legs wouldn't allow it. "Whoa, careful mate!". Aron exclaimed, as he held his hands out to steady Martin as he wobbled around, having lost all control of his legs. "That must have really taken it out of you!". "You're not wrong there!". Martin replied as he bent over double with his hands on his knees.

It wasn't until later that morning when Martin was at home that he realised the time he had completed the run in. Upon clicking on the results, he was somewhat astounded to find out that he had completed the 5k in a time of 18 minutes and 14 seconds. "Abi!". He shouted excitedly; "Come and have a look at this!" …

Chapter 9,

There were three small blue chairs situated in the corridor, facing a blank wall. Chris had been sitting in the middle one of the three, fiddling with his phone for what seemed like an eternity before he heard footsteps approaching and looked up. A rather short, dark haired individual clad in a grey pinstripe suit stopped just before he reached where Chris was sitting. "Mr Clarke?". He enquired.

Chris had found himself in this position through his own stupidity and he was both frustrated and annoyed with himself at what he had done. Ultimately, he was here today though as he had folded during the interview with P.C. Taylor; squealed like a pig some might say, spilling everything he knew about the night's events in great detail. How the break in wasn't his idea and that the others had 'made him do it.' He knew deep down though that he was easily led and that his overriding desire to fit in, have friends who cared about him and be a part of something, even if it was something bad, led to the position he was in now. He tried to lie of course; started off by saying that he knew nothing about the break in, told his planned story of how he was out with his friends that night for a drink in the Turks Head and then headed home about midnight and went to bed shortly after. It wasn't long though before his lies were starting to catch up with him and upon further probing from the young P.C. he was getting tongue tied and backtracking and it was soon obvious to P.C. Taylor that Chris was involved. "Chris if you do know anything about this", she had informed him in her soothing tones, staring at him with those big brown eyes of hers, "it's better to be honest and say now rather than for it to come out in court". Maybe it was because Chris found her so attractive, maybe he just couldn't have lied to such a kind face, or maybe it was just the final straw and he didn't want to live a lie anymore; he had done it throughout his childhood and now he was an adult it was surely time to start with a clean slate and to tell the truth for once whatever the consequences might have been. P.C. Taylor had said that if he told the truth she would try and 'help him', she would 'see what she could do' to see that they were lenient with him, particularly given the fact that he was trying to make a clean start and had admitted his part in the operation.

Chris had his day in court and had indeed come clean. He had stood in the dock alongside his co-defendants Paul and Mike and listened as they both told their warped side of the night's events, firmly placing the blame on Chris's shoulders and outlining how he had meticulously planned the whole thing in minute detail and cajoled them to join him once everything was already planned. They were so convincing that Chris for a moment almost believed it himself and could see no logical reason why the judge wouldn't do likewise. Chris's barrister had briefed him well however and instructed him to tell the truth 'however hard it may be and whatever consequences it may bring'. 'The truth will always stand'. He told him.

Fortunately for Chris, he was appointed a good barrister and the Judges summing up relayed an accurate picture of the night's events. Mike was perceived as the ringleader and being slightly older with a prior conviction was given a custodial sentence. Both Chris and Paul were spared a custodial sentence but given 500 hours of community service each.

Chris looked up. "Yes, that's me, I'm Mr Clarke". "Follow me please sir". The man in the pinstripe suit gestured to Chris to come with him. Chris got up and stood to his full height, towering at least a foot over his charge as he followed him along the bland corridor, turning right into a larger lobby area faced with a number of dark mahogany panelled doors. The man stopped outside one of them before knocking twice and waiting a moment in anticipation. He then pushed open the door and half entered, putting his head around the door. "Mr Clarke to see you". He stated, before stepping back and informing Chris that he was free to enter.

Chris did as he was asked and closed the heavy door behind him. John Barnes, the Probation officer was sat behind a green leatherette topped desk that sat in front of the middle sash window of three. Chris had met him before; an elderly man, stocky with a bald head and tanned skin as wrinkled as the leatherette on his desk, which Chris surmised was as a result of too many foreign holidays. Whilst Chris wasn't in the least surprised to see John there, he was somewhat surprised to see who was sitting opposite. It was none other than PC Taylor, and although today she wasn't in her police uniform, Chris recognised her immediately and his face lit up, almost even succumbing to a smile. "Have a seat Chris". John gestured. "And presumably you know PC Taylor here?". "Yes". Chris replied, holding his hand out and shaking hers in welcome. Whilst his by now were sweaty and clammy, hers felt warm and soft to the touch and Chris felt somehow reassured by her presence.

"Well you know the score by now Chris". Stated John, "We're here to discuss the terms of your probation and exactly how you are going to spend these 'five hundred hours' doing some good for the community. Chris noted the intonation in John's voice and the emphasis on the 'five hundred' made his heart sink. Chris had worked out that it would take him well over a year of Saturdays to work it off or over six months if he gave up his weekends in their entirety and he wasn't looking forward to it one bit.

"Except this time Chris, we may be able to do things slightly differently and I've got a proposition that I'd like to discuss with you". He took some notes out of a folder on his desk and scanned the top sheet briefly before placing it on the desk in front of him. Chris strained his eyes but wasn't close enough to be able to make out any of the wording. "First of all, tell me what's happening about this job of yours at Tesco's, are you still there?". John asked. "No, strangely enough they fired me!". Chris stated forlornly. "Anything else in the pipeline?". John enquired. "Not at the moment". Chris shook his head. "In that case, have a listen to P.C Taylor then as she's got something that may be of interest to you".

Chris turned and looked towards the female officer as she started to speak. "OK Chris, this is a bit unorthodox, but John and I have run this past the necessary people and we have indeed got a proposition that we would like you to consider!". She looked towards John who handed Chris the piece of paper from his desk whereby he had a quick scan through it. When he had a grasp of his contents, P.C Taylor elaborated; "From what I'm hearing Chris you were somewhat of a talented athlete in your younger days; two times UK under 16 cross country champion if I'm not mistaken?" "Yes, I used to run a bit". Chris replied. "Any reason you gave it up?". "Well when I had to move foster homes, things all got a bit hectic and the running got lost along the way as well somehow. John and Jenny; John and Jenny Ratcliffe that is, who were my foster parents at the time were mad keen on running, particularly John. He was a good runner in his day and used to take me with him when he went training. He encouraged me to take part in events and it was through him that I got quite good. Unfortunately though after that things got a bit unsettled again and I was moving from place to place so sort of drifted out of it". PC Taylor nodded in acknowledgement. "Well how would you fancy another crack at it?". John asked. "Another crack at what?". Chris enquired. "Running of course!". P.C. Taylor interjected. "I don't know I've never really thought about it". Chris answered, shrugging his shoulders "Well I've spoken to John Ratcliffe, who asked me to pass on his best wishes by the way, and he showed me some of your achievements in the athletics field and to be honest Chris they are pretty impressive. You've obviously got some natural talent there, so it would be a crying shame if you didn't put it to good use!". Chris thought about the proposal in more detail; "So what would I actually be doing then?". He asked.

Between the two of them John Barnes and P.C.Taylor explained the proposition to Chris. On face value it did sound a bit bizarre and it was something that he had never really come across before. His options were limited however and given the fact that he had no job to return to, no settled home life to speak of and wasn't looking forward to carrying out a years' worth of community service he decided that he had little to lose by giving it a try. A week later he formally accepted and had signed the necessary paperwork to enable the plan to be put into operation.

Chapter 10,

"This course is a bit shit isn't it?". James Freeman leant across and whispered to Martin as the two of them were sat at the back of the class doing their best to try and look interested. James was sat fiddling with his phone, attempting to find anything that would provide a few moments distraction and respite from the tedium of the day. The morning coffee break had long since passed and the two were trying hard to reach the next milestone of the lunch break before dropping off entirely. Martin was struggling to keep his eyes open but looked up to acknowledge James with a wry knowing smile. Both had been 'asked' to attend the mandatory Customer Relations training and neither had managed to muster up a good enough excuse to wriggle out of it. The course was being delivered by two Human Resources and Customer Relations 'experts' specially drafted in for the day to a cold village hall just outside Exeter. After the introductions, the cohorts were informed by one of the senior managers how lucky they were to have secured the services of two such 'experts'. Martin certainly wasn't feeling lucky that morning though and after the participants had been ritually subjected to a series of 'death by PowerPoint' presentations, he was feeling less lucky with every second that passed. Martin hated PowerPoint. 'what's the point' would have been a more appropriate description in his eyes. It appeared though that PowerPoint had become the standard default for anyone that didn't have the nouse and charisma to stand up and deliver something off their own back without subjecting the audience to mind blowingly pointless slides of graphs, bar charts and pie charts purely for the sake of it. Martin may have been somewhat of a dinosaur, but his approach was completely different, being able to deliver a witty and engaging half hour presentation with notes written on a piece of paper not much larger than a postage stamp.

As time wore on all Martin could hear was a dull monotone droning noise coming from the front of the room. It's said that the average adults' concentration span is around twenty minutes, but Martin was struggling to get anywhere near that today and even twenty seconds was a hard push. Martin's thoughts drifted, he looked around the bare brick walls of the building and wondered just how many bricks they actually contained. He wondered if counting them would be moderately more interesting than enduring the further delights of the course; well it couldn't be any worse could it! The cold of the building and the uncomfortable plastic seats were the only things preventing him from falling asleep but as he looked around the room he noted that several his colleagues had somehow managed to overcome these particular obstacles and appeared to be sleeping soundly. Some were hiding it better than others, but some were blatantly asleep, open mouthed in full view of the facilitators. It reminded him of scenes from the House of Lords that he had seen on TV with copious quantities of elderly peers of the realm fast asleep in the background when a debate was taking place in open view of the cameras. The two 'experts' must have seen them sleeping but perhaps like Martin they didn't actually care anymore. They were being paid to deliver the training so what did it matter to them if people were asleep or awake. Someone a few seats down from Martin started to openly snore only for the person next to them to give them a swift nudge to wake them up. Martin laughed to himself, resisting the urge within to do so out loud.

James, being a rather canny individual, had noted well before the first break that the course was a complete waste of time and shortly after the presenters had moved on to 'dealing with difficult customers' his cup of tedium had runneth over. He headed out of the room to take an 'urgent' phone call after his distinctive 'meowing cat' ringtone filled the room, much to the others amusement. Martin slipped out to the 'toilet' shortly after. It was apparent that the two ladies taking the course both knew little about the reality of customer relations other than the theory of it. They had never actually had to run the gauntlet day in day out of dealing with angry customers; but here they were preaching the 'gospel according to the textbook' to the staff of the organisation who had to deal with this day in day out. Martin and James had the dubious pleasure of carrying out similar jobs in different areas of the organisation and knew what it was like in the real world which was a million miles away from the rose tinted one the two instructors were living in. The two were reunited having both found solace in the adjoining kitchen area, each presuming that no one would be too worried about their absence, if indeed anyone had even noticed that they were gone!

"Hi Martin, cup of tea? The kettles just boiled". James puffed his cheeks out and gave a large sigh, shaking his head in despair. Although the two didn't know each other particularly well they were certainly on the same wavelength about the pointlessness of it all when it came to work and the never ending daily drudge of wading through treacle to try and get even the simplest tasks completed through the never-ending stream of bureaucracy policies and red tape. "Yeah go on then, why not indeed. You managed to sneak out with an urgent phone call then?". Martin observed. "Well not really". James replied, "I'll let you into a little secret shall I?". He confided to his colleague, giggling to himself like a guilty schoolboy. "When things get a bit heavy going, I just play one of my ringtones on the phone and pretend that someone is calling me. I then just get up and walk out, it works every time. Once you're out no one really misses you. If you had a look around the room most of them were asleep anyway from what I could see of it". Martin smiled, it was nice to meet a kindred spirit. "Nice one!". After the usual moans and groans the conversation soon moved away from work and turned to the weekend and what they had planned. Martin knew that James was into his running so told him about his exploits in the parkruns and how he was going to take part in his first 10k race later that year.

James was significantly younger than Martin, indeed at 32 years old Martin had nearly twenty years on him and could even have been his father. Martin remarked as much before jokingly assuring him that he wasn't. Well not to his knowledge anyway! Having sported similarly long hair in his younger days, James reminded Martin of a younger version of himself and was of a similar stature and build but perhaps an inch or so shorter. James was a bit of a maverick when it came to work and had a distinctive style all of his own. He seemed to get away with things that others couldn't, invariably dressing in jeans and a t shirt, often emblazoned with a logo of some various rock group or another. Today's T shirt of choice was a retro Iron Maiden 'Trooper' design which the majority would have deemed wholly inappropriate for the work environment. Whilst others, Martin included, had succumbed to the more socially acceptable regulation collar and tie coupled with a pair of smart trousers, James had carved a different furrow and was certainly an unconventional conventionalist! Martin had seen photos in the local media of James running; his trademark red and white bandanna tied around his head and his long dark hair flowing in the wind. Today he was repeatedly brushing it aside from his forehead with a flick of his wrist only for it to fall lazily back down over his dark brown eyes again. "No bandanna today then!". Martin observed. "Ah you've seen the photos as well then!". James replied with a smile. "No not today, that's mainly for running! I can use this to my advantage though as well". He stated, pulling his hair down over his forehead and onto the tip of his nose. "Brush this forward and no one even knows you're in there let alone asleep or awake. Nobody can say anything about it these days can they, what with political correctness and all that, I could come in with my hair dragging along the ground and no one could do a thing about it! May slow my running down a bit of course and there's always the possibility that I could trip over it as well, so I think I'll keep it in check a bit. I may be glad of it later though if this course doesn't perk up a bit!". Martin laughed, and indeed it was the first time he had really laughed at work for some considerable time.

"So how long have you been running then?". Martin enquired of James. "Probably four or five years now, I would have thought". James replied. "I used to be quite a good runner at college and in my younger days I ran a bit for 'Team Bath' which was the Uni I went to. You know how it is though; start work, get married and then life takes over doesn't it, there's never enough time to do the things you want to do for yourself is there. I got back into it though through a friend of mine who was a member of the Summerfield Roadrunners; went out with him a few times, got a bit fitter again and really started to enjoy it. And the better I got at it the more I enjoyed doing it. I look after the training side of things now and know a bit about it as I did a degree in sports science before I ended up working here. And before you ask how I managed to end up here, don't ask! It's a long story and even less interesting than being back out there!". He stated, gesturing to the other room. James explained a bit about the club to Martin and told him about their facilities, what nights they trained on and what different things they worked on at any given time. Martin had a bit of an insight from his playing days, but it appeared that things had moved on a bit since then. "You should come along sometime, you'd love it". James concluded. "Don't forget, we meet every Tuesday and Thursday, we're a friendly bunch and everyone is welcome, well as long as they pay their subs anyway!" He smiled.

The two finished their tea and subsequently took it in turns to slip back into the room, James first followed a few minutes later by Martin. The two chatted some more over lunch before enduring the afternoon session and joining the inevitable stampede for the door once it was all over. "Don't forget to come along next Tuesday". James shouted after Martin as he beat a hasty retreat out of the door. On the journey home Martin reflected on the conversation and decided that he would at least give the club a try to see how things went.

The following Saturday was again parkrun day. "Only one more sleep to go Dad!". Abi exclaimed as the three sat down to their Friday night meal of fish and chips, cooked by Martin's own fair hand. Well, taken out of a box and placed into the oven by him anyway! "It's not Christmas again is it?". Martin enquired. "No… one more sleep until parkrun Dad". Abi explained, holding up her phone proudly displaying the Facebook page that proclaimed the information. "Ah right, I see! Max do you fancy coming along tomorrow?". Martin asked his son, eager for him to join in with his and his daughters exploits. There was however an emphatic "No" from his son. "Looks like just you and me again then Abi!". Martin exclaimed.

Chapter 11,

It was just before 7 pm when Martin pulled his car up into the car park. The building it contained certainly looked more impressive than he had imagined; two storeys high with a resplendent partial stone and partial rendered front façade sporting an aluminium stair case and aluminium and glass balcony above the main entrance doors overlooking the car park and rugby pitch beyond. There were several other vehicles already there that night, but Martin couldn't see James' camper van amongst them. Rather than go in unannounced he decided to sit in the car and wait a while to see if James turned up. He fiddled with the radio, flicking between the channels but couldn't find anything to his taste. He ultimately shoved in a CD; Status Quo; Aquostic, to while away the time and provide some easy listening motivation. After about ten minutes or so and listening through tracks one to four, Martin switched off the CD player half way through 'Whatever you want' and decided that he would proceed in anyway. There wasn't much point in his eyes to have driven the twenty-mile journey only to turn around and head back home with the night's entertainment having consisted solely of listening to a few tunes in a random car park. He got out of the car and felt like a kid attending his first day of school again, only this time he didn't have the comforting hand of his mother to pat him on the back and wish him well as she waved goodbye to him and watch him walk innocently into the abyss. He swallowed hard, wondering why he should have been so nervous; fear of the unknown perhaps. 'Come on Martin don't be so bloody stupid, you're a grown man'. He told himself as he headed across the car park towards the front door.

As he approached and was on the brink of entering, a red and white VW T4 campervan turned into the car park. Martin immediately recognised it as James'. It was his pride and joy and did indeed look immaculate with its five spoke alloy wheels, red pearlescent paintwork and distinctive white stripe down the side. James had purchased it two years previously for just under £30,000 from a local VW dealer with a high spec conversion and a full-service history. It had all the bells and whistles on it including leather upholstery, leisure battery, swivel passenger seat, fitted fridge, cooker and sink, built in storage, reversing sensors, central locking, side bars & bike rack. Martin was later to get the guided tour from James who looked after the machine better than he did his own kids and quite possibly loved it more too!

Martin turned and headed towards the vehicle and upon approaching it James alighted wearing a red and white t shirt that matched perfectly the colouring of his camper van with a VW logo on the front. Martin raised his eyebrows and had a small chuckle to himself. As well as a black pair of running shorts and his trainers, James was also sporting his trademark bandana.

"Bloody hell!". James stated as he greeted Martin in surprise. "I never actually expected you to turn up!". He smirked. "Well you know how it is". Martin replied, thankful that James had arrived and that he didn't have to go in on his own unannounced. "Most people say that they will but then never bother do they! So, on that basis I thought that I'd give it a go rather than wonder what might have been! I'm glad you've turned up though as I wasn't really looking forward to going in on my own and introducing myself to a load of strangers!". Martin admitted. "Well good on you for turning up, and don't worry about this lot they're all friendly and don't bite. And remember that strangers are merely friends that you haven't met yet!". James put his hand up to high five Martin. "Come on let's go in and I'll introduce you to everyone".

As they reached the front door, James took out a key from the inside pocket of his shorts and unlocked it. "There's a few of us who have keys". He explained to Martin. "But if you turn up any time on your own just ring the bell and someone will let you in. Although having said that, there have been times in the past when rather than let me in they've chucked a bucket of water over me from the balcony up there. There are a few jokers in the pack here, but you'll soon get used to who they are if you decide to come along more regularly. We're upstairs". James gestured to Martin as he turned left and headed up the staircase that greeted them. "I wasn't really expecting anything quite so grand to be honest!". Martin exclaimed. "I don't know if you saw the pitches across the road, but we share this with the rugby club, and the football club as well so there's three main clubs using it and contributing to the upkeep. It also gets let out for functions and stuff as well, the main room's through there". He paused on the stairway and pointed back down to a set of double mahogany fire doors that led through to the main function room, complete with dance floor, bar and kitchen area and adjoining toilets. He turned and proceeded up the stairs. "I think it was built initially with a grant from lottery money though as I don't think the income from the 50 or so spectators of the local footy and rugby on a Saturday would have been quite enough to build this somehow! I'll give you a bit of a tour later if we get time. In through here". He stated, as the two reached the top. The door opened onto a lobby area with three doors off of it. James stopped and turned to Martin, lowering his voice slightly as the low buzz of conversation could be heard coming from one of the adjoining rooms. "We're a bit late tonight…. well I am anyway, to be honest I'm nearly always late!" James chuckled. "I'll take you in though and introduce you briefly to the others before they start heading out onto their various training runs. Generally, Tuesdays are speed training nights, but it does depend really on whether there are any particular races coming up and what anyone is aiming towards. I don't suppose you really know at the moment what you want to do, do you?". James asked Martin. "No not really, I'll be happy just to join in with one of the groups to see what they do". "I tell you what". James declared. "I'll introduce you briefly to the others and then we can have a bit of a one to one session on the treadmill to see what you are capable of. Once we know that I can work out what group you are going to fit into best. No good putting a tortoise in with a hare is there or vice versa for that matter. You'll get the best benefit really by running with people who are around the same pace or preferably slightly faster than you are, so we'll try and gauge where you are at so you can get the most benefit".

The door opened to reveal a large room; one side set out with various chairs and tables and the other with several pieces of different gym equipment. Martin noted at least three running machines, a couple of cross trainers and numerous various other items of apparatus, some occupied and some not. Various groups of both male and female members were scattered around the room either chatting, stretching or generally working out. Martin's eyes flicked around the room and of the twenty or so occupants he was seeing if there was anyone there he recognised. There wasn't initially but out of the corner of his eye he could see the outline of a familiar silhouette walking towards him. He turned to see that it was Dave Macready who was heading over, hand outstretched and beaming from ear to ear. "Hello mate". He stated shaking Martin's hand. "Got your passport! You're a long way from Bridgetown!". Martin smiled back at Dave, pleased to see both a familiar and friendly face. "I didn't realise you knew old 'Speedy' here Martin?". James enquired. "Well sort of". Dave interjected. "I know him from behind anyway, which is the main view I get of him over at Bridgetown parkrun on a Saturday morning. If you want to know which group to bung him in James, make sure he's in with the first team as he's fairly quick! I'll catch you both later". Dave turned to re-join a group of five males who looked as though they were just about to head out for their evening session. James looked at Martin as the two of them stood there. "You generally beat Speedy in the parkrun then?". He enquired, somewhat surprised. "Well I wouldn't say that I 'generally' beat him, I have beat him on occasion, but he's also beaten me plenty of times as well. I think you could probably say that we are of a similar ability". Martin replied modestly. "Well". James enthused "Dave is certainly no slouch when it comes to running so if you're up with him already that's certainly a good start".

Dave put his hand up to Martin as he and the four other males exited the room and Martin did likewise in response. James then went around meticulously introducing Martin to the other members there that night. Martin was a 'faces' person and whilst it was highly likely that he would recognise all of these people if he saw them again, it was highly unlikely that he would actually be able to remember any of their names, no matter how hard he tried.

After the introductions and a ten-minute warm up on the treadmills, James decided to take Martin out for a one to one session to see what he was capable of.

The two headed out of the building and onto the streets of Summerfield. "I'm going to take you on what the club call the 'streetlights' route". James announced to Martin as the two headed out of the club's headquarters. As it was relatively dark James decided that it would be best if the two of them stuck to a route that James and the club used regularly; a 5k jaunt that circumnavigated the town but was predominantly lit by street lights so that they could see where they were going. James showed Martin his warm up routine and after an initial 10 minutes running at an easy pace James decided that it was time to ramp it up a bit. "OK Martin I'm gradually going to increase the pace a bit now for a kilometre or so to assess where you're at. If it's too fast for you let me know". Martin nodded in response and James increased the pace, looking at his watch regularly to see how fast they were running. He started at a four and a half minute per kilometre pace which the two both felt comfortable with, before increasing it to four and a quarter and then four minutes per kilometre. "This is a 20-minute 5k pace, are you OK with this?". James asked Martin as the two of them ran along the main street through the town centre side by side. "Yes, that's fine". Martin responded. James increased the pace again up to 3.45 per kilometre. Martin was breathing smoothly, exhaling on every fourth stride and he knew that he still had a lot more to give. When operating at full capacity his breathing would intensify to exhaling on every third step and he wasn't anywhere near that yet. He was however when James increased the pace again and Martin could sense that James was nearing his limit, a fact borne out when he pulled up around 200 metres prior to the athletics club and bent forward with his hands on his knees gasping for air. Martin too stopped. After a few minutes James looked up, his face still distorted in pain. "OK." he spluttered, still panting, "I think I know which group I need to put you in!"

Martin hadn't particularly liked running in his younger days, in fact, if asked he would probably have said that he hated it. He had done it in abundance of course as part of his football training but he saw it more as a means to an end rather than as a sport in itself and was merely something that he had to endure in order to get fitter so that he could improve his football skills and keep competitive. This time around it was different though, it was as if the running was almost something spiritual, something that lifted the soul and took him to a different place, a place where all the troubles and woes of everyday life were swept aside, and his mind was free of the burdens and shackles of work, his troubles and the trials and tribulations of life in general; and the further and faster he ran the better he began to feel.

Following a few visits to the club Martin would now run at every given opportunity; before work, after work and sometimes even in his lunch break. He had set routes that he had mapped out of different lengths ranging from 5k through to 10k and half marathon distance. He had specific hills of different gradients for hill work and leg strengthening and a specific set kilometre along the sea front for his speed work. This was his favourite run. He would run from home the mile and a half or so to Wildewater beach and then run along the sand to Wildewater village where he would stop his watch and carry out some one-kilometre speed runs along the front. There he could really let rip, really put the hammer down and run for all he was worth with every sinew in his body straining to propel it faster than it had been before. He did this numerous times; sprinting in one direction and then jogging back, sprinting again and then jogging back, time and time again until his lungs were bursting and he was spent of energy and had no more to give. He would then jog home at a steady pace before carrying out at least ten minutes of stretches as James had instructed him.

As part of his training Martin was also continuing his parkruns on a Saturday morning and to him and Abi it was somewhat of a ritual that had become engrained into their weekly schedule. They both loved the competitive nature of battling not only against the other athletes but also against themselves and trying to better their own times. They also loved the spirit of friendship and camaraderie that existed between the athletes; they all wanted to do well but also encouraged each other and were genuinely pleased when others they knew had done well too. "There are no egos here!" a fellow runner had stated to Martin after completing the run one Saturday morning, and he was certainly right! Martin's progress had now meant that he was regularly a top three finisher although he had never yet actually won the race. He had come second to Rob Williams on a few occasions but never yet come close enough to trouble him. There was one morning; the day before the local marathon, that some of the quicker runners weren't participating in the parkrun and Martin's usual time would have possibly given him a first-place finish but that particular morning him and Abi were helping out as volunteers with Abi marshalling and Martin handing out the finish tokens, so it wasn't to be.

Martin by now had all his running gear sorted out on one small shelf on his wardrobe; three pairs of shorts, black; three pairs of long compression socks, black and grey; two pairs of short running socks, blue; two running vests, teal. two long sleeved running tops, luminous yellow. Along with these essentials there were a few additional T shirts of assorted colours as a back-up; all folded and stacked neatly next to two pairs of identical bright blue Nike running shoes which Martin meticulously cleaned after every race and training session, so they always looked in pristine condition. This shelf in the wardrobe was now by far Martin's favourite and although it only made up about ten percent of his wardrobe, he wore something from it in around ninety percent of his spare time. Today was no exception and after taking off his work clothes he decided that due to the temperature today was a day for the long compression socks and long sleeved luminous yellow top. He donned the attire before heading out of the door and closing it firmly behind him.

Today was a 10k day and as he headed out into the cold evening air and sucked a lungful in, he looked up in awe at the purple evening sky above with the sun setting behind Lundy island in the distance. It felt good to be alive.

# Chapter 12

Mike Shannon arrived at the club in plenty of time that Tuesday evening. James was already there to let him in and gave him a hand in setting up his equipment; a laptop and a projector and an old-fashioned flipchart on a tripod. By the time the remainder of the club members had arrived the seats had been neatly assembled in rows facing the front of the room and the projector was wired up and ready to go. After helping out with the teas and coffees in the kitchen Martin and Abi settled down in one of the middle rows, with Abi on the end of the aisle and Martin seated next to Dave Macready.

"Evening everyone". James announced as he was stood on the makeshift stage at the front of the room adjacent to the somewhat rickety projector screen that looked as though it had seen better days. He hoped it would at least see out the evening. "Tonight we've got a bit of a treat for you and I'd like to introduce you all to Mike Shannon; one of the country's leading coaches and renowned sports scientists. Mike has trained some of the world's top athletes in his time and we're very lucky to have secured his services for tonight's event. So, without further ado I'll hand you over to the legend that is Mr Mike Shannon". James stepped back; hand outstretched to welcome Mike to the stage to a polite round of applause from the attendees. "Not so sure about 'legend' James". Mike raised his eyebrows and smiled as he looked at James and stood up to face the eagerly awaiting audience.

The room itself was jam packed that night and Mike had indeed attracted a lot of attention. The club had widely advertised the event and despite the £10 admission fee to cover expenses there wasn't an empty seat in the house with chairs packed in tightly from front to back, to the limits the fire regulations allowed.

"Good evening Everyone". Mike stated authoritatively as he took the stand. "First of all I'd like to say what a pleasure it is to be here this evening and thank you for inviting me along. I hope that you'll find the evening both entertaining and informative and that you'll leave with just that little bit of extra enthusiasm for your running than when you came in!". Mike went on to introduce himself, giving a brief overview of his upbringing, his qualifications, and his background as an athlete. He spoke freely about some of the races he had won and subsequently about some of the athletes he had successfully trained. It read like a who's who of anyone who was anyone in the world of athletics and it wasn't long before those watching were nudging each other in the side, in awe of the man stood in front of them. James' 'legend' tag didn't appear to be too far off even if Mike was too modest to admit it. James had known him from way back when Mike was working part time as a tutor at Bath University and the two of them had struck up a friendship and ran together regularly. James had been there for Mike when his parents were killed in a motorway accident some years previously and the two had kept in regular contact. Mike had helped James out with training and advice whenever he could and unknown to James, he would also be donating his fee for the evenings talk back into the club's coffers such was his determination to put something back into the sport at grass roots level. "This evening though I'm going to talk to you about sports science". He eventually announced after the introductions were completed and an interesting tale or two had been delivered.

"What even is sports science?". Abi whispered to her dad. "Well I know what Weird Science is!". Martin replied, recalling to himself the 1985 film of the same name whereby Kelly Le Brock played the stunning beauty created on a computer and brought to life by a pair of geeky high school outcasts, thus bringing them overnight kudos as the coolest kids in school! Abi looked at him somewhat puzzled. It was the kind of off the wall bizarre comment she had come to expect from her dad, but it didn't prevent her shaking her head in despair. "It was a film back in the day…never mind I'll explain it to you later!".

Martin protested. 'They don't make them like that anymore!' He thought, smiling to himself at the memory of the film. "Dad I swear you're losing it!". Abi riposted.

"So, for those of you wondering what sports science actually Is". Mike continued. "It's all about how a healthy human body works… or should work!". He teased, peering around the room over the top of his titanium framed Cartier glasses at the various shaped and sized individuals sat before him. "How it works during exercise that is and about how physical activity promotes and enhances the health and performance of an athlete from the basic individual cells right through to the whole body make up". Mike started on the main bones of his talk and it was soon apparent from his demeanour and knowledge of the subject that he spoke with a great deal of gravitas. He paced up and down, first taking his glasses off and waving them in the air as if to extenuate his already grand hand gestures, before placing them back on again only to remove them again moments later to do likewise. Occasionally he stopped and faced the audience, pausing for thought and stroking his well kempt beard before pacing back and forth again. "Psychology, anatomy, biomechanics, all these areas are incorporated within sports science and there's a growing demand now from athletes and coaches to work with sports scientists if they want to reach the top of their game. Indeed, without one it's unlikely an athlete will ever be able to achieve their peak performance however hard they tried." "That's where you've been going wrong all these years then Speedy!". James smiled to Dave Macready as he dug him in the ribs. Dave smiled sarcastically in return. "Yes, very funny!".

Martin meanwhile was listening intently to the man now stood still again for a moment at the front of the room. Mike was around 5' 10" tall and of slim but athletic build. He wore a crisply ironed blue and white checked shirt, open at the neck over a pair of black chinos. His shoes of choice today were a pair of size nine and a half black leather brogues, hand made in England by shoemaker of note, George Cleverly. On his left wrist he wore his favourite Rolex Submariner time piece, a non-date version which was a present he had bought for himself many years ago after he had won the marathon at the 1976 summer Olympics in Montreal when he was 24 years old. His greying hair was still thick with an expensive cut and on his tanned and well-lined face he sported a neatly trimmed goatee beard. And then there were those glasses; Martin could tell they weren't your typical two for the price of one at Specsavers but wondered whether there was actually any lenses in them or whether Mike just used them solely for the purpose of aiding gesticulation. He would have to have a closer look later! As well as knowing his facts and figures though, Mike's talk was delivered with copious quantities of wit and humour thrown in thus making it both informative and entertaining. Martin had no desire to count bricks today and it was obvious that Mike was a well versed and prolific public speaker and the experience the viewers were having this evening showed this to be the case. Top athletes that were well known household names were slipped effortlessly into the conversation and it soon became apparent that there wasn't really anyone of note that he hadn't worked with and had some involvement in their success. In short, the guy oozed charisma from every pore!

"Today though". Mike stated. "We aren't going to get too carried away with world class athletes; to me, you are the most important athlete in the world right now". He pointed to several individuals emphasising the fact. One of whom was Abi and she felt a warm sensation come over her knowing that someone of Mike's stature held her in a similar esteem to some of the world's greats. I'm going to talk to you about two basic things that effect all of our running and what we can do to make ourselves just that little bit quicker". Mike looked around the room at the audience sat in front of him. "Can you put up your hand please if you don't want to run any quicker than you do now?". Mike enquired. Martin looked around to see that no hands had been raised in the air. Mike smiled, a big broad toothy grin. "Excellent, that's what I though; it's good to know that we're all on the same wavelength then. Of course, we all want to be able to run faster don't we! After all we're all athletes aren't we; yes, we all have different abilities but we all get the same feeling of elation when we beat our personal best times don't we. That could be something as simple as knocking a mere one second off your parkrun time on a Saturday morning, but it still feels good doesn't it?". Heads were nodding around the room; people were on his wavelength and it was apparent that Mike had got everyone hooked.

"Now I'm going to talk to you about the two most important things for every runner. Anyone got any idea what the first is? I'll give you a clue, it's in this box". He stated picking up a large plain brown cardboard box from the floor and shaking it vigorously before placing it on the table. "Shoes". someone shouted out from the audience. "Well done that man!". Mike pointed to the person who had responded; Mark who was sat attentively listening in the back row. "Yes shoes". Agreed Mike. "Fairly obvious really isn't it? Think about when you're running and how many times during a race your feet are in contact with the ground and the pounding you are putting your body through. You need a decent pair of shoes to suit your running style and posture; to cushion your feet, to protect your ankles, your shins and knees and the shock to your body in general. Anyone here suffered from shin or knee trouble?". Mike asked. Quite a few nodded. Dave Macready put up his hand. Mike acknowledged him. "Well to be fair Dave, in your case it's probably just old age and there is only so much a pair of shoes can do!". He joked. Dave took it in the spirit it was intended, and Mike proceeded to take a number of different pairs out of the box, passing them around the audience to examine their different weights and styles.

"People often ask me what the best make of running shoe is. Anybody got any idea what that might be?" Mike gazed out at the audience in anticipation. "Nike". "Asics". "Adidas". People shouted out various shoe makes randomly from the floor. Mike acknowledged each one before pointing to the next person and asking them to do likewise. There was a momentary lull as most popular makes had been exhausted. "Anyone else?".

Mike asked, looking around the room. A few more names were shouted out before Mike responded. "OK, I want you to all stand up for a moment please". The audience did as they were asked. "Now take a look around the room at your fellow athletes. What do you notice?". "They're all ugly!". James shouted out. "Touché!". Stated Dave. "That's as may be!". Mike laughed, "But as well as being ugly you are all different; you're all different heights, different weights, different build, different sex; all which will have a bearing on what type of shoe you need. Just because Mo Farah wears a certain type of shoe it doesn't mean it's the best shoe for everyone! It may be the best shoe for him but not necessarily for you. Having said that though in his case it's more likely that he's wearing the latest model laden with carbon fibre soles because some firm is paying him an extortionate amount of money to do so!". Mike laughed. They all looked around and acknowledged the fact that they were all indeed of significantly different stature.

"OK". Mike continued, "So we've established that we're all different and that we all need different shoes, but how do we know which shoes are best for us? What do we need to look for when we go shoe shopping?". Those two words; 'shoe' and 'shopping' immediately resonated with Martin and led him to instinctively think of his wife and her passion for shoes; countless pairs of shoes, many of which she never even got to wear. "Mum used to like her shoes Dad, didn't she?". Abi whispered to him, knowing exactly what he would have been thinking at that moment as though she had some form of sixth sense that was wired directly into his brain. Perhaps it was just the father and daughter bond that had led them to know instinctively what the other was thinking at any given time but sometimes it was just uncanny. "She certainly did Abi!". Martin replied with a warm smile of the fond memory. His daughter gently squeezed him on the leg as if to say, "I miss her too Dad".

Mike went on to show a video that explained the merits of different types of shoe and the differences between pronation, supination and a neutral gait when going through the running cycle and how different styles were designed for the various ways in which different athletes run. Once this was finished Mike explained that any good store with knowledgeable staff should be able to assist in the process of guiding you towards the most suitable shoe. "Make sure they understand what it is you are looking for though but if in doubt and you are currently injury free in your current shoes my advice would be to stick with what you have or a newer version of the same model if it works for you. If you're looking for an increase in overall speed carbon fibre soles are something to seriously consider but they can be a bit on the pricey side. If any of you are struggling though and getting pain in your shins or knees always seek some advice from your GP".

James announced that there would be a short break before the second part of the talk and the tea and coffee along with custard cream biscuits were dutifully dispensed from the kitchen by the willing volunteers. After ten minutes or so of the audience generally putting the world to rights the second part of the evening commenced.

"Everyone OK?". Mike enquired, once the hum drum had died down. "I hope I didn't bore you to death too much during the first part of the talk!". He smiled. Mike looked around the room and did a quick head count confirming that there were no empty seats so at least no one had left or snuck out at the break! "So now we've got the basics taken care of and you've all got the right shoes for your running style. Shoes that will give you the correct support and give you the best chance of running well and preventing injuries as your feet pound along on that hard tarmac for mile after mile putting untold pressures on your joints!". He emphasised the fact by jogging to and fro along the room bringing his knees high into the as if he were reenacting a scene from Monty Pythons Ministry of Silly Walks. "Now, the next thing you need to do is train". He proffered, as he stopped and once again faced the audience, using the forefinger of his right hand to push his glasses back up on his nose. "Given that you all belong to this lovely club, I'd hazard a guess that you're probably all on some sort of a training programme already, depending upon what level you're at and what events you have coming up; am I correct?". There were several nods from around the room. "Even if you come to the club once a week and jog for 5k around the block, that can still be classed as training, right?". Again, there were several nods of agreement from around the room. "But what is the actual point of all this training, why do we do it?". Mike looked around the room. "To get fitter". Someone shouted out. "Yes". Mike agreed, nodding his head enthusiastically. "Anything else?". There was silence, no one wanted to commit for fear of saying something stupid. The majority knew that it was obvious that you had to train if you wanted to run faster or run longer distances or be competitive in races but weren't quite sure what Mike was fishing for. "What's the fundamental most important thing we need to improve if we want to run faster?". Mike asked. Again, there was silence. "Anyone?". Mike enquired. "Increase muscle performance". Old John at the back replied. "Yes, in a way". Mike confirmed but what's that one thing we all need to increase to run faster?". Again, there was silence. Mike took his marker pen and turned to his flipchart. He wrote the words; 'VO2 MAX' on it in large letters. He turned to face the room. "Anyone ever heard of 'VO2 max?". He enquired. There were a few nods but also a lot of puzzled faces, Martin's amongst them.

"Let me explain". Stated Mike. "As VO2 Max is one of the most important contributors to being able to run fast, particularly over distance. Think back to when you were at school and your sadistic ex rugby playing sports teacher announced that next week it was going to be cross country week. What sort of thoughts were going through your mind? It was probably somewhere on the spectrum between; 'Great I can't wait' to 'Sod that, I'm going to be off ill next week!'. Some kids loved it in my class and for others it simply filled them with dread. If you were one of the slower kids, you probably wondered how the hell it was that some of those kids were running so much faster than you. You were all the same age and probably of a similar build back then and you were busting a gut to run as fast as you could but getting nowhere near them. They seemed to be flying around the course with virtually no effort and when they were at the end they were barely out of breath whilst you and the rest of the mere mortals were left reaching for the oxygen cylinder! Some of you may have been lucky enough to be one of those fast kids and have grown up into the finely-honed specimens you are today!" Mike beamed with a smile and a hint of irony in his voice. "Even now though as you've got older you'll probably have been training for all you're worth and there always will be some guy, or gal of course, of similar age and size that will just waltz past you with seemingly no effort and beat you to the line. How is it that two people of roughly the same age, size and stature that train similarly can run at such different speeds?". Mike was pacing up and down the room again and was on a roll. "I'll tell you!". He exclaimed, answering his own rhetorical question before anyone had had a chance to interject. "VO2 Max!" He stated emphatically. "The Holy Grail of any distance running!".

Mike went on to explain that VO2 Max was the body's ability to use oxygen efficiently; measured in units of oxygen per kilogram of bodyweight per minute and that the higher the score you had the more efficient your body was at using oxygen. "The more efficient your body is at using oxygen the faster your muscles can work and the faster you can run. Simple!". He stated emphatically. He handed out some sheets of paper with a VO2 Max calculator printed on, based on race times and age so people could see theoretically how they measured up; announcing that he himself had recently done a test and was a '57'.

Mike paced up and down thinking about his presentation and where he was going next with it, getting the words ready in his head before he delivered them making sure he was able to inspire those sat waiting onto greater things.

Martin was looking at the chart and putting his recent parkrun times into it to see where he was. He noted that he wasn't too far off from where Mike was and although he was younger than the great man himself, began to wonder what he could have achieved if he had started running at an earlier age as Mike had done. He surmised that it was all about the football back then for him though and running was never really in the equation. Others were also fervently working out their scores according to the figures placed before them and comparing notes with their neighbours. After a couple of minutes Mike stood back in front of his flipchart. "OK, anyone think that they've got a VO2 Max of 90?". He asked, smiling and pointing to the figure at the top of the chart.  90 was the highest score on there so unless Mo Farah had snuck into the room whilst he wasn't looking there wasn't going to be a hope in hell that anyone would be anywhere near that score. Unsurprisingly no one raised their hands. "Now I'm not going to embarrass anyone by asking what your individual scores are but I'm guessing that you're all going to be somewhere around these middle figures, give or take". He stated, gesturing to the mid ranges of the table. "But what do you do if your score sucks? Do you just give up and say that I'm never going to be any good as I have a low VO2 Max, so I might as well call it a day? No of course you don't!" Up and back the room Mike strode purposefully once more.

"Luckily, it's not all bad news and if you do have a low score, or indeed whatever your score is for that matter, there are a few of things you can do to improve it." "Yeah like get a heart transplant!". A voice from the back shouted. It was old John again, who ironically many thought had already had a heart transplant! "It's a thought!". Mike laughed, nodding his head in agreement with John and taking on board the proposition. "And it is true that VO2 Max is largely genetic; some of you may have heard the term; 'a runner's heart or an athletes' heart?' that simply means you have a large heart with the capacity to pump blood around the body efficiently. This could be inherited from your parents so if you can run fast you may have them to thank for it. Fortunately though the heart can also be enlarged through regular aerobic training as it's a muscular organ and responds just like your other muscles do when exercised regularly". Mike was on a roll again; he paced up the room, swiveled on his brogues and returned to the middle of the room before continuing.

"So, the first thing you can do is run more, or swim more or cycle more or whatever it is that floats your boat; do more of it and you'll find that you become more efficient. The more you do it, the more you repeat something, you'll find that your body will do it more economically and eventually you'll be able to run at a faster pace for the same amount of effort".

"The second thing you can do is to perhaps try losing a bit of weight. I know it goes against the grain a bit when we're trying to build up our muscles, particularly for the guys, but it's no coincidence that most of the top athletes have got less meat on them than a butcher's pencil. They're stick thin aren't they without an ounce of extra weight on them than they require?".

"And finally, remember you can't run faster unless you actually run faster, if you know what I mean!". Mike paused, looked to his right and raised his eyes in thought, pursing his lips together contemplating if the words he had spoken had come out correctly. "What I mean by that". He emphasised. "Is that it's no use going for your runs at a steady pace and then expect to blitz it at your next race; you have to get your body used to running faster and the only way to do that is to actually run faster than you do now. Makes sense really when you think about it! Do it gradually though, in short intervals first then build it up. But let's remember it's not all about winning is it; it's about having fun, keeping fit, and running with your mates. 'Run for fun and anything else is a bonus!' Thanks for listening and good luck to you all for whatever the future holds".

Mike passed out some training notes that he had tailored for a number of different abilities and provided a link to his website which contained a further plethora of information on the subject to be perused at the attendee's leisure. James wrapped up the proceedings, thanking Mike to a rapturous round of applause before the delegates retired for further refreshment.

"Custard creams aren't exactly what you would call the healthiest of options are they Dad for a group of runners that have just been told that one of the ways they can improve their speed is to lose weight!". Abi joked to her father. "No not really Abi!". Martin replied. "I don't think it will stop me from having a couple more though!" He stated as he dunked one of what had always been his favorites into his awaiting brew.

"Hi you two, how's it going then?". James enquired of Martin and Abi as the club members milled around chatting after the evening's presentation. "Yeah we're fine". Martin stated, as Abi smiled and nodded in agreement. "And you?". "Yes, all good here mate thanks, all in all it was quite a successful evening really". James looked around to see a plethora of club members vying for Mike's attention and in his usual inimitable way Mike was doing his best to try and attend to all their needs; handing out training plans, answering questions and posing for selfies with his Olympic medal "Listen mate, I'd like you to have a chat with Mike as I've told him a bit about you and he'd like for the three of us to get together if you're OK with that?". "OK, yes I suppose so!". Nodded Martin in agreement, somewhat surprised at the request, "He certainly seems to know his stuff doesn't he." Martin continued, looking over towards Mike who was now literally being mobbed by the other members. "It looks like he may be a bit busy for a minute though!". "Yes, there's probably not going to be time tonight unfortunately, I might have to scrape him up from the floor later by the looks of it! He's back in town again in a couple of weeks' time though and if you're OK with it I'll see if I can set something up for one of our club nights; we can use one of the other rooms, so we get a bit more time with him to ourselves". "Sounds good to me". Said Martin. "Just let me know when you want me, and I'll be there".

"I think I'll have to get you an award Dad". Abi stated to her father as the two of them bade their goodbyes and headed down the steps of the building towards the exit. "What do you mean Abi?". Martin enquired, turning towards his daughter with a somewhat puzzled expression on his face. "Well perhaps we could call it 'Mike's aspiring young pup of the week award!' as he must have taken a shine to you for some reason to want to meet on a one to one basis!". "Yes, it does seem a bit strange doesn't it.... it's probably got more to do with James than Mike though I would have thought as Mike doesn't even know me really does he! Still nothing ventured, nothing gained I suppose and anyway what's the worst that could happen". 'Where you're concerned Dad, it could be anything!' Abi thought to herself.

Chapter 13

Abi Rose first that Sunday morning. Upon opening the front door she was greeted by the early morning sun already blazing like a beacon in the cloudless blue sky. She looked out beyond the garden and the rose bushes gently swaying in the breeze, towards the beach and to the Atlantic rollers breaking along the shoreline, caressing and tugging the infinite grains of sand back into the watery depths. She yawned and extended first her left arm and then her right towards the sky and arched her back to stretch out her limbs before returning inside to knock on her dad's bedroom door. "Looks like it's going to be a hot one for the race today Dad, how are you feeling, are you up for it?". Abi was certainly up for it, so much so that she had hardly slept a wink the previous night in anticipation. Martin on the other hand was out like a light, he glanced across at his alarm clock to see that it was only 7.30 am. "Blimey Abi it's a bit early isn't it, the race doesn't start till ten o'clock!". "Well I thought we could have a decent breakfast and then go for a bit of a jog around the block and do a few stretches before we go in. You don't want to be all stiff and unprepared, do you? I'm having some protein waffles; do you fancy some?". "What's protein waffles?". Martin responded, curiously. "Well they're like normal waffles but made with powder from one of my protein shakes". "I may try one, but I think I'll stick to my tried and tested Weetabix and a banana with a strong black coffee. Give me ten minutes to wake up and I'll be there". Martin flicked on the radio that was sat on the bedside cabinet. It was an old Roberts Radio with a black leatherette front and a broken aerial that had belonged to his wife. He remembered how she had chastised him some years earlier when he broke the aerial whilst listening to the football commentary and as such the reception on it wasn't that good anymore. Despite its reception issues he didn't have the heart to throw it out as it reminded him of her and the times they had listened to it together. He fiddled with what was left of the aerial and tried to tune it in to his preferred station as best as he was able but was still incapable of getting the volume absolutely right with the dodgy controls. He eventually settled for too loud rather than too quiet and listened to a couple of tunes before the presenter announced; "And good luck to everyone running in the Bridgetown 10k today, keep an eye out for our very own intrepid reporter Tyler Anderson who will be running the race. Tyler reliably informs us that he will be trying to beat his previous best time and aiming to break the fifty-minute mark. He'll also be interviewing some of the runners prior to the start of the race and if he's got the energy; which is highly unlikely, afterwards as well. So, this next song is for Tyler and indeed all of you running in the Bridgetown 10k today. Good luck everyone". 'Keep on running' by the Spencer Davies Group rang out. Martin turned it up slightly and shouted to his daughter. "Hey Abi, this song is for you!". She came into the room and started to sing and mimic the act of running in slow motion. "Apparently that BBC presenter guy Tyler Anderson is running in it as well, he's hoping to break 50 minutes; I think he must be crawling around!" "Hey, behave, that's not a bad time, I'm hoping to get somewhere near that myself". Abi reprimanded her father before returning to the kitchen. The song finished, and Martin got out of bed, and headed to the Kitchen himself to make some breakfast. Abi had finished making her waffles, so Martin had a taste; upon realising that they tasted a bit like cardboard though he turned his nose up at them and decided to stick with his original plans. The two of them finished breakfast, tidied up and then headed out the front door for a light jog around the block to loosen up a bit leaving Max still fast asleep in bed.

"How far do you want to go Abi? We don't want to burn ourselves out before the race, do we?". "Just around the block, probably about ten minutes or so, then well do a few stretches and drive in. We can also go into the park first if you like and do a bit of a pre-race warm up there as well". The two did a brief lap of the neighbouring streets, discussing as they ran how they felt and what their tactics were going to be for the day. Abi planned to run at a set pace that she hoped would bring her in at just under the fifty-minute barrier. She had her gps watch to record her pace as she went along so she knew what she had to aim for and had worked out the pace she needed to keep up. Martin had run with her on several occasions and knew that a pace of five minutes per kilometre was something that she was more than capable of on a good day. Martin's tactics for the day however consisted simply of running as fast as he was able for as long as he was able and to try and keep up with or overtake as many of the other runners as he possibly could! The two pinned their running numbers onto their T shirts, bade their goodbyes to Max, who was still in bed but promised to be there at the finish to watch them come in, and left the house.

After parking up in the supermarket car park, it became evident that there was indeed a lot of interest in the race. With over 1200 competitors alone, coupled with numerous spectators and race officials all milling around on the Quay awaiting the start, any spare room to warm up was certainly at a premium. As such Martin and Abi retired to the park for some last-minute preparations and wishes of good luck before ultimately returning to the Quay and taking their places in the starting line-up. Martin edged his way as close to the front as he was able, eventually getting the cold shoulder from the some of the other athletes who quite rightly weren't willing to give up their place to any late arrivals. He wasn't as far forward as he would have wished but felt he had pushed his luck as much as he had dared and resigned himself to the fact that this was as good as it was going to get. Both pavements were now lined with spectators and the start time was edging ever closer. Abi settled for a spot nearer to the middle where the crowd was a bit thinner, realising that it would ultimately take her a while to pick her way through the throng.

The Bridgetown 10k was renowned as being a particularly fast race and the course itself was predominantly flat with only two slight elevations and drops, both fairly close to the start of the race, just beyond Bridgetown's ancient longbridge. As such it attracted a number of competitors both locally and nationally trying to run a fast race and beat their best times. As the athletes continued to jostle for position on the starting grid Martin clearly noted the plethora of different vests and T shirts being worn by athletes from the numerous running clubs represented that morning. As well as some of the familiar sky blue, red, and green and white striped vests from the clubs of the local area, he also noted running vests emblazoned with such names as; Southampton, Barrow and Furness, Enfield and Haringey, and even one from the Edinburgh Athletic Club. A few rows in front of him Martin noticed a young slim male wearing a distinctive yellow vest with a black stripe down the side coupled with a contrasting pair of black shorts with a yellow stripe. Martin immediately recognised it as the strip worn by athletes from the Newham and Essex Beagles, the club of none other than a certain Sir Mohamed Muktar Jama Farah, or "Mo" to his friends and just about everyone else in the country! Martin had no idea how tall Mo Farah was but the guy in question looked quite short at about 5' 5" tall so in his mind Martin had immediately dubbed him 'Mini Mo' as was his want. Martin felt it an honour though to even be lining up with someone from the same club as the great man himself and supposed that it wouldn't be long before he saw the familiar yellow and black vest disappearing off far into the distance. Not far from Mini Mo was the ever present black and white striped vest and familiar silhouette of top local man Rob Williams.

The start time was rapidly approaching, and the gent tasked with starting the race ascended the two steps and took his position on the podium that had been fashioned from scaffold poles and plywood adjacent to the road. He started to bark some instructions to the athletes but by now Martin was totally oblivious; he had butterflies in his stomach and was suddenly nervous, fearful of lack of success and what others would think if he didn't do well. Today he would be unable to enjoy the run for the sake of running as he did with his training runs. There was the added pressure of the competition and pitting himself against others and pushing himself as far as he was able; and in some cases, perhaps just that bit too far. He remembered some tips that he had gleaned from a TV programme some weeks earlier in relation to stress and how top athletes managed to turn the stress of a race day to their advantage by recognising it as a trigger for excitement rather than fear, thus boosting the adrenaline levels in the body. There were so many thoughts going around in his head that he wasn't quite sure what he was feeling; excitement was probably in amongst them somewhere but so too was that deep over riding fear of failure coupled with his own expectations of what he was able to achieve. He wasn't sure if there was anything there though that he could use to his advantage however much he may have wished.

He took one last look at the athletes around him: tall, short, male, female, all clad in their own specific attire and probably feeling similar thoughts to those of his own. No doubt they too all had their own dreams and aspirations as to the outcome of the race and had put in the necessary hard work to give themselves the best possible chance of doing well. As for the outcome of the race however, at that point no one knew, and it was down to everyone to do what they could to make their own mark. Martin turned and looked back and could just make out his daughter some way behind him in the middle of the crowd. He put his hand up to wave to her, but it was apparent that she too was lost in her own thoughts prior to the start of the race and no doubt as keen as he was to try and do well.

Ultimately the time had come, the dull murmur dropped, and it wasn't long before silence fell upon the start line. The starter raised his arm and pointed his pistol into the air. Athletes were poised and ready; the majority with their finger planted over the start button of their GPS watch in anticipation; "Three…, two…, one" …. "Bang" the starting pistol signalled the start of the race and the athletes burst into life.

The first of the athletes sped away immediately at the sound of the gun with those behind filtering along and over the start line, automatically engaging the timing chips embedded in their race number as they did so. Although Martin was fairly near the front, he noticed how far the front runners were already ahead of him as he turned left onto the Quay and surmised that there must have been at least fifty athletes preceding him. Mini Mo, Rob Williams and a highly rated local athlete, Mark Sampson, led the field on the opening stretch of the race as they ran parallel to the river. They had already opened a clear gap as they turned left across Bridgetown's ancient longbridge, after which the town's name was derived. They were almost half way across it by the time Martin made the left turn onto it, swinging out wide to avoid the numerous clapping spectators as he did so.

The ancient longbridge spanned the river near its estuary and had for many a year connected the old part of Bridgetown on the left bank to the newer part on the right. It was renowned as being one of the longest medieval bridges in England, made up of 24 individual arches all of differing size. Martin recalled to himself that the last time he ran across it was one New Year's Eve some years previous; a local tradition whereby revelers started off at one end of the bridge when St Mary's church clock rang the first chime of midnight and tried to get to the other end before it reached the twelfth. No mean feat for those that had achieved it given that the length of the bridge was in excess of 200 meters. Martin's endeavors' that particular night however hadn't gone quite so well and with the local council's ultimate realization that the mixture of excess alcohol and too many people running in a confined space was a recipe for disaster, it wasn't long before the events demise came about with the bridge being closed altogether on a New Year's Eve. An inevitable consequence of Health and Safety legislation taking precedent over people simply being allowed to enjoy themselves! Today though people were again running across it for fun. 'The next time I cross this bad boy' Martin thought to himself 'I'll be nearly at the finish.' He puffed out his cheeks and pushed on across the bridge, recalling to himself the New Year's Eve in question with a wry smile as he breezed past a number of runners who had gone off quickly but hadn't the stamina to maintain that pace for the duration.

It wasn't long before Abi too was turning left onto the bridge, engaged in her own personal quest for fortune and glory; or if not that at least a personal best!

At the end of the bridge the route swung left heading up the first incline of the course. Martin managed to kick on up the hill and passed two male and one young female competitors. He reached the brow of the hill and did a quick head count of ten athletes in front of him; just catching sight of Rob Williams' black and white vest as he disappeared around the corner at the bottom of the incline. He passed the first kilometre marker and looked at his watch; three minutes fifteen seconds per kilometre. Excellent by his standards but obviously not good enough to keep him in contention for the top spot. He hadn't quite anticipated the level of the opposition and after only a kilometre in was finding it difficult. He knew that he had to up his game to keep in contention and couldn't afford to let the leaders slip any further in front than they already were. The next kilometre was about consolidation, the initial adrenaline rush of the start and the jostling for positions had gone and he now had to get into a steady but hard pace, one that he could sustain for the rest of the race, but which would still leave something left in the tank for a sprint finish if it came to it. Up and down he went through the second incline but was unable yet to make any headway against his competitors and as he turned the corner onto the long straight road section ahead he sensed that there was already around 200 metres between himself and the leader. Martin consciously changed his breathing rate, inhaling on every third pace and exhaling rapidly on alternate left and right strides. He started to get into a systemic rhythm and could sense the gap slowly closing between himself and a group of three of the top local club runners who were running together pushing each other on. Martin eventually managed to catch them up and tucked in with them for a while, feeling the small benefit of running in with a group and soon visibly noticed that his addition had also spurred them on collectively to run quicker.

As they neared the halfway point at Meadowbridge where the course did a u turn, transitioning from the road onto the MeadowbridgeTrail and heading back towards Bridgetown, Martin could see the first of the athletes heading back. It was Rob Williams, about twenty yards or so in front of Mini Mo, who himself was a similar distance ahead of the third placed athlete, Mark Sampson. As the group of four neared the gate by the level crossing Martin caught sight of the other three athletes that were ahead of his group, one of them being the first of the female runners. At the water station just after the turn Martin grabbed an already opened 500ml bottle of Highland spring water and doused his head in the cool liquid, discarding his bottle once depleted. The other athletes rejected the option, not wishing to break their stride. Martin dropped to the back of the group and knew that the homeward 5k would have to be significantly quicker than the first if he was to be a contender, and he was already feeling the strain of the initial 5k. Running well however wasn't all about physical strength and he knew that many races were won and lost on mental ability and resilience. He felt his watch vibrate and steadied his arm to see his 5-kilometre time flash up on the screen. 'Not good enough Price!'. He told himself. 'Come on, you can do better than that!' He urged himself on. A friend had once told him that the secret of success was to tell your brain not to let your body know it's dying. Nothing could have been truer than that today; although Martin had no idea how to actually go about achieving this! The advice was sound enough but like an Ikea shelving unit devoid of instructions Martin had no idea how to go about putting it together. Martin's brain today though was as sharp as a razor and focused on the task in hand, refreshed and reawakened by the cool liquid that was by now running down his face and neck and mingling with the sweat already present on his teal running vest.

He gritted his teeth and consciously upped his pace, putting a few yards between him and his former running compatriots. He set his sights firmly on the athlete in front; the first female competitor of note he had come across in the field; her slim athletic body clad in white vest and blue shorts seemed to be flowing effortlessly with her long dark hair streaming behind her. As he got closer however he could hear her somewhat deep and erratic breathing and he quickly surmised that even though all appeared calm on the surface she too was hurting underneath and all wasn't as first appeared. He approached her on her left shoulder and as he did so could feel her trying to increase her pace. He glanced across to see the pain etched on her face. She glanced to her left feeling Martin's presence and although she was finding it tough, with gritted teeth and determination she tried to go again.  Martin however was in the ascendency and after running alongside her for a couple of hundred metres to gain momentum he could tell that she had little more to give and would have to settle to let him go. It was a shame as he was looking for someone that he could latch onto to push him on, but it wasn't to be and if he was going to make any further progress today, he was going to have to do it the hard way, by doing it alone.

The 6km mark came and went and following the turn the wind was now blowing directly in his face. He didn't really notice any advantage from it on the way out when it was blowing from behind him and although it was relatively light it still took him extra effort to maintain his pace whilst running into it, particularly during the not infrequent gusts that blew in off the river.

He focused on the track ahead, keeping his head up and his chest out, breathing in deeply during two strides and exhaling quickly during the third, trying desperately to suck as much precious oxygen in to his lungs as he was able so that his body could convert it into the kinetic energy it needed to propel him ever faster towards the finish line. Ahead of him on the straight one time railway track he could now see all the athletes in front of him strung out in a line. The clapping and cheering crowd lining the route spurred him on and a loud 'come on Martin you can do it!' shouted from an old school friend on the wayside gave him an extra boost of encouragement. He acknowledged them with a thumbs up, not having the spare lung capacity to acknowledge them verbally and risk losing the precious intake of a few millilitres of oxygen.

He quickly came alongside and subsequently overtook a runner from Cornwall before focusing the cross hairs firmly on a senior male competitor wearing the colours of Edinburgh Athletic Club; a white vest with two horizontal stripes, blue over black. 'You're a long way from home' Martin thought to himself, as he edged ever closer to the young blonde male, concluding that the runner in question must have fancied his chances of a achieving a decent position to have travelled the length of the country to get here. By now the front runners were flying and on target for a finish time of around thirty-one minutes. By rights Martin knew that he shouldn't be running this fast; it was at odds with his VO2 Max score of 57 which on a good day would have brought him home in a time of around 35 or 36 minutes. This wasn't a good day though, it was a very good day, and the further he ran and the harder he ran the more he felt his body flood with feel good endorphins; the bodies happy chemicals, activating his bodies opiate receptors and initiating an analgesic effect that made him feel like he was running on air. The pains in his legs and knees were gone, the aches and crakes were nowhere to be seen now and were just a distant memory as he was driving forward like an out of control machine whose engine was running at full speed, red lining and about to overheat and explode at any time. Except this was different, Martin could at last control the machine at will; he could turn it on and off again in an instant by the flick of a switch; in short, he finally knew what his friend meant, and he had now mastered the art of telling his brain not to let his body know it was dying. In fact, never before had he felt so alive as he did in that particular moment, not until he took the next step, and the next and the next, and with each one he felt more and more alive as if everything that came before just paled into insignificance, getting higher and higher on endorphins and the pure ecstasy of running. He left the blonde male trailing in his wake, veritably eating his dust, and was now reeling in the next runner like an angler landing the next big catch. This one was a big one, it was a prize specimen, it was local runner Mark Sampson. Martin was playing him, edging him ever closer and closer and letting the line out again to tire out his prey before reeling him in again, the ultimate aim to pull him from the sanctuary and safety of the water to aimlessly flap around on the ground until his lifeless cold-blooded body had no more to give. Martin now knew he had him; he was in his favoured position on the left shoulder of his prey. Mark attempted to kick on again, but it was no use; a pointless exercise as Martin was stuck to him like a barnacle on an ocean-going liner and he wasn't letting go. Mark tried in vain to kick again but Martin was closer to him now than his own shadow. 'Is that the best you've got!' Martin thought to himself, as he glanced sideways at the look of despair etched on Mark's face as he slammed the machine into top gear, adding insult to injury by switching on the afterburners at full tilt; pulling away with every stride and leaving Mark flailing in his wake as he did so.

Only three more kilometres to go; Martin knew that he had a quick finish but the two guys in front of him were certainly not your average everyday runners. These were class athletes who had run at national level and picked up first places in local runs like this for fun. Mini Mo and Rob Williams were now all that stood between Martin and the finish line. The two were around 50 yards ahead of him and now running together side by side. Martin knew that it wouldn't be easy to catch them with the relatively short distance left to make up the ground, but it was now or never, do or die, and he knew he had to give it his best shot. Mo and Rob meanwhile were pushing each other on and had just completed kilometre number eight in three minutes and five seconds which was an awesome pace even by their high standards. The previous year's winning time was over 34 minutes but these two were on target to smash that out of the water. Both running side by side, aware of each other's presence, the others breathing, and every tiny move they made, but ignoring each other completely and shutting everything out and focusing solely on their own race, wondering what the other had left in the tank and how it compared with their own reserves. Mini Mo had run under 30 minutes on two previous occasions, Rob had done likewise so on paper there was little to choose between them. Which one of them wanted it more today though that was the question that needed answering. One person who wanted it was Martin, and he was gradually closing the gap, running as if his life depended on it. At the nine-kilometre marker Mini Mo had expended his reserves and dropped off the pace slightly and it appeared to be local athlete and North Devon's finest Rob Williams who wanted it more and was once again going to take the honours today. Martin could sense Mini Mo flagging and caught up with him just before they got to the longbridge. As the two turned and hit it for the second time that morning Martin could see Rob around ten metres in front of him. He could even smell a waft of the Calvin Klein aftershave he had donned that morning lingering in the air as he ran into his slipstream. They were now only 800 metres from the finish and Martin knew that he would have to make his move now and really sprint for the line to have any chance. He changed up a gear and by the time he reached the end of the bridge he had latched on to Rob, not only smelling his aftershave but tasting it as well such was its liberal application. There were 600 metres to go to the line. Rob sensed Martin and made his move, Martin responded, digging deeper into his reserves than he thought possible, well beyond his lactate threshold and sapping every last ounce of energy his body possessed. Rob responded again but Martin threw in everything he had and put in one final all-out effort, pulling away a few yards. The noise levels from the spectators was rising and the crowd were cheering and clapping, and Martin knew that victory was now his. He turned to see how much distance he had put between him and Rob and as he did so he could see the look of panic and despair on Rob's face as the realisation set in that he wasn't going to win this one. Suddenly Martin realised that something wasn't right; he felt something that he had never done before; an overwhelming flood of empathy towards his fellow athlete. He shouldn't be coming home first, he knew that he wasn't a better athlete than Rob and he felt like an imposter. He hadn't done his time, he didn't deserve to win this, Rob was the top athlete in these parts not Martin. He switched off, there were so many things going around in his head and he subconsciously shut down and turned off the engine allowing it to freewheel the remaining distance to the finish. Rob passed him with around 50 metres to go and Mini Mo pipped him just before the line. Martin coasted through the finish line and looked up to the LED display to see his time of 30 minutes 15 seconds. He was exhausted and staggered through the finish funnel before lying down on the grass flat on his back breathing deeply trying to recover. He closed his eyes.

"You had me there, what happened?". Martin opened his eyes some time later to see Rob stood over him offering a hand out to pull him up from the ground. "That was your race!". He reiterated "What happened?". Martin shook his head. "No, I just didn't have the energy come the end unfortunately, it just wasn't to be. I'm more than happy with third place though and that time is a new personal best for me and much quicker than I thought I could run so all in all it's a pretty good day". "That was your race mate, you had the better of me and you know it". Rob could see that Martin wasn't telling him the truth, but he wasn't sure why. The other person who wasn't sure why was Martin himself, perhaps he just wasn't ready to be the person everyone wanted to beat, he wasn't sure. He did know though that he had run a good race, he was pleased with his time, ecstatic in fact, although he was too tired to let it show, and third place in a time of just over 30 minutes was more that he could ever have dreamed of at the start of the day. He also knew though that this race wasn't the end, in fact it was only the beginning. He knew that despite everything and all the effort he had put in today that he still had more to give, he could feel it. He also knew that there were only three occasions in his life that could have ever compared to the feeling he experienced when he was running that race; the first was the day he set eyes on his wife all those years ago in a local night club and the second and third were being there to see the birth of his children, and those were certainly very special times indeed! He patted Rob on the back as he walked away "Well done mate". He declared "Perhaps I'll catch you next time!". Rob put his hand up, smiled back at Martin and shook his head, still in disbelief at what had happened. Martin walked back down to the finishing straight to cheer his daughter home.

# Chapter 14

"Dad come here quick, you're on the news!". Abi shouted to her father later that evening. She was settled down in the lounge with her brother watching the telly. The three of them had just finished their tea and Martin was in the kitchen doing the washing up. He stopped what he was doing, put down the dish cloth and joined them in the lounge. "What is it?". He enquired as he entered. "Sit down here a minute". Abi gestured. Martin joined them on the sofa. "You know that guy from the TV was running the 10k today". "Yes". Martin replied. "Well they're doing a bit of a feature on the race in the local news. They've followed his progress through it and showed a few shots of him as he's been going around". "Not that he looks like much of a runner though". Max interjected. "He must weigh about twenty stone!". "Max that's a bit of an exaggeration isn't it, he's obviously just big boned!". His sister replied. "Anyway, they've just showed a shot of the first finishers coming in and you were quite clearly in the lead coming down the home straight Dad, but you seemed to ease off a bit at the end. That's not like you?". Max hadn't got there in time to see his dad finish and although Martin had told Abi and Max that he had finished in third place he hadn't elaborated on it any more than that. "Well you can't win them all can you!". Martin replied. "No but you could have won this one Dad, couldn't you?". Abi enquired somewhat puzzled. "I just don't think it was my time darling, not to worry, I'm more than happy with third place, not to mention a first in the 'old gits' category!".

The three watched some clips of the prizes being given out with Martin receiving his third-place trophy and one for finishing first in his age category. Martin turned to see the trophies sat where he had placed them on the sideboard, next to a photo of him and his wife on holiday in Ibiza. He smiled a knowing smile and rubbed his daughters head lovingly as he exited the room to return to his chores.

"Third place, that's bloody amazing!". James enthused. "Thirty bloody minutes and fifteen seconds!". It was shortly after 9am the morning after the 10k race and Martin had managed to gingerly make his way in to work despite the fact that his legs were barely functioning. They felt as stiff as boards; as if someone had snuck into his bedroom overnight and gaffa taped a length of four by two timber to each one as he slept. He could barely bend his legs at the knee. The actions of putting on his shoes and socks that morning wouldn't have looked out of place in the finest of comedy routines, with many aborted one-handed attempts to try and reach the end of his toes before 'mission sockable impossible' was finally completed. It seemed to take an eternity and he would never have believed that the simple act of bending over could have been so difficult. This morning he certainly felt the pain of every one of his 51 years on this planet. The endorphins and adrenaline that had carried him along so sweetly during yesterday's race had now drained from his body and all that was left was an empty shell and he felt like a shadow of the man he was less than 24 hours previously. He had been transformed from a veritable flying machine to an old man overnight and to top it all he had the mother of all headaches.

He picked up his cup from the desk and took a sip of the strong black coffee within; three spoonsful to try and kickstart his day but somehow it didn't seem to be having any impact. "Yes, it was a good day yesterday". Martin replied, somewhat subdued, "But to be perfectly honest with you mate I'm feeling like shit today! I can barely move my legs, I'm aching in places that I didn't even know existed and my head feels like it's about to explode. I could do with going back home to bed really and sleeping for about a week!". James laughed. "Nonsense mate, hair of the dog is what you need! When you get home tonight get your running gear on and go out and do a gentle jog around the block. Around 5k or so should do it and tomorrow you'll be feeling as right as rain again! You've heard of a recovery run haven't you, well that's what you need to be doing!". "I think I'll probably need resuscitation and recovery if I go out tonight and someone will probably find me collapsed in a crumpled heap on the pavement! Anyway, I'll see how I feel later, hopefully I'll loosen up a bit as the day progresses". Running was the last thing on Martin's mind and his immediate concern was that of how he was going to survive the day. "I've already spoken to Mike about your time mate". James continued enthusiastically. "And he's keener than ever to get together now; he can't believe you ran a 10k that quick!" "To be honest neither can I!". Martin replied. The two finished their conversation and said their goodbyes, with James planning to contact Martin again when he had arranged something with Mike. Martin saw out the day at work with the aid of a few painkillers and more cups of strong coffee. He gradually felt better as the day went on but even in the evening was still in no fit state to undertake James' suggested recovery run. He retired to bed directly after tea with copious quantities of ibuprofen gel applied to his legs and a couple more tablets to boot. That night he slept like a baby.

It was three days later, the Thursday evening, when James rang Martin again. "It's all sorted mate". He stated, in his customary enthusiastic manner. "He can do it next week, either Thursday or Friday but we've got to get back to him tomorrow to let him know which one!". "Let who know what exactly?". Martin enquired. "Mike of course, he wants to get started on you as soon as he can!". Martin wasn't particularly over enamoured with the fact that someone wanted to 'get started on him' and joked with James that it made him sound like a three-course meal there to be eagerly devoured, but he knew where James was coming from! "Sorry bad turn of phrase!". James apologised. "What I should have said is that he's really excited about the prospect of working with you!". It was all moving a bit fast for Martin and he wasn't really sure where all this was going and even if he had the will or inclination to work with Mike, or anybody else for that matter. After all, to all intents and purposes he was a man in his fifties who currently had a lot of aches and pains, who had done relatively well in one local race and who had a few parkruns under his belt. He stated as much to James. "Yes, I understand where you're coming from mate but there's no pressure, all he'd like to do is to spend one day with you and put you through your paces and run through a few tests. Are you up for it?". "Can I have a think about it first?". Martin enquired. "Yes of course you can mate, as I say there's no pressure and no one is going to be holding a gun to your head or push you in to doing anything you don't want to. All I'll say though is that you know who this guy has trained in the past and if he's interested in you he must see some potential. Most runners would give their right arm to be trained by this guy, me included". James proffered. "May make the running a bit more difficult though eh!". Martin replied. "Hilarious!" James dead panned. "Have a think about it, sleep on it and let me know in the morning". "Presumably he's coming down to the running club then?". Martin asked. "Ah no, sorry mate, I didn't explain properly did I, he wants you to go to Bath University next week as they've got all the facilities there. He said that he wants to wire you up like Frankenstein's monster and pass massive charges of electricity through your body to see if it will make you run faster!". "Very funny!". Martin replied. "Are you going to come along with me?". "Try stopping me mate!". The two spoke for a while longer before winding up the conversation. "Thanks for ringing James, I do appreciate it you know, and I am grateful, but it's just that you've taken me a bit by surprise that's all, I'll sleep on it though and give you a ring tomorrow morning".

Sleep was unfortunately the last thing that Martin did that night and come the next morning he was no further forward towards deciding. Yes, he was excited, but he was also wary that if something sounded too good to be true, it usually was, and after all why him? There must have been hundreds, even thousands of athletes out there in their prime that could wipe the floor with him. He showered and got dressed for work and thought about the proposition further as he made the car journey into work, arriving in a blur, not recollecting any of his journey as if the car was on autopilot. He turned on his computer, made a cup of coffee whilst waiting for it to load up and returned to his chair to ponder what his next move was going to be. Oh well what's the worst that can happen! He thought to himself as he picked up the phone and started to dial James' number.

## Chapter 15

"Thomson, Flight 6278 to Gran Canaria is now boarding at gate seven, that's Thomson, Flight 6278 to Gran Canaria, gate seven, thank you". Martin picked up his bag and headed down the terminal towards gate 7 along with the throngs of other passengers all heading off for their one or two weeks of winter sun. It felt strange for Martin to be in an airport on his own. In fact for him it was a first and he wasn't sure that he liked it. 'What if something happens to me on the plane, who'll take care of the kids?'. He thought to himself. It dawned on him though that they weren't actually kids anymore, they were grown adults who were perfectly capable of looking after themselves without his intervention. He had simply become too engrossed in looking after them and catering for their every need to notice. The time had seemed to pass so quickly and with so many things to do all the time the years had whizzed past so fast that it had all become a blur. 'I'm doing this with their blessing'. He reassured himself, but he still felt guilty about leaving them, such was his strong paternal instinct. Tears had been shed earlier when they had both accompanied him on the journey to the airport, both wishing to be there to start him off on his journey and wish him well with his endeavours. He wondered if they were now still feeling the same way he was or if they were sharing the car journey home already planning their first house party in their old man's absence. The thought that it was probably the latter gave him some consolation and he had a chuckle to himself at the prospect. After offering up his passport and boarding pass for inspection, he navigated his way through gate seven and headed out onto the tarmac towards the awaiting Boeing 737 that was going to be his and one hundred and eighty-eight other passengers' mode of transport for the journey down to Gran Canaria. It was a relatively new plane; the type with the upturned wing tips and looked resplendent in its white and blue livery. The distinctive roar of the CFM built engines could be heard loud and proud as Martin headed out towards the rear steps and made his way up to the plane.

Martin paused at the top of the steps as he always did and placed his hand over the top of the plane's rear door. He patted the palm of his hand twice onto the metal outer skin of the plane, noticing the thousands of tiny rivets that held the outer panels onto the planes superstructure as he did so. Martin wasn't superstitious; however, this process was something he always undertook before boarding a plane ever since his first flight to Florida some thirty years previously. He thought about the physical size and weight of the plane and how theoretically it should have been impossible that something of such an immense size could even get off the ground. Thankfully for him and the other passengers it did, and it wasn't long before the plane was in its preferred location and cruising at 35,000 feet above the ground. A utopian environment above the clouds and the weather and in a place where it never rains and never snows and there are no storms. A place in existence for time immemorial simply waiting for the moment that mankind eventually caught up and invented the aeroplane to whisk passengers across the globe through the void that existed between heaven and earth.

Martin had an aisle seat on the plane and was sat next to an elderly couple heading off for their annual two-week winter break. They had informed Martin that they had done this every year for the last ten years and had always stayed in the same hotel; even stayed in the same room if they could; room 510 on the fifth floor, because it was a corner room and had the largest balcony in the hotel! It was lost on Martin though and he wasn't really in the mood for making small talk. He was polite though, as ever, and nodded and tried to say yes and no in the right places so as not to upset them or spoil their holiday but all he really wanted was a bit of peace. "I think perhaps we should let this young man have a bit of a rest now dear". The husband eventually stated, realising that they had talked non-stop to Martin for about an hour. Martin smiled, and the lady proceeded to pull out a somewhat dog-eared book of crossword puzzles which the two of them knuckled down to try and tackle.

Martin put his head back onto the headrest and closed his eyes. The last few weeks had been a bit of a blur and he tried in his mind to unravel and comprehend the events in the preceding months that had got him onto this plane to Gran Canaria and what he was actually going to do next.......

"Oh well what's the worst that can happen!". Martin thought to himself as he picked up the phone and started to dial James' number. He took a sip of his coffee, it was steaming hot, made his preferred way with one sugar and whitener rather than milk. The taste was sweet to his lips and as he gazed out of the window, phone in hand, he placed his cup down and began reflecting on his life up until that point. It had been a bit of a mixed bag really, consisting both of some very high highs and some very low lows. He thought about the low points; the death of his parents and grandparents were lows but the death of his wife was a real low; a deep abyss, a chasm that he had found impossible to clamber out from. It was something he had never really got over and was never likely to. He thought about the high points; generally things had been good in relation to his childhood and upbringing, yes, his family wasn't blessed with enormous wealth, but they had always been happy and had a tight bond. He had never gone hungry or wanted for anything and his parents' stance of always making sure his and his brothers needs were catered for before their own was one that he had taken forward into adulthood himself and applied to his own family. His footballing career hadn't really taken off as he may have hoped but there was many a young kid that would have dreamed of playing professionally even at a lower league level, so at least he had that to be thankful for and would always have the memories. There were his children of course, he had nurtured them and was proud of them and loved them more than anything else in the world. They had been the main focal point that had kept him going through the long dark days and nights when he was at his lowest point and ready to give it all up and throw in the towel. Together they had traversed the long dark tunnel and emerged into the glimmer of light at the other end ever stronger as a unit. All these thoughts were whirling around in his head and he wondered perhaps if he should just be contented with his lot; continue with his work and his job until retirement and ride away graciously into the sunset. Age was catching up with him however and after much deliberation he finally concluded that it was now his time. He didn't want to ride away graciously into the sunset, he wanted to go out with all guns blazing; more 'Sundance', as in 'Butch and', rather than 'sunset'. And so, it was decided, he looked at his watch to note the time. It was 9;47 am. '9;47, flying over heaven', he remarked to himself to etch the significance of that moment into his brain. He entered the remaining digits into the phone and pressed dial. After a few rings James answered. "Hi James, it's Martin; OK I'm in, let's do it!". He stated emphatically.

Chapter 16

After Martin had mulled things over in his mind and decided to accept the offer of undertaking the tests at the university, James made the necessary arrangements and that following Friday, the two of them made the trip up. Martin was doing the driving and entered the Bath University postcode into his Sat Nav before he set off from home so as not to get lost. He made a slight deviation from the programmed route to pick up James from his house in Summerfield and the two of them were soon on their way. Martin was both excited and apprehensive at the prospect of the day that lay ahead, but his own emotions paled when compared with those of James', whose excitement and enthusiasm soon managed to extinguish any doubts that Martin may have had. James of course knew the way to Bath University off by heart through his former years as an employee there and was looking forward to getting back again, if only for a day's visit. "You won't be needing that one Martin!" James stated, pointing at the Sat Nav stuck to the front windscreen of the car. "It's all up here!". He marvelled, pointing to his head. The car continued up along the M5 and crossed the Devon border into Somerset heading towards the county's largest city. "Got your passport Martin?". James enquired with a smile as they hit the sign proudly proclaiming, 'Welcome to Somerset'. The two laughed as they read an impromptu addition that had been bolted on by some practical joker in relation to the recent flooding the county had experienced; 'Twinned with Atlantis!'

As they neared the University, James instructed Martin to turn off Claverton Down Road and onto the main entrance road of the campus. "We'll need the East car park". He explained to Martin. "So we'll need to go down here". He pointed. "Past the sports training village and bear right; then the car park is on the left". 'Sports training village!' Martin thought to himself. 'All sounds very grand!'. It was indeed grand, as was the whole campus and as they drove down the entrance road Martin was in awe of the size of the complex and the buildings and facilities that were unfolding in front of him. The first building of the University, a large self-enclosed square building initially known as the 'preliminary building' was completed in the mid-sixties and was coincidentally around the same age as Martin. James remarked as such as they pulled the car up into a free parking space in the already busy car park. He also informed Martin that the 50 plus-year-old building looked in significantly better condition than he did, something which Martin found hard to argue against! The campus now though had expanded at least twenty-fold since its opening and had grown to become the well-respected institution it was today.

Martin caught a glimpse of the impressive athletics track as the two grabbed their bags and headed in through the entrance of the East building to the reception where they were politely greeted and logged in and given their visitor passes. They were asked by the receptionist to take a seat and informed that someone would be with them shortly.

It wasn't long before that someone arrived and the double doors to the reception area swung open as a big bruiser of a guy swaggered through and made his way over. Clad in black trousers and a short sleeved white shirt, Martin immediately noticed his physical presence, not only his height but more so the size of his arms that he surmised must have been around the circumference of a six-inch drainpipe. Martin observed how the sleeves of what should have been a loose fitting casual white shirt were digging into the bulging biceps beneath, almost cutting off the blood supply to his lower arms. Martin stood up and raised himself to his full height, but he was dwarfed by the man that stood before him. James however had met him before and stood up to greet him. The man mountain in question was Lee Stockley, an ex-Saracens and Exeter Chiefs pro; a fellow student that had been at the University when James was there in his younger days and now held a position as a lecturer in sports science and head coach of the Bath University rugby team. "Hi James, I've been expecting you, long time no see!". Lee beamed, as he stepped forward to give James a big old man hug, enveloping him in his grasp. "Hi mate, good to see you again, looks like you've grown a bit since we were last here!". "Well not in height but probably in girth a bit!". Lee boomed, as he held his hands to his stomach and rubbed it up and down to emphasise the fact that now his playing days were over it was harder to keep the weight off. "This is Martin, he's the one Mike has been telling you all about!". Lee held out his hand towards Martin, nodding his head in appreciation. "Good to meet you mate, I've heard a lot about you!". Martin extended his hand towards Lee and felt it shudder under his grasp. He was only relieved that Lee hadn't afforded him the same greeting as James for fear of crushing his somewhat fragile frame. After the formal introductions had been made and pleasantries exchanged, Lee led the two of them out of the reception and down an adjacent hallway. He continued past the indoor athletics training area and the fifty-metre pool towards the sports training village. The three entered one of the common rooms off of the main corridor where Lee made them all coffee whilst they waited for Mike's arrival.

It was around ten minutes hence when the man in question arrived. "Apologies that I'm late." Mike stated, as he entered the room. "Car trouble I'm afraid! Anyway, we're all here which is good, and I trust that you've had a chance to meet Lee and have a bit of a chat with him?". Martin and James acknowledged that they had, and Mike pulled up one of the comfy chairs set around the room to join them. "OK.". He stated, now sat directly opposite Martin. "You know why you're here Martin don't you?". "Well sort of!". Martin responded. "You want to do a few tests and things to see how quick I can run?". "Well yes that's part of it!". Mike replied. "James here though thinks you've got the ability to achieve something in the world of athletics, despite being, shall we say…. of more senior years!". "I see, does he now!". Martin responded. "James is usually a pretty good judge of things so when he comes to me with something like this I take notice". Mike went on to explain what was in store for the day. "What I'd like to do with you this morning, if you're in agreement of course, is run you through a few tests. After that we'll have some lunch and a bit of a rest and later on I'd like to put you out on the track with some of the students we have here to see how you measure up to them. I know it's only a snapshot and everything can't hinge on one day, but it will give us a good idea of whether it's worth considering you for an accelerated training programme. Of course, it's entirely up to you if you want to pursue it or not, our purpose is merely to see if we think you've got the ability to do it". "OK, sounds good to me, I'm here so we may as well give it a try". Martin responded enthusiastically. "What sort of tests are we going to do?". "Over to you Lee, you'll probably be able to explain that side of things a bit better than I can". Declared Mike, handing the proverbial baton to his man mountain of a colleague. It was one of Lee's functions within the university to carry out the tests in question and he was indeed conversant and proficient in the set up and workings of each. "Three things this morning Martin; the first will be a V02 Max test. We'll wire you up to the machine and put you through your paces on that one to see what your capacity is. You'll then have a bit of a rest and we'll do what they call a 'beep test', have you ever heard of that? Martin hadn't, but when Lee explained the concept to him of running end to end in a room to the timings of a beep that got ever shorter, requiring the athlete to increase speed to keep up with it, he recognised the format. "Oh, and we'd like to take some videos of you on the running machine as well, so we can have a look at your running style and your pronation to see if there's anything there we could improve upon. After all that we'll have some lunch and you can relax for a couple of hours to get your energy back. At five o'clock I want to get you out on the track; get you warmed up again with some jogging and stretching exercises before putting you in a race against some of the students here". Martin was taken aback, it had all been planned with military precision and he was humbled to know that these three had gone out of their way to sort it all out just for his benefit. "Do you think you'll survive the day Martin!". James joked. "Oh, and by the way James." Lee interjected; "I wouldn't get too smug as you're going to do it all with Martin as well, so we've got someone to compare him against! And don't say that you aren't dying to have a go cos I know what you're like!". Martin and James headed off to the changing rooms to don their running attire and returned shortly after whereby Lee led them into Room AV12 which was where the first test was to take place.

The room itself was relatively small and clinical looking at around twelve feet square with whitewashed walls and a grey linoleum floor. Two 'Matrix fitness' commercial treadmills sat in the centre of the room, both independently wired up to their own lap top which in turn were sat on two small desks either side of the room. The treadmills faced a large window which overlooked the road that Martin and James had driven down to get to the complex.

"OK, one machine for each of you then, choose your weapons!". Lee exclaimed. Martin took the one on the right as they faced the window and James the one on the left. The two stood on their respective machines and Lee instructed each in turn to remove their running tops whilst he wired them up with the necessary electrical monitors to be able to record the readings from the test. There were eight in all for each athlete, stuck to the chest and upper body at strategic locations so that heart rate and other vital signs could be plotted directly onto the computers. The two donned their tops once again after the process was complete and Lee placed a mask over each of their faces, asking that they test them out whilst walking slowly to ensure the air was getting through to them. The masks were also wired up to the computers to monitor the various volumes of gasses that each was inhaling and exhaling.

Lee then gave them a briefing of what to expect during the test. "I'll get you to do a short warm up." He explained. "Walking briskly for three minutes to get the legs moving. Then I'll be increasing the speed of the machine and the incline every three minutes after that, so it will get progressively harder as the test goes on. There will be seven three-minute stages in all, so the test will last for twenty-one minutes. Just keep running for as long as you can, but if you've had enough at any time just hit that red button and the treadmill will slow down and stop in line with your pace. OK if you're ready and there are no questions then we'll begin?". Both athletes nodded in agreement. Mike took his position next to James' machine and Mike made one final check of the laptops to see that all was in order before setting up next to Martin. "OK; three, two, one, begin!". Lee instructed the two to commence.

Phase one was indeed a steady walking pace for three minutes before the incline was raised and the treadmills set for seven miles per hour. Both athletes jogged along steadily and after another three minutes the incline was again raised with the speed increased to seven and a half miles per hour. On through the next increases of eight and eight and a half miles per hour and Martin was finding it comfortable. Both he and James had run much quicker than this for relatively long distances and were at relative ease. Martin was enjoying the view out of the window, across the road and beyond where he could see a small lake in the distance with a water fountain squirting copious volumes of the liquid high into the air. "Heart rate 178 beats per minute Martin". Lee advised him. "Nine miles per hour now please Mike". Lee gave the instructions and the next stage commenced. Lee shifted positions and had a check of both computers to ensure all was in order. Martin glanced over at the computer to see a range of different graphs displayed with lines that seemed to be increasing ever upwards as the test progressed. He had no idea of their significance though and just dug deep and continued with his running. It was suddenly starting to hurt a bit now and he glanced to his left to see that James was noticeably struggling a bit too, lolling from left to right rather than running in his usual effortless style. "Heart beat 182......187......189", Lee advised Martin as the load on his body and lungs intensified, forcing his heart to react by pumping more oxygen enriched blood to the muscles to keep them working. Mike and Lee were giving words of encouragement to the two and shortly after Lee finally announced that they were entering the last phase of the test. "Nine and a half please Mike!". He stated. It wasn't necessarily the speed they were running at but more so the incline which made it so hard. Nine and a half miles per hour was the equivalent speed of running a 10k race at around thirty-eight minutes or a marathon in under two and three quarter hours. This would have been no mean feat on the flat but when running on a hill of a moderate incline it was near on impossible to sustain that pace for any significant length of time. Martin was by now sucking in air like it was going out of fashion, trying to keep up with the relentless pace the treadmill was flying around at. "197....199......two hundred beats per minute!". Mike exclaimed, as Martin's heart was now on overtime. "Two minutes to go, come on Martin you can do it!" Lee shouted out as both he and Mike were giving encouragement to the two athletes, urging them to keep going. Those two minutes seemed like the longest two minutes of Martin's life but he somehow managed to keep going and breathed a heavy sigh of relief when Lee finally counted down the last seconds from ten to zero to signify that it was all over. Martin placed his hands on the arms of the running machine to support his weight and gradually slowed down to a walking pace before eventually stopping altogether. He was by now panting heavily and sweating profusely. He was unaware that James had stopped before the test concluded and as Martin turned to him he saw that James had sank to his knees on his machine. Mike was bent over him attentively checking he was OK.

"Well that was a nice little warm up!". Lee smiled wryly, once the two had recovered enough to be able to stand upright again. "Are you both ready for the next test then?". Luckily for Martin and James he was only joking and the two of them were afforded the opportunity to rest easy for a while and have a sit down whilst Lee and Mike analysed the results.

They weren't long coming, and Lee printed out four copies of each so that they could all have a look. Whilst a lot of the information didn't mean a great deal to Martin or James, their overall VO2 Max scores; the main purpose of the test, were received with much interest. James' score was read out first and at sixty-eight was fantastic. However, when Martin's came in at an unbelievable eighty-one, Lee was unable to hold himself together. "Bloody hell!". He exclaimed, as he quoted the two digits printed out on the piece of paper in front of him, squinting to ensure that he hadn't in fact misread them. "Excuse my language but eighty bloody one!". He exclaimed again. "I've never tested anyone who's come out that high before; eighty one!". Lee was flabbergasted. James gave Mike a knowing nod as if to say, "I told you so!". Mike examined his copy of the results in closer detail and asked Lee out of curiosity if there was any way that the test could be wrong and that the results had been artificially inflated in some way. Lee assured him that there wasn't. "Eighty one Mike, come on that's pretty amazing isn't it!" Lee enthused.

Martin modestly congratulated James on his score knowing how good an athlete he was in his own right and that as a young man in his prime with a score in that region he could still easily have got the better of Martin on a good day. Martin wasn't getting overly excited about his own score though; indeed, he was the kind of person who never got too excited when things were going well but also never got too low when they weren't. He liked to try and rub along at an even pace, knowing that if you got too elated about something it wouldn't be long before somebody inevitably came along to knock you off your perch. In his eyes if you didn't get too high you didn't have so far to fall. To him at the moment though that eighty one was just a number; it didn't mean he was any different a person than when he woke up that morning, and he still had the same throbbing pain in his right knee and his lower back was still playing him up. At least he knew one thing though; despite the fact that he had a known heart murmur and a slightly irregular beat to it, it was certainly functioning well for a man of his age, and he at least had that to be thankful for.

Mike, Martin and James retired to the small kitchen area in the complex to make a cup of tea whilst Lee set up the room for the second test. It was somewhat easier than the first and merely consisted of one of the running machines being set up with four video cameras focused on it from all angles so that a film could be taken of each athletes running cycle for analysis. Martin and James spent ten minutes each on it whilst their actions were recorded onto the laptops for analysis. After this had been completed and there was another short rest period, the two athletes were led into the sports hall of the complex where they were to be subjected to the 'beep' test

Lee led them through the double doors that led into the hall, its sprung wooden floor adorned in multiple coloured lines depicting the courts of the many sports that were played within its walls. The hall was empty today though, save for two large yellow cones strategically placed about half way along the floor towards the middle of the room. Lee outlined to his charges what the test consisted of; "You have to run continuously back and forth between the two points indicated, in this case the wall of the sports hall and the cone; at a pace predetermined by the beep". "Seems simple enough to me". James stated, "We just keep running up and down between the wall and that cone keeping up with the beep!". "Yes, you got it, easy as pie!". Lee smiled. Mike grinned to himself. He had carried out a number of these tests in his time and whilst athletes often started off laughing and joking at the slow starting pace, their bravado was soon diminished as the timing between the beeps got less and less, meaning that the eventual speeds needed to keep up were quite phenomenal. It was indeed a rare occurrence for anyone to complete the test, with even the best athletes dropping off a minute or two before the end. Lee explained that there were 23 levels to the test, each of which lasted a minute, and that at the end of every minute the interval between the beeps would reduce. "This'll mean that you have to run faster and faster to try and keep up, but you'll probably find that as the test goes on it'll be impossible for you to keep in sync and this is when you need to drop out, so Mike and I can record the number of reps you've done". "Basically this is another way of measuring your VO2 Max". Mike interjected. "So in theory if this morning's test was accurate you should be able to go a bit further in this one than James can Martin!". "Come on James don't let that old timer beat you!". Lee remarked, as he high fived James before the test commenced. James and Martin wished each other luck and Lee positioned each of them in line with their respective cones some twenty metres away in the centre of the hall. He counted them down from three to zero and the test began. The two jogged back and forth at a steady pace through the first few levels with no problems and even when they reached level ten they were both relatively comfortable. By level 14 however James was reaching his limits. Mike remarked as much to Lee as the two studied the chart showing that someone with James V02 Max score wouldn't get much beyond this limit. James hadn't seen the charts though and was determined to beat Martin in this test. Both men continued through level 14 and on to level 15 with the beeps seeming to come quicker than they could reach their markers. They both tried their hardest to get back in sync but after a few more attempts they both realised that they were falling too far behind and had to give up. "Come on you two, what are you playing at there's another eight levels to go yet!". Lee joked. They had both reached the top of level 15 which indicated a V02 Max score of around 67.5. "Almost identical to your score earlier this morning James, well done". Mike stated, as he analysed the number of repetitions completed on level 15 against the chart. "Same score for you Martin, very respectable but not as good as this morning! Just for your information, David Beckham has actually completed a beep test and got all the way to the end!". "Obviously old 'Golden Balls' is fitter than us then!". Martin exclaimed.

"So, what do you think then Lee, do you think it's worth taking a punt on Martin?". Mike enquired as the two were back in room AV12 looking at the results of the tests and viewing the videos they had taken earlier. "Well I have to admit that his first V02 Max score was pretty amazing, but what is it you're actually planning on doing with him?". Lee asked. "I mean he's no spring chicken is he. He's a very good athlete for his age but the question is, is he seriously going to be able to compete against some of the young athletes that are around today no matter what distance he runs over? Sure, he'll win his fair share of veterans races I'll give you that, but who's really interested in that!" "You don't think even with his scores then that he could be a serious competitor?". Mike asked. "Take a look at the video, his right leg is all over the place when he runs, his knee is dodgy and he's rolling out on that right foot to compensate for it". Lee's initial fervour had died down a bit following the beep test and studying the videos, he had landed back in the real world, the world where athletes in their fifties are put out to grass and not given lifechanging opportunities. He finally concluded; "I just think he's too old really to put that much time to. It would take a couple of years of solid training for any athlete to be seriously competitive and by that time he'd be.... what fifty-five or so? His score in the beep test wasn't that great either was it. Have you really got the time and energy to put to him? I admit he seems like a nice enough guy and a genuine bloke but it all seems like a bit of a thankless task if you ask me". Mike had worked with Lee numerous times in the past and knew he was a good judge of character when it came to those who would make it or not. He liked Martin though and sensed that there was something a little bit different about him. Maybe it was his quiet unassuming nature that he had warmed to, or his sense of self-deprecation and modesty, he couldn't put his finger on it, but there was something. He also trusted James' judgement and he also thought Martin had something about him worth trying to develop but he wasn't quite sure. He pondered the predicament for a while before eventually asking Lee; "Who have we got lined up to race against them this afternoon then?". Lee reeled off the names of six of the top athletes in the university running squad; all fit, in their early twenties and on the top of their game. "What distance are we racing them over then?". Mike enquired. "I was going to go for 5k, that should be a fairly good test and it's a distance that Martin runs regularly isn't it?". "I'm not really sure that Martin runs any distance regularly to be honest". Mike replied. "Other than the parkrun on a Saturday morning, but that is 5k I suppose. He hasn't really done any trackwork either, so all this will be new to him. Maybe I was a bit over enthusiastic trying to fit it all in in one day, maybe we should have stretched it out over two days to give him a bit more chance for recovery?". "Yes perhaps!" Lee mused. "Realistically then where do you think he would come in a race against the line-up you've got ready for us?". "Realistically?". Lee replied. Mike nodded, rubbing his chin as he pondered where the afternoons event would take him. "Well realistically I would expect him to come last, and probably be at least a hundred metres or so, possibly more, behind whoever is the slowest of the Team Bath runners". "That far off the pace eh?". "It's the age Mike, even if he ran the race of his life there's no way someone of fifty plus can keep up with a top athlete in their twenties. Think back to when you were that age; you had energy to burn didn't you, and you didn't know what an ache or pain even felt like. How does your body feel now in comparison?". Mike nodded. "Yes, I suppose you're right! We've got to give him a crack though, after all I've dragged him all the way up here and he's performed well in the tests so far so let's not right him off completely. I tell you what, seeing as you don't think he'll get anywhere near the pack this afternoon we'll make a deal that if he finishes within five seconds of the pack I'll take him on and train him up". "Within five seconds of the pack!" Lee exclaimed "So what you're saying is that you want to put time into training an old fart who can't even keep up with some university students. These guys are good, but they aren't Mo Farah or Usain Bolt you know. I would say that he needs to come in the top three or it isn't worth pursuing!". "Top three!". Mike replied, "You just said that he won't get anywhere near the pace". "He won't, but sometimes you've just got to give it up as a bad job, if he isn't in the top three he isn't worth bothering with!". Mike thought about it for a while and reluctantly realised that Lee was right; he couldn't put sentiment in the way of business, and after all coaching was his business. He held out his hand and shook Lee's in agreement. "OK top three it is if I'm to take him on!". They decided however not to mention this to Martin so as not to put undue pressure on him, they would just let the race take place and see how things panned out.

"How's work going then Martin?". James enquired as the two of them were relaxing in one of the universities Jacuzzis in a room adjacent to the Olympic sized swimming pool. The room also housed a sauna, steam room, small plunge pool and two hot stone bed loungers which the two had eyed up as they entered and already availed themselves of. They had eaten earlier with Mike and Lee and had been given free rein to use the facilities of the pool complex to unwind in whilst the two coaches analysed the mornings results. As they lay back and relaxed in the hot water and the vigorous air jets massaged their respective bodies, the two were totally oblivious to the conversation that Mike and Lee were engaged in, and to the fact that potentially Martin's future hung on the results of this afternoons event. "Well you know how it is mate!". Martin responded, before telling James a story about one of his colleagues who over the course of a year noted in his diary whether each day at work was a 'good day' or 'bad day'. At the end of the year he noted the results, vowing to leave his job if the bad outweighed the good. The first year of recording erred on the side of 'good' by three days but the balance tipped significantly in the second year and he was gone the following January. "So, let's put it this way". Martin stated. "If I did the same and added up the results as I went, you probably wouldn't see me much after July!". The two of them laughed. "It's all about quality of life really for me now James, the kids have grown up and I'm on my own so the last thing I want to do really is work my nuts off every day when I don't know how long I have left!". "God don't go getting all morbid on me mate!". James sighed. "Just being realistic mate; my parents died relatively young and you know what happened to the wife, so I've got to make the most of what time I've got left, and no one knows how long that may be do they! Sitting in front of a computer screen for eight hours a day wishing I was somewhere else isn't really my idea of living; existing perhaps, but is it living? Not really is it?". "No, I suppose you're right". James agreed. "Anyway let's make the most of today shall we and enjoy this Jacuzzi whilst we still can!". Stated James, placing his hands in the water and scooping up a large handful to throw over Martin's face. "Get out of it!". Martin laughed, before doing likewise.

It wasn't long before Lee entered the room to see Martin and James stood up in the Jacuzzi chucking water over each other laughing and joking like a couple of small kids. He stood and stared at them for a while with his arms folded before the two noticed his presence and stopped what they were doing. "I can't leave you two alone for a minute can I!". He stated, shaking his head and wagging his finger. "Anyway, if you two can drag yourselves away from your antics and get dressed we'll head out onto the track for the final session of the day". The two did as they were told, still giggling to one another as they headed off to get changed.

"I hear you two got 'busted' by Lee then!". Mike exclaimed, looking up at them from his seat over the rim of his thin framed glasses. "Messing around in the Jacuzzi by all accounts!". Mike continued, doing his best to wind the two of them up as they arrived back in the common room, now showered and changed back into their athletics gear. The two merely looked at each other, smiled and remained silent.

Chapter 17

After some warming up on the track, Martin and James were introduced to the six other athletes they were to be pitted against that afternoon. Whilst a couple of them specialised in 5k races there were two who considered 1500 metres to be their best distance. They had been training hard though and were stepping up to have a crack at the 5k today at Lee's request. One athlete was a 10k specialist looking for a bit of a speed workout and one was proficient at everything from 1500 metres to the marathon. One thing they all had in common though was that they were all class athletes, and amongst some of the finest young distance runners the university had to offer. They also had one other advantage over Martin, as whilst James had done a fair bit of trackwork in his time, the last time Martin ran around one was in the 400-metre event at his school sports day over thirty-five years ago. The track that day was somewhat different than the pristine clay one he would be running on this afternoon though and consisted of an uneven grass track that doubled up as both a football and rugby pitch. A successful race on that track was deemed to be one where the athletes managed to make it around without turning their ankle!

James had informed Martin that he would probably need a strategy for the race if he wanted to do well in it. To date though Martin had never had any form of strategy for any race he had run in, he just ran as fast as he could for as long as he could and slowed down when he had no more to give. "I don't think that's going to cut it today I'm afraid Martin!". James informed him, as the two chatted before the race got underway. "Look". He began to Martin, as he placed his hands behind his head checking that the knot on his bandana was secure. "Mike and Lee probably don't think you've got a cat in hells chance against these guys but if you want to prove to them that you've got what it takes, you're going to have to be in the mix somewhere at the finish and not lagging behind like an also ran. There's no way that I'm going to be able to go the distance at the speed these guys will be running but I may be able to stick with them for around 3k or so if I work hard. If you tuck in behind me and I'll try and guide you around and keep you up with them for the first three kilometres and then that'll be me done. Then you'll be on your own and it'll be down to what you've got left". James was unaware of the 'third place' proviso that Mike and Lee had agreed if Martin was to progress with them, but he knew that they weren't going to be interested in working with someone who was way off the mark, particularly when they already had so many talented youngsters coming through the ranks. He had run with Martin on many occasions though and had seen what he was capable of; he had witnessed his blistering finish and his determination to push on long after others would have thrown in the towel. In short, he believed in him, probably more so than Martin believed in himself, and he wanted to play his part in getting him to where he thought he belonged, however small that part may have been.

"There's one other thing you need to do before you start as well!". James added. "What's that?". Martin replied. "Give me your arm". James instructed, holding out his hand. Martin offered up his right arm to James, somewhat puzzled by the request. "No not that one, the other one". James indicated. Martin offered up his left hand and as he did so, James unfastened Martin's watch and placed it on his own wrist. "You'll need to ditch this one; you don't see Mo Farah running around the racetrack checking his watch do you, wondering if he's going to be home in time for tea or not!". James continued. "It's not all about how fast you run when you're racing on the track, it's about what position you come. There are times when you can run the fastest race of your life and still not get a medal, and there are others when a relatively slow time will get you the gold; it's not all about speed, it's about reading the race, sussing out the other athletes, getting inside their minds and putting yourself in the right position at the right time; make sure you don't get shut in or blocked off and most importantly run the race with your head as well as your legs, got it?". Martin had no real idea what James was on about, but he talked a good fight and delivered it with passion, so he nodded in agreement. "Yeah Got it!". He agreed. "Oh, and one other reason I'm taking this watch away is because when you see how fast these guys will be running you won't actually be able to believe that you can keep up with them so its best you don't actually know. Come on let's show these kids what a couple of old guys can do!".

Crunch time came, and Lee lined the athletes up on the track ready for the off, explaining to them that the race was 5000 metres which would be 12.5 laps of the 400-metre track. "There will be a bunched standing start and you can break for the inside as soon as you please". Lee informed them. "There will be an electronic timer at the finish line, so you can see how you're doing as you go past, and you'll hear a bell as you commence the last lap. The signal to start will be three, two, one and then you'll hear the starting pistol to signal the off. Anyone got any questions?". There was a deathly silence from the athletes. "OK we'll get started then".

Martin and James lined up together at the outside of the bunch. "Remember just tuck in behind me for as long as I can keep going". James instructed his colleague. Martin was feeling anxious as he heard Lee count down to the start and he felt a cold sweat run through his body making him shudder right down to his bones, as if someone had walked over his grave. "Three, two, one…". 'Bang!' The starters pistol signalled the off and the athletes immediately headed for the inside of the bend that was to take up the first quarter lap of the track. To Martin it seemed as if the others had gone off at a sprint and as they rounded the first bend and headed onto what would be the home straight for the first time, the eight were spaced out over a distance of about fifteen metres with James in seventh position and Martin at the back. The pace of the first two hundred metres seemed blistering and Martin was doing his best to keep as close to James as he could, tucking in behind him to get as much benefit as he could from running in his slipstream. By 400 metres Martin was beginning to think that it would be he rather than James that would be dropping out at the 3k distance, and that was even if he managed to make it that far! He knew however why James had removed his watch though as they hit the timer at the 600metre mark. "No wonder I'm bloody struggling". Martin thought to himself. James was struggling too but was managing to stick with the pack and although he was still in seventh position he hadn't lost any ground on the others in front of him and was managing to hold his own. By 800 metres Martin's breathing had become a bit more rhythmic, it was fast and loud, but he was managing to get enough air in and allow his body to convert it into the precious energy required to keep on the pace. By lap five however and the 2000 metre mark there was a distinct gap between the first and second runners and the rest of the pack and barring a miracle both James and Martin knew that it was going to be nigh on impossible to catch them. On lap seven and hitting the 2800 metre mark James shouted behind him to Martin; "That's all I've got mate, it's up to you now!". He pulled off the track totally exhausted and collapsed onto the ground to recover. There was now a short gap between Martin and sixth place and he knew if he wanted to make some ground he was going to have to eat away at it lap by lap. He could see that these guys were quick, and he wasn't of the opinion that his usually quick finish was going to make much of an impression on athletes of this calibre. He recalled the words that James had said to him; "Run the race with your head as well as your legs". "Put yourself in the right position at the right time". He surmised very quickly though that last position at 3000 metres wasn't the best position to be in at any given time and that he would indeed have to think about his next move. He looked ahead. Runners one and two seemed to be pulling further away and he doubted that there was any chance that he or any of the athletes in the pack would catch them. So, it was between him and the other four as to who would be able to claim the third place. 'That's still a bronze medal theoretically'. He told himself. 'So still worth fighting for'. He consciously tried to up his pace, difficult as that was, given the already immense speed at which he seemed to be running. His breathing quickened and deepened, and he pushed his legs to breaking point as he sped around the next 400metres of the track. He moved up on the outside of athlete number six and as he did so felt; as he so often had with other athletes before, him too increase his pace. It was well documented that two athletes of a similar ability running together spurred each other on, and the combined total was greater than the sum of their individual parts. Martin was panting loudly, like a dog left in a baking hot car on a summer's day, gasping for air. His counterpart on the contrary was barely making a noise as he ran seemingly effortless around the track. Did it mean he was coasting? That it wasn't hurting? Martin wasn't sure, perhaps it was just the age difference that made it so. "Come on Martin let's see what we can do shall we?". The younger man acknowledging the elder's presence. It was Mark Scoines, the 1500 metre specialist looking to step up a distance and he was certainly flying today. Martin didn't have the energy to speak to him but gave him his usual thumbs up, glad of the encouragement and for someone to assist with dragging him along over the remaining laps. For three laps they ran side by side and edged past athletes four and five before they were on the shoulder of athlete number three heading into the last 400 metre lap. "I'm out now Martin, good luck mate!". Mark shouted, as they took the bell for the final lap and he pulled off the track. It was all down now to what Martin had left and as he hit the bend hard there was only a metre or so in it between him and Jock Barrow; a young Scotsman from Aberdeen. At the start of the back straight Jock kicked and started to put some distance between the two of them. Mike and Lee were watching the race unfold from the finish line, both somewhat amazed that Martin was still in the running for that coveted third place finish. "He's put up a good fight, but I don't think he's got it in him now Mike!". Lee stated as Jock pulled some five metres clear by the time they were half way down the back straight. Mike knew that Lee was probably right but was desperately hoping that Martin would prove him wrong; that he would still have something left inside to give, after all he had come this far, and he was only a whisker away. "COME ON MARTIN!" He screamed out at the top of his voice. Martin heard the shout, and something clicked in his brain. He could feel the cogs going around. "Run the race with your head as well as your legs!". "Put yourself in the right position at the right time!". He could hear the words echoing around in his head. He wasn't in the right position at the right time, but he also knew that to kick with 300 metres to go and bring it on home would take some doing. He knew if he was on the shoulder coming off the bend and heading into that last 100 metres he still had a shot. He sucked in a lungful of air and gritted his teeth and started to sprint for all he was worth, the fast twitch muscle fibres in his legs were awakened and being forced to respond by the signals sent to them from his brain. He could slowly feel himself edging ever closer and closer, bit by bit, inch by inch. Half way around the bend the gap was three metres and by the time they hit the home straight it was two. With 50 metres to go it was one. He could feel the burn, but he was flying, and he wasn't stopping now! With ten metres to go he edged in front of an astonished Jock, just making it to the line ahead of him by two tenths of a second. He made his way off the track and collapsed on to the central grass area panting like a rabid hyena. Lee turned to Mike in disbelief and shook his head. "Unbelievable!" He gasped.

Chapter 18

After Martin and James had thanked their fellow athletes and partaken of some well-earned rest and recuperation, the two of them bade their goodbyes to Mike and Lee and made their way back down the motorway towards home. Mike had informed Martin that he and Lee would go through the results of the tests and that he would be in touch in due course. Mike had also informed him not to be too disappointed if things didn't work out and that however things went he had performed well during the day and should be pleased with what he had achieved. Martin had heard the 'don't be too disappointed' spiel many times before and recalled one particular occasion to James where he knew that he had 'aced' a job interview, thinking that there was no way he wasn't going to be offered the position, only for it to go to someone else whose face seemed to fit just that little bit better than his. From that day forth he never took anything for granted, as however well things seemed to have gone there was inevitably always a hidden agenda that was at odds with Martin's aspirations. He knew that he had done reasonably well today though; he hadn't disgraced himself by any stretch of the imagination and he knew that at least he had given himself a fighting chance. He was however a bit disappointed with his results in the beep test and felt that might give Mike the excuse he needed not to pursue things further. James was more enthusiastic however; "Come on Mate let's look at the facts shall we, you've crammed in two really hard tests and a 5k race with some of the universities top athletes in one day and performed well in all of them. Don't worry about that beep test, it's no wonder you didn't do so well in that one as that treadmill test beforehand was a killer!". Martin mulled the comments over in his head before responding. "I was miles behind those first two in the race though, wasn't I?". He protested, playing devil's advocate. "Hardly a resounding success!". He paused to think for a while about the day's events before continuing and trying to make himself feel a bit better by trying to put a more positive slant on things. "If you look at it from a realistic perspective, I suppose I did OK in the V02 Max test, performed averagely in the beep test and came third in a 5k race against some fairly strong opposition! I reckon the video of me running won't show up many positives though as my foot has never been right since I broke it! I just don't know mate, hopefully I've done enough but if I haven't it just wasn't to be that's all, it's not the end of the world is it! I mean I've still got my club night runs with you to look forward to haven't I!". Martin quipped, smiling, "Yes I suppose you're right mate, life doesn't get any better than that does it!". Martin concentrated on the road ahead and gently squeezed his foot down on the accelerator as the car disappeared off into the night."

"How did it go then Dad?". Abi asked enthusiastically, the moment Martin opened the front door. It was a little after midnight and she had heard the car pull up on the drive and was stood waiting patiently in the hallway. Martin had instructed Max and Abi not to wait up for him as he wouldn't have been back until late, but might have known his daughter wouldn't have complied even though she had to be up early herself the next morning for work. He and James had stopped off on the way back for a bite to eat leading Martin to arrive home even later than he had anticipated. He wrapped his arms around his daughter and gave her a hug. "Hi Abi, thanks for waiting up darling, there was no need to you know! Where's your brother then?". Martin enquired. "Probably asleep by now I'd imagine!". Max's enthusiasm for his dad's running ability and interest in his endeavours thereof ranged somewhere between zero and one on a scale of one to ten, and Martin knew that he wouldn't mind missing out on a recap of the day's events. As such he retired to the lounge with his daughter to give her a run-down of what had taken place. Upon hearing the tale Abi was suitably impressed, even though Martin had played it down as much as he was able. "I'd like to have seen you racing against those youngsters' dad! They must have been a bit shocked when you beat them?". Well to be fair one of them did give me a hand and there were two who were way quicker than me and I only just managed to come in third so it's not that impressive really! I'll tell you what is impressive though and that's the university itself and the facilities they have there, you'd have been impressed with that! Anyway, it's getting late and we've both got work in the morning". Martin stated, looking at his watch to confirm it was heading into the small hours of the morning and far too late to be up on a 'school night'. Abi got up and gave her dad another hug, "Night Dad, see you in the morning, and well done on today, let's hope you'll hear from Mike soon". 'Yes, let's hope so!' Martin thought to himself, as he nodded in agreement before heading off to bed himself.

The following days however passed in the Price household without further word from Mike. Not a peep was forthcoming and as the time passed Martin eventually began to give up hope and supposed that like most other good things that happened in life, they only happened to other people and not him. A week came and went with no word and when ten days had passed without hearing a dicky bird he started to put all thoughts of anything happening behind him.

It was out of the blue on a Thursday morning that his mobile rang. He had only just put it down after a 30-minute call from an irate customer which hadn't put him in the best of moods and he initially thought it was them ringing back again to give him some more grief as they had eventually slammed the phone down on him. It was a number he didn't recognise, and he eventually resisted his initial urge to not answer and pressed the button. "Hello?". He answered half expectantly and half sheepishly. "Is that Martin?". A voice on the other end enquired. "It is". Martin replied. "Hi Martin, its Mike here. Look firstly I must apologise for not getting back to you sooner, I'm not sure if you heard or not but I got taken into hospital a couple of days after we met, unfortunately I picked up some sort of virus. There were some extra complications, which believe me you don't want to know about, and I only came out yesterday". "Oh right, sorry to hear that Mike". Martin responded. "I should have tried to get hold of you earlier, you must have been wondering what the hell was going on?". "That's OK". Martin responded. "I understand. Are you better now?". Martin felt awful; all this time he had been thinking that Mike had merely dropped him like a hot potato when in reality he had been ill and laid up in a hospital bed. "Yes, much better thanks, I've lost a bit of weight, but I'm sure I'll soon put that back on again! Anyway, enough about me, you've been waiting long enough, and I've got some news for you!". "Go on then, break it to me gently!". Martin responded, fearing the worst. "Well I've been through the results with Lee and its actually all looking fairly positive. What I'd like to do though if it's OK with you is to make a couple of enquiries with some people I know and then sit down with you and Lee to go through the test results and see what we can do, would you be up for that?". "Yes of course". Martin responded. "It will probably mean going back up to Bath University though to go through them, are you OK with that?". Mike added. "Yes, that's fine". Martin responded. "Right if you can leave it with me for a bit and I'll give you a ring again next week with some potential dates and times".

Two weeks on from Mike's phone call and Martin was back in Bath University again, in the same complex as before but in a classroom this time sat behind a desk with Mike and Lee going through a presentation that Lee had put together. Little known to Martin, all the tests he had taken part in during his previous day at the university had been filmed and Lee had edited them into a video that the three went through. Mike and Lee had already studied it meticulously, pointing out every minute detail to Martin where improvements or changes could be made. The results of the tests were intertwined with video footage of Martin running on the treadmill; carrying out the beep test with James and running the 5k race on the track. At the end of the session Mike leaned forward to Martin, looked him directly in the eyes and offered him a proposition.

The following couple of weeks at work were tough for Martin. It was now heading towards autumn and this was always a busy time with numerous complaints and problems literally flooding in. Mike's offer had been weighing heavy on his mind but the reality of what it entailed meant that Martin was becoming ever closer to writing it off as a realistic possibility. Mike had told Martin to take his time though and there was no pressure on him in that respect. The previous Friday he had picked up the phone and began to ring Mike. He had decided to thank him for the opportunity but decided that perhaps it wasn't really for him. He had started to dial the number but couldn't quite bring himself to enter the final digit and actually hit the call button, there was still something, some small element that was holding him back, perhaps he realised that once he had done so the final grasp of him achieving his dreams would have been prised from his hands. At the moment, he still had the last embers of that dream flickering away in the darkness and there was still a glimmer of hope that they could be reignited. He hadn't been quite ready yet to let go.

As well as his running, something that gave Martin a respite from the pain and drudgery of everyday life was his guitar playing. He wasn't a particularly good guitar player by any stretch of the imagination, but he could strum a tune or two if the mood took him. After a particularly bad day at work Martin had been seeking solace by listening to the radio on the way home and had heard the song 'Piano Man' by Billy Joel being played. It was a song that he had heard before many times, but today for some reason the words were resonating strongly around his head and in particular one certain verse. Upon arriving home, he unlocked the front door and placed his bag down in the hallway before going into the lounge and turning on his computer. He was the first home that evening, so the house was empty. He typed the words; 'Piano Man, chords', into a search engine and hunted for a version with the chord pattern best suited to his limited skills. He found one that he deemed to be appropriate and printed it out. He placed it on his music stand, drew up a chair and picked up his guitar. He started to strum out the chords, initially making a few mistakes and then starting again before he got the chord pattern and the tempo right. He got to the verse in question and played it repeatedly as he couldn't get the words out of his head.

He heard the front door open and his daughters voice shout out; "Dad I'm home". "Abi quick come in here!". Martin shouted to her from the lounge with a matter of urgency in his voice; "Listen to this!". Abi came into the lounge to see her dad sat there, guitar in hand. "What is it Dad, what's the matter?". She enquired. Her dad asked her to listen.

Martin sang the words of the song as his daughter stood attentively and listened. Once he was finished he put down his guitar and looked towards his daughter. "That's me that is Abi, I'm John at the bar, aren't I? It's describing me and my job…it's killing me Abi!". Abi looked at him somewhat surprised but deep down she knew he was right. She had seen him deteriorate over the years; she had felt his pain and witnessed his gradual demise since her mums sad passing and as usual in her unique way she knew exactly what to say. "Well Dad it's not a movie star for you is it". She stated, referring back to the song. "You know what your destiny is; it's right there in front of your face isn't it. What do you love doing? What are you good at? Better than anyone you know of your age or virtually any age come to that; its running isn't it. Give up that bloody job Dad, you're right it is killing you! I don't even know if you're still in there sometimes Dad, you've lost your spark, lost your mojo, your zest for life! That job is turning you into a soulless zombie and you're right Dad, one day the stress of it will kill you. You've done a good job bringing me and Max up Dad, but you need to do something for yourself, life's too bloody short to be doing something you hate every day, it's just not worth it. Go on Dad, do a Billy Joel, go on do it!". She flung her arms around her dad and squeezed him as hard as she could. "Thanks Abi". He responded, wrapping his arms around her and gripping tightly "You're the best daughter anyone could have wished for, you always know how to cheer me up".

Max came in through the front door and heard the commotion so came into the living room. "Max we're having a group hug". Abi stated. "Dad's job is killing him and he's going to do a Billy

Joel!". "My job's bloody killing me as well, can I do a Billy Joel too?". He laughed. "Oh, and by the way what is a Billy Joel anyway?". Abi laughed and explained the concept to her brother whilst Martin got out his guitar again to play the verse of the song in question. After playing it through once he amended the words slightly for effect and the three of them sang in harmony; "Now Dad says that his job is killing him, and the smiles gone away from his face, well he swears that he could be an ath-a-lete, if only he could win a race!".

That night Martin picked up the phone and dialled Mike's number in its entirety. He paused for a few seconds, took a deep breath and then pressed the call button.

Chapter 19

"Come in". Martin heard the response following his knock on the door and pushed it open to reveal his boss sat in front of him at his desk; Fred Short; Short by name and short in stature. Generally, quite short in temper as well unless you managed to catch him on a good day! As well as temper and stature, most employees, Martin included, would also have said he was short on brains as well! Yes, in general if ever there was a name that was well suited to an individual, it was certainly Fred Short's. What Fred lacked in height though he more than made up for in girth with his brown leather belt struggling to bursting point to keep the large stomach that protruded over the top of it in check. Fred had had the belt for years and the marks could clearly be seen etched into it where he had had to let it out a notch at a time over the years as his waistline had expanded. Of the many different management styles Fred could have adopted he had opted very strongly for the 'Laissez Faire' approach. Loosely translated from its French origin to 'let them do as they will', it was very much leadership by delegation and taking a hands-off approach and letting others make the decisions. Fred's staff however often referred to him as 'Slopey Shoulders' or 'Teflon Man' as nothing seemed to stick with him for long. To be fair though Fred made few mistakes, after all the man who has never made a mistake has never made anything and this was never truer than in Fred's case. Martin gazed at the red faced rotund individual and looked him up and down with a mixture of sympathy and despair. 'If this is the future of the company God help us all!' He thought to himself. Fred's grey hair was thinning to the extent that he was all but bald save for a few wispy strands straying unkemptly at the front. Martin had always wondered why he simply hadn't just cut them off, as to all intents and purposes they looked completely ridiculous and served no purpose whatsoever in their vain attempt to cover up the volume of skin on show beneath. Martin's eyes were immediately drawn towards them once again, much as they were every time they met. He tried hard not to stare, and each time made a conscious effort not to do so but each time his gaze was drawn in their direction, like some form of crack cocaine addiction he was incapable of dealing with. He finally managed to avert his gaze but not until it had become obvious to Fred what he was staring at. Fred subconsciously reached to his back pocket for his comb and wet it with his spit before running it through his hair and pressing it down onto his head with the palm of his hand. Martin wasn't sure which was worse, the strands of hair sticking up or the thought of them having been effectively stuck down to Fred's scalp via his own bodily fluids!

Martin often wondered, undoubtedly like most employees, what their bosses did with their time all day; other than the inevitable dumping of crap on those lower down the food chain of course! Martin didn't get to see his boss very often; there was the inevitable annual appraisal process of course, both of whom knew that it was simply a waste of their respective time although neither had the honesty to admit to the other that this was the case, pleasantly going through the motions and ticking the right boxes as corporate policy dictated to show that the employer was indeed a 'caring' one that had the best wishes of its employees at heart. Other than that, there was the odd occasion when Fred did the rounds of the other offices on an ad hoc basis just to show willing. Fred's own office was somewhat larger than the small desk space Martin occupied and the panoramic view it afforded over the river Exe was somewhat more resplendent than the parked lorries covered in tarmac residue that Martin had the pleasure to admire on an almost daily basis.

"Have a seat Martin, do you want a cup of tea?". Fred enquired, picking up from the desk and raising his own cup in gesture. Fred never gave a great deal away and Martin could detect that he had caught him in a relatively good mood today, so he took the opportunity to at least whet his whistle at Fred's expense whilst he was there. He surmised that there might even be a biscuit in it for him if he played his cards right, but that fantasy was soon exhausted when Fred returned solely with two cups and nothing else in sight that remotely resembled a custard cream or chocolate digestive. It wasn't long before Martin also realised that the tea itself was little more than a lukewarm cup of milk that had barely been blessed by the insertion of a tea bag. Fred seated himself down and enquired of Martin as to how he could assist. In his e mail to Fred requesting the meeting, Martin hadn't given much away in relation to his intentions but merely stated that he wanted to have a chat about a few things.

"Well." Martin responded, shuffling himself trying to get comfortable in the almost threadbare brown swivel chair, and leaning forwards, "The truth is that I'm not really enjoying things here that much at the moment!" "Join the club!". Fred interjected, smiling. Martin paused and looked down thinking of the best way to try and broach the subject. "Go on". Fred stated, noting his anxiousness. "Well I've been thinking about taking some time off". Martin went on. "That's no problem, you've still got a fair bit of annual leave left, haven't you?". Fred replied. "Yes, but it's not annual leave I'm after really, I want to take a bit of an extended break, I know that it won't be paid but I'd like to take a sabbatical if I can". Fred rocked back on his chair until it was perched on two legs, balancing on the tipping point. He quickly pulled himself forward before going completely over. Corporate policy did allow sabbaticals, but Fred was inherently lazy and knew the hassle it would require both to advertise the job and interview the candidates and then potentially train someone up to take Martin's place. It wasn't what he wanted to hear but he also knew he had to play the 'caring employer' card.

"How long is it you want to take off then and is there any particular reason for wanting time off?". 'Mid-life crisis perhaps!' Fred thought to himself. "This may sound a bit strange". Martin explained. "And I'm not sure if you are aware or not but I do quite a lot of running in my spare time". "No, I wasn't aware of that". Fred responded, neither knowing or particularly caring about Martin's running exploits. He looked

Martin up and down and surmised that it didn't look like he had enough energy to even run a bath let alone run any distance. In his eyes what he looked like he really needed was a good cooked breakfast inside him. "So, what are you going to do then?". Fred enquired. "Are you going to do a Forrest Gump and run across America or something?". Fred started laughing. 'That's actually not a bad idea!' Martin thought to himself. 'Perhaps I should actually be doing a Forrest Gump instead of a Billy Joel!'. "No not exactly but I do want to take some time off to put in some serious training to see if I can improve my running. It's been coming on quite well and I've had an offer to go abroad for a while to undertake some training over the winter in a bit of a warmer climate". "Really?". Fred inquired, screwing his large red face up in disbelief. "Yes really!". Martin stated emphatically.

Fred took a sip of his tea before placing the cup back down on the desk. He turned around and pulled out an orange cardboard folder from some shelving behind him, its outer edges faded by the sunlight that had strewn in through the window over time. He opened it up and pulled out its contents, flicking through page after page of now off white A4 paper. "Here it is". He stated, upon finding the piece he was interested in. "Blimey this goes back a bit, fifteen years in fact, that was the last time anyone in this department went on a sabbatical. It was Andy; do you remember Andy?". Martin nodded. "He had a six-month sabbatical when he went to Australia to see his mum. I think she was ill at the time and he thought that may be the last chance he got to see her. Turns out he was right as she died whilst he was over there if I recall correctly. So yes, it's a possibility". He stated, slipping the piece of paper back into the folder and closing it. "But I'll have to look into it in a bit more detail and consult with personnel. We've also got to think about the needs of the business as well, so I can't say for definite that it will be approved. There's probably an application form required to start the ball rolling so I'll look it out and send it to you".

The two finished their respective drinks and exchanged a few pleasantries, before saying their goodbyes and going their separate ways. It was obvious however that the two had little in common save for their place of employ.

'What an idiot!' Fred thought to himself, shaking his head as Martin left the room. 'Runner, my arse!'

'What an idiot!' Martin thought to himself, shaking his head as he left the room and closed the door behind him. 'Boss, my arse!'

"Plymouth Argyle today then Max, should be a good game!" Martin exclaimed to his son as they patiently sat in a queue of traffic behind a slow-moving tractor and trailer laden with hay, bits of which were blowing all over the road and the following vehicles. "That's if we ever get there!". Max responded rolling his eyes. It was the day of the Devon Derby, Exeter City versus Plymouth Argyle, the Grecians versus the Pilgrims and the first fixture that was looked for by every fan of both teams as soon as the fixtures were announced. Today it was Exeter City who were playing at home and the two were heading up for their bi weekly football fix. Martin himself never had the pleasure of playing in a Devon Derby during his time at City but he certainly knew the importance of them, not only to the players and staff but more so to every city fan who lived and breathed as there was no better feeling than putting one over on their green chums down the road. "Hopefully we can do the business today!". Martin stated, as even he himself was starting to feel nervous even though his role today was no more than that of a spectator.

After the two had discussed the possible outcome of the game and mulled over some of life's major issues; such as whether it was better to view the match from the Old Grandstand or the IP Office stand, the subject turned to Martin's running. "I haven't mentioned it to your sister yet Max, but you know that I was going to try and get some time off work to go and do some training?". "Yes". Max responded looking towards his dad. "Well I heard yesterday that it's been approved, I've been given a year's sabbatical to pursue my training. I was just wondering how you felt about that?". "Well who's going to drive me to the Exeter City games now then?" Max responded, indignantly. Martin wasn't sure if his son was joking or serious but supposed that there was probably an element of both in his response. "What are me and Abi going to do then?". Max continued, his voice sounding more concerned. "Well you can carry on doing the same as you are now. I'm not saying that I'm going to go away for the whole year; in reality it may only be for a few weeks. I'm not really sure how it will work out yet and anyway the start date is open, so It may not be for a while yet so don't get too concerned about it".

Max sat in silence for a while and pondered all the things that his dad did for him and how much he would miss him if he wasn't there. Martin could sense his unease, so he decided to share something with him;

"I had a dream a while ago Max, it was about me and you and we were out walking, it was a lovely summers day and we were just walking hand in hand across a field. The long grass was swaying in the wind, the sun was warming our backs and we didn't have a care in the world. You weren't the age you are today though; you were a young child, sweet and innocent with those long blonde locks you used to have, and we were just skipping along happily across the field laughing and joking. Then all of a sudden as we were walking along you turned in front of my eyes from a young boy holding their dad's hand into a butterfly; a gorgeous Red Admiral. I continued to walk, and the butterfly followed me everywhere I went. This went on for days. The days turned into weeks and then months, and everywhere I went and every which way I turned the butterfly was by my side. One day though as I was out walking I looked around and suddenly the butterfly that was by my side, the one that always followed me everywhere I went, was gone. I searched and searched everywhere but no matter how hard I tried I couldn't find the butterfly, and I returned home with tears streaming down my face at the loss of my beautiful friend. For days after I searched, but I couldn't find you, and then the days turned into weeks, and it wasn't long before I spent every waking hour of every day searching for my beloved butterfly but try as I may I never found it again and my life was never the same. I never really realised what the dream was about, but I know now that it was a metaphor really for you growing up and turning from a boy into a young man and leaving the family home and going and making your way in the world. I guess there comes a time when every parent must let go and I suppose I've got to realise that that time has now come. I know it will be a change for both of us, and for your sister as well, but just think of it as starting out on a new chapter in our lives. It's still the same book of life but were just turning over onto a new page".

Max looked somewhat perplexed and was unused to such philosophical musings from his dad. Comedic wit and sarcasm possibly but philosophy no! "So, what you're saying then Dad is that I'm a butterfly right!". Max knew the point his dad was making but couldn't resist the urge to wind him up a bit. "Well no, that's not the point I was trying to make really Max!".

"Chill out Dad, I get it, Yes I suppose you're right!". Max responded, equally philosophically. After a moment of silence, he perked up; "Anyway come on Dad lets go and watch City smash those Janner's!"

# Chapter 20

"OK that's not bad; your quickest time to date in fact. Now I want you to go ahead and do it again to see if you can better it". Alberto instructed the young man stood in front of him without so much as averting his gaze from the large heavy stopwatch in his hand. It wasn't a modern stopwatch, not by any stretch of the imagination, in fact it was anything but modern and certainly not any of the digital rubbish that the coaches and athletes of today put so much faith in. Alberto wouldn't have dreamed of using one of those, as like his equipment, Alberto was old school. He was a famous and successful runner back in the day and if the equipment and techniques in place were good enough to get him to the top back then, in his eyes they were still good enough today. He felt the weight of the shiny object in his hand, caressing the buttons with his fingers as he did so, losing himself in the memories it brought back to him of days of former glory. The watch to him said everything about quality and standing the test of time. It was a rare piece indeed; a swiss made Hanhart, dating back to the 1930's and one of the world's first timepieces capable of measuring hundredths of a second. It had been given to him by his own father and it was one of his most treasured possessions. Three days earlier, Chris, the young athlete Alberto was training had described it as 'a pile of old crap' much to Alberto's disdain and unfortunately for Chris he was still paying the price. Chris fixed him a hard stare. "I've been doing this non-stop for seven days now and I'm getting fed up with it, this is pointless!". Alberto looked up from his watch. "Remember Chris, it was you who came to me not the other way around, do you want me to help you or not?". "Well yes but can't we do something different, this is ridiculous!". "Off you go Chris, one more time please." Alberto held his trusty stopwatch aloft so that Chris could clearly be reminded of his insubordination; "Three, two, one, go...". He pressed the button on the top of the watch with the thumb of his right hand and raised his eyebrows in Chris's direction as the second hand started to sweep around the dial. Chris breathed a sigh before reluctantly setting off over the rough terrain of the crater once again.

Alberto had been one of the top marathon runners in the world during the late seventies and early eighties and was a former Olympic champion at the distance as well as a silver medallist in the half marathon. His list of accolades was long and distinguished and although Spanish he was a former coach to the Great Britain team meaning he still had a lot of connections within the UK. Since formally retiring from UK athletics though he had built up a good reputation as a coach who could get the best out of individual athletes who may not necessarily have come through the ranks in a regular format. Not all however agreed with his training regimes. He was now based in Gran Canaria and trained athletes that had been sent to him by clients on an individual basis. His training camp was a somewhat unique if not bizarre location being based in the Bandama Crater in the mountains of Gran Canaria, so named after the Dutch merchant, Daniel Van Dame who grew vines in the crater back in the 17th century and who was the first to adopt the land for agricultural purposes. Alberto had been looking for somewhere isolated with a climate that would suit his 'semi-retired' lifestyle but also somewhere that could be utilised for year-round training should it be required. This location met the criteria perfectly. The land at the base of the crater was farmed for many years until the previous occupant eventually became too old to work it and had to move on. Some years later the single storey farmhouse at the base of the crater and the land associated with it was put up for sale and Alberto managed to pick it up for a good price as the house had become somewhat dilapidated and the land overgrown. He had renovated the old house lovingly however and installed a gym complete with running machines for indoor use when the weather wasn't as kind as it may have been. In relation to the crater itself, whilst the majority of the base remained predominantly overgrown, he had fashioned a gravel and cinder running track around the perimeter, firstly by using a chainsaw to remove a number of trees and then by digging out the track with a wheeled digger and bulldozer before importing the necessary gravel and cinder and rolling it in to provide a firm base. It wasn't an Olympic stadium by any stretch of the imagination but at 800 metres long the track was equal to two laps of a standard 400metre athletics track and suited Alberto's purposes. He was proud of the fact that he had completed all the works himself even though it had taken him around two years to do so. During this time, he had taken a break from training but now he had his set up as he wished he was back in the market for taking on recruits again.

Chris however hadn't yet been afforded the opportunity of using the track and his training to date had consisted solely of a week's regime that Alberto had dubbed 'the soul breaker' which consisted of repeatedly running across the base of the crater over the rough terrain and then up the side of the crater via a narrow winding track and then beyond to the 1,867 ft high peak; the Pico de Bandama, before coming back down again. Chris had been impressed with the stunning views from the top over the entire north and east coast of the island and the mountainous centre to the west, but that was on his first ascent and the repetitive nature of the training now only made the views a tiresome experience that merely marked off one more lap of training. Whilst Chris was indeed close to breaking point, he had been warned that Alberto was a strong taskmaster that wasn't to be questioned. "As long as you do what he says, you'll be fine!". He had been informed by his probation officer as they parted ways at Bristol airport. Alberto was certainly a stickler for discipline and a firm believer in the proven regime he had built up over the years.

Alberto sat back in the old blue and white striped deckchair that was positioned just outside the low stone garden wall of the farmhouse and kicked back and relaxed. He placed his feet upon a strategically placed large lump of volcanic rock which made for a perfect natural footrest and started to drift off in the sunshine. Sometime later the familiar sound of Chris picking his way throughout the undergrowth could be heard and Alberto picked up his shiny stopwatch and held it aloft as Chris sprinted the remaining fifty metres or so towards the old man. 'Click', Alberto stopped the watch and shook his head in Chris's direction. "Not so good on that one Chris, almost twenty seconds slower than your personal best! Come on time for a break and to have some lunch". The two of them retreated into the cool of the farmhouse where Alberto whipped them both up a high protein lunch of grilled chicken and assorted vegetables.

"How are you enjoying the training so far then Chris?". The old man asked his prodigy, taking another slug of his white wine and swilling the remnants around in the glass, as the two of them sat down to the meal. Alberto drank wine with everything and his favourite tipple was a Testamento Malvasia dry, a pale, straw-coloured white from south-east Tenerife. If he couldn't get his hands on a bottle of this his back up choice was the equivalent Lanzarote Malvasia. Following his meal, he always took a tot of the Canarian 'Ron Miel', a sweet Honey Rum produced locally in most of the Canary Islands and widely available at a reasonable price. Chris had quickly surmised that the old man was both an alcoholic and a complete nutter and presumed this was the reason that his training regimes were so off the wall. He looked across the table at Alberto, who was now draining the remnants of his glass between his thin craggy lips, and thought carefully before he gave his measured response, still reeling from the effects of his previous badly chosen words. "Well I am enjoying it in a way". He started, "But I just wish there was a bit more variety in the training; I'm getting a bit fed up just running across that rough ground and up and down the mountain. Can't I do something a bit different as it's a bit boring. I've been here for a week now and that's all I've done". "All in good time Chris, all in good time". The old man laughed. "That's the trouble with you youngsters today". He stated, getting up from his chair and patting Chris on the shoulder as he did so. "You want everything straight away; instant gratification; no one's prepared to work for anything these days. Just bide your time lad and do what I tell you and you won't go far wrong!". Alberto turned from Chris and walked into the kitchen of the farmhouse, its units fronted in traditional pine. He ducked his head as he did so underneath the low doorway and crossed the slate floor to the large chest freezer situated adjacent to the back door of the property. He brushed some parched brown leaves from the top which had blown in through the adjacent open window and opened its lid. He pulled out the ice tray and placed two lumps into his glass before heading over to the bottle of Honey Rum on the shelf and pouring himself a generous helping. He returned to the table with his glass and sat down to enjoy the sweet nectar. "Cheers Chris". He nodded, raising his glass in his direction. "Stick with me son and you'll do fine".

Once lunch was finished and after Chris had somewhat reluctantly completed the washing up, Alberto allowed Chris some time off from his training regime and let him borrow his old Seat Arosa to get out and have a look around the island. "Don't forget what I've asked you to do after that though and make sure you're there on time". The old man instructed Chris as he handed him the keys to the somewhat battered and bruised old automobile.

The afternoon respite from training was indeed a welcome relief and an opportunity that Chris was keen to exploit before the old man changed his mind.

Chris climbed into the driver's seat of the car and adjusted it accordingly to suit someone of his stature. He put the key in the ignition and after cranking it over a couple of times with no end result the engine eventually fired into life on the third attempt, emitting a large cloud of black smoke in Alberto's direction as it did so. Alberto handed Chris three twenty euro notes through the open driver's window of the car as he was about to head off and instructed him both to fill it up with petrol on the way back and to pick up a couple bottles of his preferred wine. With that Chris gingerly eased his foot down on the accelerator for the precarious drive up the winding track that led up the side of the crater and on to the open winding road beyond. 'Freedom at last!'. Chris thought to himself as he steered the aging vehicle through Tafira Alta and onwards towards his destination which was the islands capital of Las Palmas.

Upon approaching the capital, he stopped the car on the roadside to take advantage of the view over the city and the harbour beyond. The last time he had travelled through there was in a taxi after dark following his flight out from Bristol Airport a week previously. Las Palmas was a heady mixture of both low and high-rise buildings, old and new interspersed with no seeming logic. The harbour in the foreground a haven, speckled with the whites and pale blue hues of small leisure craft, yachts and cruisers gently bobbing up and down on their moorings, their chrome and stainless-steel fittings glinting intermittently in the sunlight. The industrial part of the port beyond was somewhat less enchanting and picturesque with its industrial cranes and oil tanks busy loading and unloading and refuelling the awaiting merchant ships moored patiently. Two cruise liners took centre stage with the 150,000 tonne Independence of the Seas dwarfing the 30,000 tonne Marella Celebration in the foreground. Chris paused and looked and took in the ambience of the place reflecting on his decision to come and decided that despite Alberto's somewhat strange ways and unorthodox training methods he had probably made the right decision after all.

He continued his journey on through the outskirts of the city and through the main thoroughfare to the harbour, managing to find a parking space close to Las Canteras beach, a long swath of golden sand sweeping down one side of the capital, and one of five beaches Las Palmas was blessed with. He had a look around at some of the sites and took in a jog along the main promenade before picking up the old man's provisions and heading off to his instructed destination. As he drove into the fading sunlight of the day it allowed him to refocus his thoughts and appreciate how fortunate he was to have been given the opportunity.

Chapter 21

Martin was awoken from his thoughts by the Captain's voice over the tannoy. "Ladies and gentlemen, we are beginning to make our descent and shall be landing at Gran Canaria airport in approximately twenty minutes time. Could you all ensure please that your seats are in the upright position and that your seatbelts are fastened. The weather in Gran Canaria this evening is a balmy twenty-two degrees with barely a cloud in the sky. Upon landing and exiting the aeroplane could you all make your way to gate five please. Finally, on behalf of myself and the crew we would like to thank you for flying with Thomson Airways and we look forward to seeing you all again very soon. We wish you all a very enjoyable holiday". There was a brief pause followed by; "Cabin crew, final checks please and positions for landing". The three stewardesses made their way down through the aisle, checking that seats were in the upright position and that all passengers had their seatbelts fastened, before folding down their own seats and strapping themselves in. The cabin lights were dimmed shortly after and as Martin awoke he smiled to the old lady next to him; offering her and her husband a boiled sweet as the plane made its final approach towards the runway.

Chris felt a bit awkward stood there holding a piece of A3 paper aloft with the name 'Martin Price' written across in large letters in black marker pen. He had no idea who Martin Price was, how old he was or what his purpose was with Alberto. All he knew was that the old man had told him to be at the airport by seven o'clock and to wait in arrivals to pick him up. As people filed past Chris, he tried to pick out potential candidates as they approached him, but each merely ignored him and walked on past. Chris had been waiting for about twenty minutes or so and was getting a bit fed up of holding up the paper when a tall slim male in his fifties approached him. He had a blue rucksack draped across one shoulder and was pulling a large black Dunlop suitcase behind him. "Hi, you must be Chris?". Martin enquired, as he approached the young man and held out his hand in greeting. Mike had informed him previously that there would be a young tall dark-haired male going by that name who would be at the airport to meet him, "Yes that's me." Chris smiled, extending his hand to shake Martin's. "I guess that you must be Martin? If so that means that I don't have to hold up this piece of paper anymore thankfully!". "Yes, that's me, and yes you can indeed put it down now, unless of course you are expecting two Martin Prices to turn up!". Martin replied. "Nice to meet you too". Martin was as in the dark as Chris was though as to the identity of his young taxi driver for the evening. All Martin had been told by Mike was that he was going to go to Gran Canaria for three months of initial training by a colleague of his who was one of the best in the business. When Martin had heard the words "three months" and "Gran Canaria" he didn't need a lot more convincing. He was initially disappointed that it wasn't Mike himself that was doing the training but when Mike had explained Alberto's pedigree and the fact that he had had unbridled success in training athletes that couldn't really be classed as 'run of the mill', he was sold. Also, whilst the prospect of running the 'streetlights' course with James on a wet and bitterly cold January evening in Blighty had a certain appeal to it, it paled into insignificance when compared with the milder winter climate of the 'Islas fortunas' and the opportunity of spending three months warming his bones in the winter sun of the canaries. If Martin had the idea that it was to be some form of extended vacation however, any thoughts he may have had along those lines were soon to be extinguished!

Chris led Martin back to the car and opened it up so that Martin could stow his luggage away into the boot. "Nice car!". Martin exclaimed ironically after cramming his suitcase into the tiny boot and giving his ride the once over before he climbed into the passenger seat. "Yes, it's a bit of a dog isn't it!". Chris replied. Its Alberto's only form of transport I think, but it will get you where you want to go...well just about!" "So, are you training with Alberto as well then?". Martin enquired. "Yes,

I've been here for about a week now but I'm hoping to stay quite a bit longer yet all being well". "Bit of an extended holiday then eh?". Martin implied. "Unfortunately, I don't think you would class staying at Alberto's as a holiday in any shape or form I'm afraid; the old guy is a bit of a taskmaster and keeps you on your toes". "What's he like then?". Martin asked, as by all accounts the old man was a bit of an enigma. Chris didn't really want to give too much away at the moment though, either about his own background or about what he thought of Alberto, as for all he knew he and Martin may have been long lost brothers and at the moment he didn't know Martin from Adam. He decided to play it a bit cool and be a bit non-committal for the time being; he would wait until he got to know Martin a bit better before he decided whether to impart a bit more personal information to him. His history and background had made him wary of trusting people and often in the past he had made some poor decisions and couldn't really afford to make too many more. Chris resisted the urge to tell Martin that Alberto was a miserable old bastard and if asked a week ago that would have indeed been his first impression of him. As the days had passed however Chris had warmed to the old man, yes, he had some strange ways and unorthodox methods of training, but he was a likeable old guy who had grown on him the more time they had spent together. "Yes, he's OK". Chris eventually replied. "He's a nice old guy who seems to know his stuff when it comes to training. Unusual methods though and a bit old school but yes I think you'll like him". Martin had heard from Mike that Alberto was indeed 'old school', it went with the age and the territory though he supposed. "How was the flight?". Chris asked Martin, making some small talk after a few minutes awkward silence. Martin relayed some information about the trip to Chris and told him of the two elderly travellers he was sat next to which brought a small nod of appreciation and a glimmer of a smile to Chris's lips.

Martin sat back and enjoyed the scenery on the short journey up to the crater. In the dimming light he could see the spectacular views over the northern side of the island unfolding as Chris took the car up the steep and winding road to its destination. Martin was wary of the inevitably steep drop off to the side of the road and that the only thing between that and the car coming off the road were several intermittent palm trees planted along the side, coupled with an occasional low white rendered block wall where the drop looked particularly precarious or the road took a sharp bend. Martin hoped that Chris's driving skills belied those of most young men his age and his fingers whitened as he tightened his grasp on the rucksack on his lap as if it would make some miraculous difference should the car leave the road before reaching its destination. Thankfully for Martin's nerves the trip from the airport to the Caldera de Bandama was a relatively short one with the distance between the two points being no more than fifteen miles. After less than half an hour from Chris pulling out of the airport and onto the Avenue La Avacion the car had arrived at its destination and Chris turned carefully off the road and back onto the precarious track that led down to its base. Martin could just about make out the lights in the small building below him and turned to Chris with a somewhat puzzled look on his face as if to say, "Where the hell are you taking me!". Chris had felt the same way upon his arrival at the somewhat unusual destination and reassured Martin that all wasn't as bad as it seemed!

As the two entered the farmhouse the old man was sat on his favourite chair, feet up and reading a book. He was halfway through 'The Dogs of War', a 1974 novel by Frederick Forsythe depicting the antics of mercenary 'Cat' Shannon who was hired to assassinate the president of an African country so that a British businessman could gain access to their platinum mines. Alberto wasn't a great reader and had picked the book up many times in an attempt to press on towards the end however he had had little success in doing so. Tonight was no exception and if truth be known he was grateful for the excuse as the two entered the room. He folded over the top corner of his current page and placed the book back down on the heavy oak coffee table before him. He stood to greet Martin. "Good evening, you must be Martin, I'm Alberto, pleased to meet you". Alberto said, offering out his hand. Martin eyed up the old man; he wasn't a lot to look at but then neither was Martin and he surmised that Alberto was probably having thoughts along the same lines. Alberto however never judged a book by its cover and had trained too many unorthodox athletes to let first impressions dictate his feelings. "Evening Alberto, nice to meet you". Martin replied. The two exchanged pleasantries before Alberto instructed Chris to show Martin to his room. Chris led him through the hallway of the single storey dwelling to what was a small room, no larger than eight feet square. In it were a single bed with a bedside cabinet adjacent to it, a wardrobe and a small chest of drawers. On the wall opposite the bed there was a solitary picture that depicted a silhouette of a runner heading off into the sunset. "Well it's hardly the Hilton is it Chris!". Martin stated as Chris opened the door. "No, mines about the same size, the bed's really comfortable though!". Martin was tired after the journey and a comfortable bed sounded like all he needed at that particular moment. He quickly unpacked his things and placed his clothes in the wardrobe and chest of drawers before heading back into the living area. Alberto had made the three of them some tea and toast for supper and they exchanged some further introductory chit chat before Chris and Martin retired to their respective bedrooms. On occasion, before Alberto went to bed, he liked to take his guitar out into the night air and play himself a few tunes to relax before eventually retiring. He was an accomplished player and his guitar of choice was a 1969 J-45 Gibson acoustic in a sunburst finish. It was now somewhat the worse for wear but still delivered the smooth mellow tone that the iconic guitar was renowned for. His go to tune was 'Cavatina' by Stanley Myers, made famous by the film the Deer Hunter. Alberto had played it so many times that he now could recite it to perfection, with the notes of the beautiful melody floating off into the cool Canarian evening air. Both Martin and Chris lay awake in bed listening to the sweet music before the song concluded and Alberto drained the last drop of Honey Rum from his glass and retired to bed himself.

The next morning Martin was awoken by the smell of cooked bacon wafting in through the door of the bedroom. He got out of bed and put on his dressing gown and slippers and headed out to the kitchen to see Alberto standing over the oven with Chris sat at the table, cup of hot tea in hand. "Morning Martin, sleep well?". Alberto asked, turning to greet his guest. "Yes, not bad thanks". Martin replied, having one final yawn and stretch of the arms to work out the kinks. "Tea or coffee?". Chris enquired, getting up and heading over to the kettle. "Tea please, with one sugar if that's OK". Martin replied. "It's OK by me but Alberto doesn't believe in sugar, do you Alberto?". "Let him have one for now". Alberto stated. "I'm sure we'll soon wean him off it!". "Something smells good". Martin observed. "Better than any Alarm clock this is". Alberto stated. "We always start the day with something cooked, gets a bit of protein into you for the rigours of the day. It's all grilled though, we don't fry anything here and it's all lean meat locally sourced". Martin hadn't been quite sure what to expect but it appeared that the farmhouse was full of home comforts and if first impressions were to be any indication of how his time was going to pan out, at least it looked like he was going to be well looked after. Chris brought Martin's tea over to the table and Martin sat down as instructed. Alberto served up three platefuls of sausages, bacon, beans, toasted brown bread, hash browns and a poached egg and the three sat down and tucked in. Alberto even had Martins favourite HP sauce to hand, which he applied to his fare in liberal quantities. During breakfast the three found out a bit more about each other. Alberto told them of his background, his athletic achievements and how he had come to live on the island and buy the current house and unusual grounds they were located in. "Me and Mike go back a long way." He explained to Martin when asked about the connection and how Martin had ended up where he was today. It was the same for Chris and his referral, I only take on athletes who have been recommended by people I know and trust, that way I can be confident that you'll be dedicated and won't give me any grief; will you Chris!". He stated, looking at the young man and laughing. "No that's right Alberto!". Chris replied, nodding his head ironically in agreement. Chris was already aware of Alberto's methods, but Martin still had the dubious pleasure to come. Chris surmised that like he, Martin didn't appear to be the type of person that was going to give Alberto too much trouble and was probably just glad of the opportunity to be here.

After breakfast Alberto gave Martin a guided tour of the farmhouse whilst Chris did the dishes. "I do all the cooking here". He informed Martin. "But I expect you and Chris to do the washing up in turn and help out with keeping the place tidy. Sunday mornings I go shopping for food and midweek I normally pop in to the capital for a top up on the essentials like bread and milk". 'And wine and Honey Rum!' Chris thought to himself. "Apart from that we have everything we need right here. There's a gym in this room". Alberto stated, opening the door to what would have been the fourth bedroom of the single storey dwelling. Martin clocked a basic running machine, a cross trainer and a weightlifting bench along with a couple of racks of different sized weights neatly stacked. "Any questions?". Alberto asked. "Can't think of anything at the moment". Martin replied shaking his head. "Good, now follow me then". Alberto led Martin to the front door and flung it open to allow the sun to stream directly in. "And outside we have all of this!". Alberto exclaimed, the smile on his face a mile wide as he outstretched his arms to take in the tremendous sight before them. "The Caldera de Bandama, isn't she a pretty sight". Martin looked around at the steep interior of the crater and the centre with its various bushes and shrubs of varying colours. He looked to the edge of the crater to see the running track that Alberto had lovingly crafted. He walked over towards it and stepped onto its surface feeling its firmness beneath his still slipper clad feet. "Yes, it's certainly impressive". Martin agreed. "I've never really seen anything like it". Alberto patted him on the back. "Come on you need to get yourself washed and dressed and into your running gear. I also need to take a few measurements and take your weight before we get started. I need to know exactly what I've got to work with!". The two retired back inside to find Chris dressed and ready to go for the days training. "A 10k run on the track for you today

Chris and I want you to try and hit these split times". Alberto instructed Chris. He looked at his watch. "A bit too soon after breakfast yet though so rest easy for half an hour and then I'll be with you".

Once Martin was ready Alberto put him on the scales and made a note of his weight in his notebook. 11 stone 7 pounds. He took his height, waist measurement, inside leg, thigh, calf and bicep measurements and entered them all neatly into the notebook on the page immediately after he had Chris's details. "I'll use this to work out your dietary requirements. You'll need enough calories to see you through the day and for what training I've got planned but not so much so that you put on weight. I probably don't need to explain to you the effect putting on too much weight can have on your running. Not that I think you'll have to worry too much about that from the look of you". Alberto observed, looking Martin up and down and noticing how wiry his physique was. Alberto flicked his notebook back a page to where he had entered Chris's measurements the week previously. He noted the similarities between the two; almost identical height and weight. "Interesting" Alberto thought to himself as he mulled the figures over.

By the time the two had finished Chris had nearly finished his 10k run. He was on his penultimate lap as the two exited the farmhouse and Martin noticed Chris glide elegantly past them taking the bend at what appeared to be a very quick pace. "Looks like Chris is a fairly good runner?". Martin enquired of Alberto. "The lads certainly got a lot of potential and yes if he sticks with it he'll be a contender that's for sure. I'm hoping though that by having you here it will push him on a bit as there's nothing like a bit of healthy competition to get you going. From the stats Mike has sent me you should be able to give him a good run for his money despite your age!". There it was again Martin thought to himself, those magic words; 'despite his age', it once again made him regret not having taken up the sport earlier. There was nothing much he could do about it now though, after all he didn't have a magic wand

and he couldn't turn back time, he just had to give it his best shot and put his age to one side. "You're probably not going to enjoy the first week of training particularly". Alberto explained almost apologetically. "But it's a necessity as it shows me what you're made of, it sorts out the men from the boys and whittles out any timewasters. You don't look like a timewaster to me though". Alberto stated scratching his stubbly chin and staring directly at Martin with his piercing blue eyes. Martin merely stared back and shook his head listening intently at what the old man was saying. "So just do what I tell you when I tell you to and hopefully if the three of us work together over the coming weeks and months you'll see your running ability reach heights you never knew existed". Martin liked the sound of it but wondered if it was actually true or just a pipe dream and all part of Alberto's sales pitch. The old guy talked a good fight though and there was only one-way Martin was going to find out if what he was saying was true.

# Chapter 22

"OK that's not bad Martin; Now I want you to go ahead and do it again to see if you can better your time". Alberto advised Martin, standing up and holding his precious stopwatch aloft and clicking the button with his thumb as Martin terminated his run at the farmhouse. It was late that afternoon and Martin had spent most of the day repeatedly running across the base of the crater and then up its side via the track to the Pico de Bandama as Chris had done before him. Like Chris he was impressed with the views from the top, but also felt the pleasure diminish upon every repeat visit. Martin was by now starting to feel hungry and was close to exhaustion, having run the course more times than he cared to remember in the hot sunshine. He walked over to his water bottle and slugged down a generous helping of the liquid within before turning in readiness for the return trip and heading off. Chris by contrast had finished his days training and was sat in the shade adjacent to the farmhouse wall relaxing and listening to the radio. A smile crossed his face as he recalled his own first week with Alberto and the notorious 'soul breaker'. As Martin headed off back across the scrub he heard Alberto's voice shout to him; "Martin, come back!" Martin turned and jogged back to where he was standing. The old man was stood there in his shorts, bare chested, displaying his impressive torso, skin like brown leather with tattoos across his upper chest and biceps. He still sported an impressive six pack to this day and Martin surmised that he must have been some athlete in his youth. "That's enough for today". He informed Martin, nodding his head in appreciation of the day's endeavours. Just knowing that Martin was willing to do it again without question was enough for Alberto and told him everything he needed to know about his character. The younger man stood in front of him without so much as averting his gaze from the elder, thankful that the days training was finally coming to an end. "Chris put the Kettle on please!". Alberto shouted. "That's it for today!".

The first week of Martin's training came and went and with each day that passed his body began to ache more and more. Even the supposed recovery days consisted of a long run at a moderate pace which still took its toll. Martin was becoming used to the aches however and gradually found that the initial muscle stiffness that he felt in the mornings would wear off during the day as he got his body moving and into the flow of running. By week two the three of them had built up a good bond and Martin and Chris's training had been integrated so that they often ran together. It was during the long runs that the two really got to know each other and over time Chris began to really open up to Martin about his background and the hardships he had faced during his childhood. Chris was a bit younger than Martin's own children, but he could certainly empathise with his position and was only glad that he was able to be there for his own kids and bring them up and guide them on their way through life and not have to suffer a similar fate to Chris. It was obvious to Martin though that Chris was one of life's good guys and that he had a heart of gold and a maturity well beyond his years. Anyone who could have gone through all the changes in life that he had at such a young age and come through it relatively unscathed was certainly a force to be reckoned with. Yes, he had made some bad choices but hadn't everyone? And given the circumstances would he himself have really done anything any different. He and Alberto however now had a chance to make a difference to Chris's life even if they were only to be together for a relatively short time and Martin was pleased that he would have the opportunity to perhaps help him even if it was in some small way. The feeling was mutual, and Chris quickly became fond of not only Martin but Alberto as well, as strange as it may have seemed following the initial weeks training.

The three quickly formed a strong bond and as the evenings approached they settled down and shared stories of their life's experiences. Alberto's stories of his achievements were remarkable, however here he was with his feet firmly planted on the ground standing as an equal with Martin and Chris and giving freely the benefits of his knowledge and experience. Chris began to bare his soul as the weeks progressed and shared stories of his experiences in the various children's homes he had been in and out of and of the so many foster parents he had been with over his childhood years. He reminisced with fond memories stories of John Ratcliffe, his former foster parent, and how he had encouraged him with his running which had ultimately led him to where he was today. And as for Martin, well his stories inevitably revolved around his beloved wife and the happy times they shared before she was so cruelly taken from his grasp, also of his children and his involvement in their upbringing. Not forgetting of course the time spent in residence at the other great love of his life; Exeter City Football Club. As time passed there wasn't much that the three didn't know about each other and it wasn't long before the three had settled into an established daily routine.

Alberto had meticulously worked out their dietary requirements and had a meal planner on the wall outlining each day of the forthcoming week and what meals they would be eating. These were to be supplemented by protein shakes, vitamin tablets, omega three capsules and drinks containing amino acids to aid muscle recovery. On a separate chart Alberto had each day's training schedule written on it. There were even some occasional rest days pencilled in, although Martin and Chris had noted that these were very few and far between!

Each morning Alberto would get up and make the breakfast with the other two joining him and taking turns with the washing up. Morning training would be followed by a light lunch and then the afternoon sessions. By now the two athletes were carrying out a mixture of both road work and track work with Alberto fastidiously recording everything in his notebook. Regular run timings were noted, and weights and measurements of the athletes were recorded daily as Alberto worked painstakingly to ascertain what their best potential distances to race over would be. Both were good athletes and again very similar in overall times over different distances. They were however spoilt for choice in their quest for running routes, as well as doing regular track work in the crater itself the scenery they got to run over during their long runs was breath taking. They were also spoilt for choice in their routes for hill work with the geographic make-up of the centre of the island meaning that inevitably there wasn't a lot of flat ground to be seen.

Alberto generally liked the two to start and finish at the crater although there were times when they ventured out for something a bit different. They tended to avoid the capital as Alberto had little time for that area, other than to pick up provisions and he wasn't fond of the predominantly tourist areas of Playa del Ingles and San Augustin, even though Martin and Chris loved to run along the long flat promenade that stretched all the way along the sea front between the two. One session which Alberto was keen for them to undertake at least once a week however was an hour-long session in the sand dunes of Maspalomas, running up and down the large sand hills repeatedly to strengthen the legs. This was a particularly gruelling session which made an hour seem like a day and whilst the two athletes could see the benefits of the sessions, their reluctance to carry them out was evident. They never questioned Alberto though as however hard the sessions may have been they knew that all Alberto did was for their benefit. They weren't particularly impressed though when on occasion he would extend the duration of the sessions if he felt they hadn't put enough effort into them and he had an uncanny knack of distinguishing between when the two were really sweating blood or when they were just going through the motions. Alberto usually had a large smile on his face when he pointed to the section of the chart on a Friday morning that simply read; 'MASPALOMAS!' in capital letters, followed by a large exclamation mark. The only good thing however was that the three got to spend some time swimming and relaxing on the beach afterwards as a reward for their endeavours. After the session Alberto would take the car back as far as Telde, which was about twenty kilometres from the crater, and drop Martin and Chris off to do a recovery run back to base. Although it was a long run it was at a relatively easy pace and it gave the two of them a chance to chat together in the warm sunshine whilst leisurely jogging home at a steady pace. Friday was also fish day and Alberto would have a fish and chip supper on the go and ready by the time they had returned to base and had a shower. The icing on the cake was that the Honey Rum also flowed in abundance on a Friday night as well!

"OK I'll see you back at base in about an hour and a half then". Alberto stated as he stopped the car on the side of the road and dropped the two of them off. Martin and Chris watched him drive off into the distance as he tooted his hooter and left them on the roadside. The two of them started to jog for home. Neither had a watch on that day so weren't watching or recording their times and just set off at a comfortable pace to enjoy the moment. "How's your knee then Martin?". Chris enquired of his companion, as he knew that Martin had been struggling on and off with it for a while. "Not too bad at the moment, thanks Chris". Martin replied. "It's strange really, a week or so ago it was quite painful and if I was at home, I would probably have rested it up for a while; out here though I've just kept going and the pain seems to have gone away. Not sure why that is though but long may it continue!". "Perhaps the muscles around your knees are getting a bit stronger, helping to support it". It was true that Alberto had given Martin some specific exercises designed to strengthen his legs and his knee muscles in particular. Regular repetitions of squats with weights and knee extensions on the multigym had certainly made them feel more secure than they had in a long while. "Or it may just be the sunshine that's doing it!". Martin exclaimed, holding out his arms to embrace the glorious weather they were fortunate enough to be running home in. "Or maybe". Chris concluded. "That its running continually up and down those bloody mountains of sand at Maspalomas that's done the trick!". The two laughed as they made their way along the steady incline that wound its way up through the mountains. In comparison to the somewhat barren south of the island the interior experienced slightly higher annual rainfall making the surroundings lush and green. The two headed along the GC-80 which was the road that passed through the small settlements of El Palmital and Las Goteras, stretching relentlessly upwards on a seemingly never-ending highway to the heavens. The duo had become familiar with the two settlements and had often took a well-earned five-minute respite at one or other of them, stopping to chat with some of the locals they had got to know over the preceding weeks. Both settlements were low rise and constructed in the typical Canarian style, inevitably one or two stories with a flat roof and finished in either white or pastel colour washes; their front gardens inevitably adorned with a variety of cactus plants as well as low lying bushes and shrubs encased in boundary walls constructed from local volcanic rock. No mass tourism here though, purely residential dwellings with perhaps the odd holiday villa thrown in for good measure.

Today they passed through El Palmital and raised a hand to Rico and Justine who were sat, as ever, in their front garden taking in the warm sun. They passed too through Las Goteras without stopping and decided to up the pace a bit as the road started to even out. "No sign of Jesus or David today then!". Chris remarked at the absence of the two who were seemingly ubiquitous in the streets of the higher of the two settlements. Martin shook his head as they turned off onto the GC-802 and started on the last few kilometres of the run. They passed the now familiar abandoned shepherds huts and sometime impromptu toilet stop for the two and before long were racing for the line in a final descent into the crater. Martin let Chris go today though as he knew the younger man like to come in first and he wasn't in any mood to rain on his parade by challenging him. That evening the fish, chips and mushy peas complimented with lashings of Malvasia dry white and Honey Rum went down a treat and the three companions slept well in their beds that particular night.

"OK, it's the Marathon!". Alberto stated with unbridled enthusiasm one Friday evening out of the blue as the three of them sat down to share a bottle of Honey Rum after their fish supper. Some three months had passed since Martin's arrival and the companions were sat down relaxing in the evening following a gruelling afternoon at the sand dunes. Alberto raised himself from his favoured chair and handed the other two his notebook for perusal. "What's the marathon?". Martin enquired, somewhat puzzled as he looked at the small blue book he had been handed. It was full of handwritten notes showing times and distances and percentages, some of which had been scribbled out and re written over. "Which way up is it even supposed to go!". Chris remarked as he tried to fathom out its contents, turning the book from end to end as he did so and giving Martin a nudge. Martin tried to stifle a laugh but failed and he too couldn't make head nor tail of the old man's etchings. "Give it here". Alberto stated, somewhat agitated, as he got up from his seat and gestured for them to move aside so that he could squeeze in between them on the small brown velour sofa. By now both Martin and Chris had taken a fond liking to the Honey Rum and Alberto was tonight regretting his decision to introduce them to it as it was apparent that both had already had more than their fill and had got a fit of the giggles. Between the three of them they usually managed to clear the best part of a bottle on a Friday night but as Alberto gazed at the current bottle of the local delicacy on the table he noted that it was nearly empty, and he hadn't yet had the opportunity to partake of more than one glass himself. "So, what's the Marathon then Alberto?". Chris asked the old man again for confirmation. "Your best distance of course! Look here". Alberto explained, pointing out the figures in the notepad, which may as well have been hieroglyphics as far as Martin and Chris were concerned. "I've repeatedly recorded your times over different distances since you've been here, right the way from 5k through to 10k, half marathon and marathon. Here's how your times rank against other athletes in general". He gestured to his notebook pointing to a particular column scrawled down the right-hand side of the page. "And more particularly". He continued, turning the page over "Here they are against the world record times for each event. For the 5 and 10k distances you are around 85 percent of the world record time. For the half marathon your average Martin is 86.2 percent and yours is 88.4 per cent Chris, but when we look at your marathon times, although they fluctuate a bit there was that day when the two of you together came in at 90.1 percent of the world record pace! OK I know that's still ten percent off but if we now were to concentrate our efforts solely on this distance I think we should be able to make some real progress; what do you think?". Martin wasn't a fan of the Marathon. To him his preferred distances were the 5k and 10k as he always found the longer distance a bit gruelling particularly when trying to maintain it at race pace. He guessed though that others probably did as well. Chris on the other hand just loved to keep going and seemed to be able to run for ever. He would probably have made a magnificent ultra-runner or iron man had Alberto been that way inclined, but he wasn't in the market for anything that long. The two of them studied Alberto's notes in a bit more detail and the figures didn't lie. Whilst it may not have been the most enjoyable distance for Martin it did appear to be the one where he had the best results. He recalled the day in question when the two of them had hit that time; it was a relatively cool day, overcast with no sun to speak of and a few light showers. The two had set off and run a fairly long downhill section initially before levelling off for the second half of the distance. Chris remarked as much to Alberto. "We were running downhill for quite a lot on that one?". He recalled, questioning Alberto's reasoning. Alberto went on to point out two other occasions, one when running in and around the capital at Las Palmas and one where they ran a long section of the promenade between Maspalomas and Playa del Ingles one evening which weren't far behind in relation to the timings. Martin also recalled those two runs and nodded his head in silent agreement. He had particularly enjoyed the Playa del Ingles one as he seemed to have had boundless energy that evening and managed to keep up well with Chris, which in itself was no mean feat. "I can see that you've had too much Honey Rum to decide tonight though so we'll sleep on it and decide tomorrow. Personally, I think it's the right decision though". To end the night Alberto broke out his Gibson guitar and gave the two a flawless performance of his favourite 'Cavatina' as well as a rendition of 'Spanish Romance', one of the most popular guitar pieces of all time, even though no one knew who actually composed it! Alberto's finger picking technique was indeed something to behold and Martin gazed in awe at the speed his fingers danced over the fretboard, wondering if there was any end to this man's talents. Martin himself was more of a strummer, and although not in the same league as Alberto, was keen to get his hands on the classic instrument and give it a the once over. Once Alberto had finished he passed it over to Martin who held it lovingly in his arms, feeling the quality of the instrument in comparison to his own vastly inferior model. He fiddled around with a few chords before ultimately serving up his offering. His first song of choice tonight was the classic 'Where do you go to my lovely' by Peter Sarstedt, and as the words were familiar to the other two they joined Martin in a good old-fashioned sing along. The clearness and beauty of the night sky that evening had put Martin in a reflectful mood and the 'starry night' sky had inspired him to play one of the best renditions of Don McLean's 'Vincent' that he had played for many a year, bringing a lump to his colleagues' throats. The night wore on and despite Alberto's attempts to restrict the flow of alcohol to his recruits that evening in the best interest of their training regimes, the seal of another bottle of Honey Rum was soon broken open and as the sun rose the next morning barely an inch remained in the bottom as the three lay fast asleep. Chris and Martin had somehow ended up back inside on the sofa and Alberto back in his favourite armchair. Upon waking none could recall how they had got to their respective positions but needless to say breakfast was somewhat late that morning.

Martin was doing some speedwork on the track that afternoon and nursing a bit of a hangover as he saw the seat Arosa edge its nose over the top rim of the crater and head down the track towards the farmhouse. Alberto had told Martin that Chris was going in to Las Palmas to get some provisions, but Martin had noticed that he had been gone for some time. Chris in fact had been sent to the airport under Alberto's instructions but had been told not to mention it to Martin. He had been asked to go and collect another visitor to the training camp. Martin took little notice of the battered old car as Chris drove it down the precarious track, however as it halted at its destination Martin could see that as well as Chris in the car there was another passenger sat in the front seat. The two exited and Alberto came out of the farmhouse to greet their guest, giving him a large hug as the two of them embraced and patted each other on the back like long lost brothers. Chris led the visitor inside and Alberto ventured out into the crater to shout to Martin. Martin headed back around the track and came back to the farmhouse. "We've got a visitor!". Alberto stated as Martin reached him, the smile on his face widening. "Who's that then?". Martin enquired. "Come inside and you'll see". Alberto replied as he pushed open the kitchen door. Martin entered the room to see Mike stood their wearing the grin of a Cheshire cat. Martin's face lit up when he saw him, and he too embraced the man that had made his journey possible. "Bloody Hell, this is a surprise!". Martin exclaimed, after the two of them had finished hugging. "Well I couldn't let you have all the fun could I. I had to come out and see how things were going, which from what Alberto tells me are quite well I understand. In fact, he thinks you and young Chris here are doing so well that you've got what it takes to become serious contenders for a marathon". "Well he does reckon that's our best distance apparently". Martin responded. "I've never really considered myself as a 'serious contender'". Chris added. "Christopher young Man". Mike continued, looking him square in the face. "I've been around this game long enough to know that if Alberto here says that you're a serious contender, believe me, you 'are' a serious contender. Alberto has told me all about you as well, and myself and Alberto have been in contact with your probation officer and they've given Alberto the go ahead to continue training you after your community service has expired if you want him to?". Mike looked at Alberto and nodded and gestured with his eyes for Alberto to continue. He went over to the top drawer of the dresser and pulled out a folded piece of white card which he handed to Chris. Chris opened it up and studied its contents. It was a list of the week days that had expired since he had arrived, each with the number '8' marked next to them along with Alberto's signature. At the bottom was a total that stated '500 hours', again with Alberto's signature next to it. "Twelve and a half weeks Chris at 40 hours a week. Your five hundred hours are up. You can either take a flight home with Mike when he goes back, or you can stay and continue with your training, it's up to you?". Chris didn't really have to think about it for too long, in fact he didn't have to think about it at all. The last three months spent with Alberto and Martin were probably the best three months of his life and he wasn't about to let them go in a hurry. He had nothing to go back home for and right now, given the opportunity, he couldn't think of anywhere else in the world he would rather be. "Yes, I'd love to stay on if you'll have me!". Chris exclaimed trying to take in all the events that were unfolding around him. Martin too was pleased, not only for Chris but also for himself as he struggled to think of how much he would miss his training partner if he wasn't there, not to mention the implications there would have been on the dynamics of the group if he wasn't around. "I've made an application for funding Chris as obviously there's a cost associated with all of this but I'm sure with my contacts it will just be a formality so don't worry too much about that side of things". Mike explained. "Now me and Alberto will need to work together to sort out a final training programme for you both and decide which event were ultimately going to enter you into". "How long are you staying for then?" Martin enquired of Mike. "Just a week unfortunately". Mike responded. "I wish it was longer, but I've got some other commitments back in the UK that I need to attend to". Alberto nudged Mike and gave him a wink before announcing; "Chris can you see if you can sort out the gym a bit please, we'll have to try and make up a bed in there for you so that Mike can have your room for a while!". Chris wasn't particularly happy about losing his room, but he was the youngest, so it was inevitable that he would be the lowest in the pecking order and he supposed that he couldn't really complain, particularly given the news that Mike had just brought for him. With that in mind he reluctantly headed off to set about his task. Mike and Alberto laughed as Chris entered the gym and stood there pondering how best to rearrange it so that he could find somewhere to sleep. "Chris!". Mike shouted to him. "Yes". Came the response. "Alberto is winding you up, I'm staying in the Hotel Continental down in Playa del Ingles for the week. That was almost as cheap as just getting the flights out and back and I thought I'd stay in comfort for a week rather than muck in here with the three amigos! I will need a lift down there later though if that's OK with you? I've got a hire car lined up for tomorrow, so I'll be self-sufficient from then onwards". Chris re-entered the room and had a wry smile as the four sat down for a chat and a light snack. Alberto instructed his two athletes that today there would be a change from their usual track work so that he and Mike could have the opportunity to go through the statistics he had gathered and plan the next months of their training programme. "So it will be a long run for you two today then guys". Alberto instructed them, and as they headed out of the door for the usual two-hour session, Alberto and Mike sat down and set to work.

Chapter 23

On the third day of Mike's stay the four got together again for
another meeting and Mike and Alberto's plans for the future
training regime were explained. "Alberto and I have put
together a training plan for you both for the next three months.
It'll be a similar format to what you're used to, but it'll be
geared up with the goal of you both achieving your best
possible marathon time at the end of the it. Alberto will also be
working out your diet plans as he has been previously, but we
may need to up the carbs a bit to compensate for the amount
of distance work you'll be doing. I'm impressed at how you've
both come on though, so fundamentally I think Alberto's got it
spot on up to now and there aren't many people who could
have got you where you are in this timeframe. Credit to him for
doing that and also credit to you two for putting in the effort to
bring it to fruition".

"So which marathon are we aiming for then?". Chris asked. "Is
there one in Gran Canaria?". There was a brief pause and
Mike and Alberto looked at each other. "Go on Mike you tell
them". Alberto nodded in his companion's direction. Mike
looked at Martin and Chris sat there at the table, side by side
in front of him, a look of anticipation on their faces. "London!".
He announced simply. "London 2020 to be precise, that's
when you two should be ready and at your peak. Well
theoretically you should have passed your peak years ago
Martin!". He added, smiling that broad smile of his, but if you
follow our training plan you'll have a realistic chance of
finishing in the top 100". "But!" Alberto interjected
"Unfortunately it's not going to be quite that simple. You can't
just waltz up and say that you want to enter the London
marathon; it doesn't work like that. And you don't want to take
a gamble on the lottery of a run of the mill application or a
charity application, as even if you do get a place you'll be
something like number twenty-five thousand on the starting
grid and it'll take half an hour or more before you even get to

the start line. To have a realistic chance of finishing in the top 100 you'll need to get an entry as either an elite athlete or we'll need to apply for a championship entry place". "What's the difference?" Chris enquired. "Well there's probably only thirty or forty places for the elite athletes; these guys are your household names and the ones that will be competing to win, these are the guys that have their names on the front of their running vests rather than a number". Mike explained, gesturing to his chest as if to emphasise the fact. "It'll be nigh on impossible to get you an elite entry unless by some miracle you can win another major marathon within the next couple of months, and by the way that isn't going to happen! Also, don't try and kid yourselves that you 'are' elite athletes, you're both getting some good times, but you aren't in the same class as these guys. The best we can hope for really is a championship entry place". Both Martin and Chris were listening intently as the two trainers explained the process. They had certainly done their homework. "So, what's a championship entry place then?". Martin enquired. "Well this is the next best thing to the elite entry". Alberto explained. "If you can get one of those you'll start in the pack immediately behind the elite runners and if you can get near the start of this group you should be able to get a fairly uninterrupted start. But even to get a championship entry you'll have to have done well in either a half or full marathon and unfortunately running around the roads of Gran Canaria, however quick you may have done it, isn't going to cut it I'm afraid". Alberto clearly outlined the position as it stood in no uncertain terms and to Martin it sounded like it was going to be a fairly tall order even to get the right entry. Mike jumped in and took over; "We need to get you into a situation where you've completed a half marathon in an hour and fifteen minutes or a marathon within two hours and forty-five minutes, those are the cut off qualifying times for a championship entry". Mike's words were at least of some comfort as both athletes knew that those were times they were capable of achieving and looked towards each other and nodded their heads in agreement that it would indeed be a realistic target.

"So, what we are planning to do." Mike continued. "Is to enter you in the Great South run back home in Exeter. That's a half marathon rather than a marathon and you should both be relatively familiar with the area given that it's your old stomping grounds. If you manage to get your times, then we can apply for a London entry as a championship athlete. Simple!". The plan did indeed sound simple enough, but it still depended on Martin and Chris putting in a lot of hard work. "One last thing". Mike went on. "We've got to get you both registered with an official athletics club and the official governing body. I've had a word with James about that back home and I'm sorting it out for you both through him". There was a lot to take in and by the end of the meeting both Martin and Chris's heads were spinning. "So, to summarise". Mike stated. "All you two have to do is run when Alberto says run and when he says jump you ask how high, got it?". They both nodded. "Good, now you two put in the miles and do the leg work and leave the planning and admin to me and Alberto and everything will be hunky dory!".

Mike saw out his week on the island and visited the three each day to check on their progress and work through a few things with Alberto, before eventually it was time to fly back home. Martin took the opportunity of driving him to the airport on this occasion and bade him a fond farewell as he headed off into the departures lounge. The following weeks and months passed with Martin and Chris sticking rigidly to the training programme and eating plan as Alberto had laid down. On Mike's instruction Alberto had also cut them down on the alcohol rations although this was relaxed on Friday and Saturday nights with Alberto insisting that the honey element was beneficial for bodily wellbeing and that it lubricated the joints. Martin didn't know about that, but he certainly looked forward to the extra rations that the weekend brought with it!

"Somethings been playing on my mind Martin". Chris confided in his colleague as they were about halfway through their regular Friday long run. They had stopped for a short breather in the village of Las Goteras and were perched on a bench, sheltered in the shade of a large palm tree, half seated, and half lied back, their legs stretched out and their eyes closed in reflection, just enjoying the peace and tranquillity. "What's that then mate?". Martin enquired, raising himself to an upright position. "Well it was something that Mike said when he came over, I'm not sure if you picked up on it at all?". Martin's memory wasn't what it used to be; in fact there weren't really many things about Martin that were what they used to be for that matter! Martin thought for a moment but couldn't really recall anything untoward. "What did he say then Chris?". Martin asked his companion. Chris sat upright next to him and looked him in the face somewhat concerned. "Well he said that we shouldn't kid ourselves that we're elite athletes and that we weren't in the same class as those guys". Martin recalled vaguely that something along those lines had been said. He also supposed that the fact wasn't far from the truth and he certainly didn't consider himself to be of that standard. "Well he's probably got a point hasn't he, we're hardly what you would call world class are we?". "Yes, but what's the point in us carrying on with all this hard work then if we aren't going to make it. We may as well give up now, with all the training we're putting in there's no way that we could do any more is there?". "No, I suppose not". Martin responded. "It's all about perception though isn't it and what you perceive to be a realistic goal, you've just got to keep plugging away and improving gradually, bit by bit, inch by inch. You're still young Chris, there's plenty of time for you to improve. I tell you what if that's what Mike thinks let's work that little bit harder to prove him wrong shall we? Show him that we have got what it takes. If we can work together as a team, lets show him what were capable of!". Chris perked up a bit and a smile crossed his face. He nodded in Martin's direction, now beginning to see things from a slightly different perspective. "Yes let's show him!". With that the two set off at a rapid pace for the run back to base. Mike however had known exactly what he was doing when he uttered those words, and he never did or said anything by accident. The comment was slipped in to the conversation intentionally to fire the two of them up, as like Alberto, Mike knew that being a successful distance runner was all about mental ability as well as the physical and although the hint was too subtle for Martin, Chris at least had picked up the bait and run with it!

Spurred on by the forthcoming half marathon, the training regime was gradually ramped up before being tapered in the final two weeks to allow extra rest periods in the build up to the event. This would ensure that both athletes were fresh and well energised for the big day. The duo flew into Exeter airport a week before the event where they were greeted by Martin's son Max, who had arranged to collect them. Chris and Martin enjoyed a week at Martin's home before the race date and continued with the planned build up in the somewhat cooler Devon climate. Both were given instructions on how to run the race and what time they were aiming for; one hour fourteen minutes and thirty seconds. Any faster and they would expend too much precious energy, any slower and they risked not making the qualifying time for London. As it played out the two ran a good tactical race on the day and cut it somewhat fine by coming in at one hour fourteen minutes and fifty seconds; still just within the qualifying time though. Mike was there to greet the two at the finish line as Chris came in a nose in front of Martin. Mike was pleased with how the day had gone and couldn't have asked for any more from his protégés.

The next few days were due to be spent at Martin's house before the two flew back to Gran Canaria on the Friday. That Wednesday morning however Martin wasn't up for breakfast at his usual time and as Max and Abi had already left for work Chris gave a tap on his bedroom door. In Alberto's absence Chris had taken on the task of preparing the cooked breakfast and although it was ready and waiting, Martin hadn't yet surfaced. As there was no reply to his first attempt, Chris knocked gently again and pushed the door open to reveal the room was still in darkness with not a sound or movement coming from Martin's bed. "Martin, breakfast's ready". Chris whispered. Martin however merely turned over and pulled the covers tighter around his face. "I'm not feeling too good today Chris, is there any chance you could get a couple of tablets for me please, they're in the top cupboard over the cooker?". He burbled from under the covers. Chris returned to the kitchen and opened the door of the cupboard in question. He sifted through the vast array of medication on offer and plumped for a couple of paracetamol before half filling a glass with water and returning to Martin's room. "Here you go mate". He gestured, holding the tablets out. Martin gingerly sat up in bed and took them from Chris, placing them one by one in his mouth before washing them down with the water. "What's the matter Martin, headache?". "I'm not really sure". Martin groaned. "I wasn't feeling too good yesterday and this morning it feels like I've got bloody toothache as there's a shooting pain down the side of my face". He rubbed his jaw with the palm of his hand, grimacing in pain as he did so. "I don't think I can face any breakfast I'm afraid, you go on and have yours and I'll see how I feel in a bit". It was mid-day when Martin woke again, the limited effects of the tablets having worn off. The toothache was still very much in evidence. Chris had been out to fetch a paper and was sat patiently reading it in the lounge as Martin entered. "I hate to say it Martin, but you look like shit mate!". Chris observed. "That's a coincidence because I feel like shit as well! I'll have to try and make an appointment with the dentist to get this sorted before we fly back out; I'll give them a ring to see if I can get an emergency appointment".

Chapter 24

"Martin Price". The dental assistant called out as she looked around the waiting room. There was only Martin and two other women sat there on that Thursday morning, so logic dictated that her eyes were fixed firmly in Martin's direction. He put down the year-old dog eared copy of Runners World he was flicking through and made his way across the waiting room, gazing briefly at his reflection in the large ornate gold framed mirror that seemed to take up the whole of the wall adjacent to the reception desk. Martin thought that he looked old; well older than he generally looked anyway but put it down to the fact that he hadn't shaved for a couple of days owing to the pain he was in. "Take a seat". The dentist gestured to Martin to sit down in the large chair at the centre of the room, tilted back and eagerly awaiting its next victim. Martin didn't like going to the dentist, never had done, and every time he visited he could never get the infamous scene from the film 'Marathon Man' out of his head; The one where Thomas 'Babe' Levy, played by Dustin Hoffman, was being tortured by the sadistic dentist in an attempt to get information from him about his stolen diamond collection. "Is it safe?". He kept asking Babe repeatedly; a question to which Babe had no answer, having no idea of the diamonds whereabouts, thus resulting in the aforementioned dentist drilling straight through his tooth into the nerve, 'sans anesthetic'. Now it was Martin who was the metaphorical Marathon Man and in the same position, putting himself at the mercy of his dentist, whom he was hoping would be somewhat more forgiving!

"You haven't been for quite a while have you?". Doctor Bowman enquired of Martin once he had him sat on the chair. The receptionist placed a bib around Martin's neck as the dentist lowered the chair back and swung the large 'interrogation' light into place. Martin started to sweat profusely. He knew there was no reason to fear the dentist but somehow, he still had an irrational uneasiness in their presence. He also hated injections and had a phobia about needles, to the extent that he almost passed out at the sight of them. He hoped today there would be no requirement for one but also wished an end to the constant pain he was in. "No, I don't think I've been for a little while". Replied Martin, not even remotely aware of the last time he had attended. "Did you not get our e mails and texts?". Doctor Bowman enquired, as he gestured for Martin to open his mouth. Martin often wondered why dentists did that; ask you a question and then expect you to answer coherently with their hands and a surgical instrument stuck in your mouth, all whilst trying to open it as wide as you were able. Martin had got the texts and the e mails but like most people of course he had simply ignored them, only going to the dentist when absolutely necessary such as in times of toothache. "You wouldn't believe the amount of people that don't come in for regular check ups!". Doctor Bowman went on. "They then come in to us with raging toothache wondering why they've got it!". "Really, that's interesting". Martin neither knew or really cared about what Dr Bowman was saying but tried to respond as best as he could in the awkward position he was in. It probably just sounded like a random noise though to Doctor Bowman such was his difficulty to speak. As the dentist peered into his mouth and started probing around with the stainless-steel surgical implement in his hand, Martin wondered if it was a requirement that all dentists had to have bad breath! He wondered if on the application form there was actually a box to tick that stated; Bad breath; Yes or No? And that only those that met the pungent requirements need apply. He screwed his face up, breathing heavily out through his nose to try and block out the odor and closed his eyes as the dentist went around each tooth in turn, tapping, scraping and prodding, before eventually withdrawing the instrument and retiring to the back of the room with the receptionist. He returned and raised his protective goggles. "I can't find anything wrong". He concluded. "I'm going to take some X rays though just to make sure I haven't missed anything, particularly with those back ones". And with that inserted the necessary plates into Martin's mouth before retiring to take the pictures. Martin was instructed to return to the waiting room upon completion and not more than ten minutes later was called back in again by the receptionist. "I've checked the X rays". Doctor Bowman informed Martin. "But there's nothing showing up there either". "That's strange, I was expecting there to be a massive hole given how much pain I'm in. Are you sure there isn't anything wrong?". Martin enquired. "I just said there wasn't didn't I". The dentist replied in a somewhat acute fashion. "What nothing at all?". Martin persisted, rubbing his jaw as if to emphasise the fact that the pain was still there and there must be something untoward. "Look if there was a problem there I would have found it OK!". Dr Bowman was obviously having a bad day and not wishing to feel the backlash of his tongue any more, Martin thanked him for his time and retired gracefully. He supposed like all people that dentists too must have their off days, I mean how pleasant could it have been to have to prod around in people's mouths all day to earn a living. Martin compared it to the customer experience he himself delivered at work, whereby the outcome probably hung on what kind of day he himself was having and almost started to feel sorry for the dentist. That feeling however soon left him as he returned to the reception to pay his not insignificant bill! He walked out of the surgery door somewhat lighter of pocket but no further forward in his quest for an answer to his problem.

"Did you get it sorted then?". Chris asked expectantly, in a matter of fact way as Martin returned from his appointment. Like Martin, he too was expecting it to be a mere formality and supposed that a quick filling would not only have saved the day but also relieved his friend of the pain he was in. "No, I didn't!". Replied Martin, shaking his head somewhat forlornly. "The dentist says that he can't find anything wrong! There's definitely something not right though, it feels like one of them needs pulling out, it's right at the side here". He complained, gesturing to Chris as to where the pain was. "So, what are you going to do now then?". Chris enquired. "I don't know, but right now I need to take some more painkillers and go back to bed for a while to see if it eases off a bit. I'll see if I've got anything a bit stronger than paracetamol though as they didn't really touch it. He rummaged through the medicine cupboard in the kitchen, pulling out various boxes to see what was in them and fished out an old packet of co codamol that by its faded nature had obviously been there for some time. He had a brief read of the instructions and then gulped two down. After half an hour in bed and with the pain in his face no better he got up and took another two just for good measure.

"Dad how are you feeling?". Martin was awoken by the soft sound of his daughter's voice sometime later. Abi and her brother had by now arrived home from work and were surprised to see their dad laid up in bed. Martin had the odd headache from time to time and occasionally suffered a bit with cold and flu symptoms, but he wasn't the type of person who was ever ill. He was the type of person who would soldier on relentlessly even if he wasn't one hundred percent fit. He wasn't one to complain and rarely took to his bed through illness. Abi could see though that this time he really didn't look that good. Martin explained the symptoms to his offspring and recalled to them how the dentist had looked but wasn't able to find anything. "Who did you see then?". Max enquired. "Doctor Bowman". Martin replied. "Bloody hell, not him, he's useless!". Max exclaimed, "He couldn't find the bloody hay in a haystack never mind the needle!". "Well he did have a fairly good look and he took some x rays. I know he's a bit miserable but he's probably a reasonable dentist". Max wasn't convinced. "Well if you're in that much pain there must be something wrong, perhaps you need someone else to look at it and get a second opinion". "Hmm yes maybe". Martin replied. "Look I'll take a couple more tablets and see how it is in the morning. His daughter was concerned; "But you're supposed to be flying back to Gran Canaria tomorrow, aren't you Dad? Max has taken the day off to give you a lift up hasn't he?". Max nodded confirming his sister's thoughts that he had indeed offered to drive his father and Chris up to the airport the next day. "I'll probably be fine in the morning, let me get some rest and we'll see how it goes. Can you tell Chris please that I'll see him in the morning?".

"Martin Price?". Dr Patek called as she stuck her head around the waiting room door, beckoning her next patient. Martin had woken up that morning with his face in agony and far from feeling better he was feeling like death warmed up. Max had rung the surgery on opening and secured an appointment for his dad for later that morning. Martin put down the two-year-old copy of Hello magazine that he had been flicking through for the prior thirty minutes, trying to find something in there of actual interest. He failed but read an article about David Beckham starting up his own fashion brand as well as reading all about Peter Andre's latest skiing holiday with his wife and two children. He supposed that the magazine itself harboured no end of germs having been thumbed through by all and sundry with unmentionable diseases. It was however the lesser of two evils as he only picked them up to avoid the gaze of the other patients in the waiting room. It was better to stare blankly at a magazine than have to try and avoid the gaze of others there who were coughing and spluttering and no doubt spreading copious quantities of their own germs around to all and sundry. He was feeling bad enough as it was and could ill afford to pick up any other airborne nasties that were floating around. As he rose he noted the sign over the door displaying the words; 'Waiting Room' in clinical black and white. 'More like God's waiting room' Martin thought to himself as he looked around at the rooms other elderly and infirm inhabitants. Wheelchairs, walking frames, crutches and walking sticks appeared to be de rigeur and as he walked past one elderly white-haired gentleman and cast him a sideways glance he swore he saw a twenty-year older version of himself staring back at him. A shudder ran down his spine. He carefully picked his way through the strange and colourful ensemble of chairs towards where Doctor Patek was waiting. She gave him a half smile and beckoned him to follow her to her consulting room, closing the door behind them and advising Martin to take a seat once there. Martin felt a sharp pain shoot through the right side of his face, abruptly reminding him of the reason for his visit.

"What seems to be the problem today Mr Price?". Dr Patek asked Martin. Martin was sat directly opposite the doctor and immediately noted how young she was. Petite and attractive with olive skin and long dark hair, she couldn't have been any older than her mid-twenties. Martin hadn't seen her before and indeed all the doctors he had grown up with and seen in his younger days had either now retired or died. She seemed pleasant enough though and at least appeared moderately more interested in his symptoms than the dentist did the previous day. "Well I've been getting these shooting pains in the right side of my face". Martin explained. "Initially I thought it was toothache, but I've been to the dentist and he's checked everything out and taken some x rays, but he can't find anything wrong". "How long have you been experiencing the pain?". The doctor enquired. Martin explained that it had come on a few days ago and that there hadn't really been any let up in it since. "You say the dentist took an x ray, but it didn't show anything?". She enquired, tapping a few notes on to her computer screen. "Yes, that's right". "Have you been taking anything for the pain?". Martin had, but he didn't really want to explain to her that he had been taking some strong painkillers that had been prescribed to his late father some years ago which were now way out of date. "Yes, I've taken some paracetamol and ibuprofen…. oh, and I also took a few co codamol which I had at home". "Did any of that relieve the pain?". She enquired. "Well not really with the paracetamol and ibuprofen but the co codamol helped a bit". "I'm just going to give you an examination if that's OK?". The doctor went on. Upon confirming his agreement Dr Patek asked Martin to lie down on the couch. She questioned him about whether he had pain on his scalp and asked him to close his eyes whilst she lightly touched different parts of his face, asking him to identify exactly where the pain was. She then asked him to smile and informed him she wanted to rule out the possibility of a stroke. She took Martin's blood pressure; "100 over 50!". She exclaimed, raising her eyebrows in approval. "Well on the positive side your blood pressure is amazing! You must be very fit; are you some sort of athlete?". "Well not really". Replied Martin, modestly. "I do a bit of running that's all". "You should definitely keep it up then as its working well for you. Do you know what strength the co codamol tablets were?". "No, I'm afraid I don't". Replied Martin. "That's OK." she continued. "I can look them up on your records". "Erm, I don't think they were actually my tablets, I think they may have been ones that my dad let me have!". She gave Martin a fixed stare, the kind a teacher gives to an unruly school child when they've done something they knew they shouldn't have. "You shouldn't really be taking other people's medication you know, it can be very dangerous!". She informed Martin, stating the obvious. 'Blimey they were only a few painkillers'. Martin thought to himself. He had also observed though that they were over five years out of date before he took them but proceeded to take them anyway as surely tablets couldn't actually go off could they! The Doctor paused for a few seconds and returned to her desk to type something into her computer. Martin strained his neck but was unable to see what it was. "Do you know if they were still in date?". She asked. Martin thought for a second…he knew they weren't. "I'm not sure". He replied.

Dr Patek gave him another knowing stare before asking him to return to the seat. She went on to explain what she thought the problem was. "Well from the symptoms you've described I think what you have is Trigeminal Neuralgia". It's quite a rare condition that affects the Trigeminal nerve in your head which in turn triggers a pain in one side of the face. The pain can be felt either in the jaw, the cheek, or as in your case the teeth. It can also on occasion be felt in the forehead or the eye". It sounded to Martin that what she had described fitted his symptoms exactly. It was a million miles however from what Martin wanted to hear. He was hoping she would say that it was simply an infection that could be treated with a few tablets and that he would soon be as right as rain again and winging his way back to Gran Canaria on the plane with Chris. This certainly wasn't what he needed at this stage of his training, or indeed at any time for that matter. His mind started to drift off as Dr Patek continued to talk, totally oblivious to the fact that Martin wasn't listening to a word she said. He was thinking merely of his running and of his training regime and how he was supposed to be catching that plane back to Gran Canaria later that day. This was something he didn't need and was likely to set him back massively. "So, what do you think then?". Asked the doctor. "Shall we get you booked in?". "Sorry, booked in for what?". Martin replied, trying to refocus his attention on the doctor sat in front of him, who was by now leaning in towards him in anticipation of a response. Martin again noted how young she was. He wondered if it was possible that someone so young and with so little experience could diagnose something just by asking him a few questions and tapping his face a few times. "Sorry". Martin apologised again. "I didn't really take all that in, would you be able to explain it to me again please". The doctor was used to the response and explained again that they needed to establish exactly what it was that was causing pressure on the nerve, and the only way to do this was initially to have a scan and then decide on the best course of action depending upon what it showed. "But I'm supposed to be flying out to Gran Canaria this afternoon!". Martin protested. Dr Patek leaned a little further in towards Martin and said softly; "Look Martin I can't stop you going on your trip but if you value my advice, I think you need to get this sorted out as soon as possible. Is it a holiday you've got booked?". Martin explained how he was on a training programme and that by not returning today it would affect all that he was working towards. "Well as I said I can't stop you, but realistically are you telling me that you are going to be able to train feeling like you are now? What happens if you get back out there and you aren't any better, do you really want to be stuck in a foreign country if you're ill?". Martin was listening, but the words were going right through him. It wasn't what he wanted to hear, and he didn't even have the energy to muster a response, he just sat there in silence and stared at the table in front of him, a million things spinning around in his head. Dr Patek knew he wasn't in a position to be able to think clearly so she offered up a suggestion. "Look Martin, it's important that we find out what's causing this, and I think I can probably get you in for a scan sometime next week if I pull a few strings. I think it's best if you postpone your trip for a week or so and see what the scan shows up. If all goes well you should be able to fly out again in a week or two, how does that sound?". 'To be honest it sounds like a pile of crap!' Martin thought to himself but outwardly conceded that he had little other option and agreed that Dr Patek would contact him when she had made the appointment. Martin left the surgery feeling somewhat dejected with a prescription for some strong painkillers as a temporary remedy to the ailment.

Max returned his dad to the house and after he and Chris had reluctantly said their goodbyes Max drove Chris up to the airport to make the solo trip back to the island. Abi gave her dad a hug and tried to console him as much as she was able before packing him off to bed with a hot water bottle for his face and another couple of painkillers. Later that night she heard the sound of sobbing coming from her father's room but decided not to venture in and disturb him.

Alberto was somewhat shocked later that evening when in Gran Canaria airport it was solely Chris that walked through the arrivals gate and he was both saddened and concerned to hear of Martin's plight. That evening as Chris lay awake in bed, he could hear Alberto on the phone having a long discussion with Mike.

Chapter 25

The following days passed, and Alberto and Mike had both contacted Martin to see how things were progressing. James had been around to see him and managed to get Martin out for a run and a chat, aided by copious quantities of the codeine painkillers the doctor had prescribed. If he took enough of them on a regular basis the pain was just about manageable, and he actually found that when he was out running it took his mind off the pain and it felt better than when at home resting up. "So, what's the plan now then Martin?". James enquired as Martin took him on one of his preferred runs out from Wildewater and along the cliff path before returning and running along the sea front. Martin was admiring the waves as the two ran past, about four feet high, and glassy; a slight offshore wind made them hold up perfectly before breaking and peeling off to perfection along the rocks. 'ideal surfing conditions' he thought to himself. "Sorry James, I was miles away there mate, for a moment I was out riding one of those waves! What's the plan? Well I heard from Dr Patek yesterday and she's managed to get me in on Wednesday afternoon to see a consultant and have a scan. I should be getting confirmation in the post, hopefully tomorrow". "Where have you got to go then, Exeter?". "No". Replied Martin. "I've got to go all the way up to Southmead hospital in Bristol, apparently that's the regional centre for neuroscience, and where all the specialists are!". "Bloody hell that's a pain, are you OK to get there, I can try and get a day off work and drive you up if you like". "Thanks for the offer mate, it's much appreciated but one of the kids is going to drive me up". "OK, hope it all goes well mate!". James empathised. "Yes, me too!". Martin responded.

That Wednesday afternoon Abi drove her dad up to Southmead hospital in Bristol where the scan was to take place. Martin hadn't been allowed to eat anything that morning and was beginning to feel hungry as the two made their way up the motorway. Before the scan, Martin was booked in to See Mr Mahmood who was the specialist consultant. "How come he's a 'Mr' then Dad and not a doctor?". Abi enquired of Martin as she manoeuvred the car into the last remaining space in the car park, nudging it back and forth a few times before resting to a halt between the two adjacent vehicles. They concluded that hospital must have been busy that afternoon as Abi had driven in and out of two car parks already without being able to find a space, only to grab the last available one in the third. Martin thought back to a conversation he had with his wife many years ago when she herself was ill and had explained the difference to him between doctors and consultants. "Your mum always knew stuff like that Abi!". He remembered fondly. "She was a font of all knowledge! It's so the surgeons can distinguish themselves from the run of the mill doctors who are probably less qualified. Years ago, barbers used to carry out surgery and as they didn't have any medical qualifications they would have to use the term 'Mr'!". "Barbers used to do surgery!". She exclaimed. Martin laughed. "Sounds a bit barbaric doesn't it, but things have moved on a bit since those days Abi………. well at least I hope they have!". "Perhaps you could ask him for a bit of a trim whilst you're in there then Dad, your hair is getting a bit long!". Abi stated in an attempt to lighten the mood. Once Abi had parked up Martin headed to the ticket machine and as he stood there reading the instructions a white Volkswagen Golf pulled up alongside him containing an elderly couple who were exiting the car park. The driver wound down the window and gestured to Martin to come over. As he did so the man offered up his ticket. "Here you go son you can have this one if you want, it runs all day". Martin thanked the gent for his generosity, his faith in human nature restored, and he returned to place the ticket on the dashboard of his own car.

After being sat in the waiting room for what seemed like an age, Martin was eventually called in by the nurse to see Mr Mahmood. At least he thought he was being called in to see him but what was actually happening was that he was merely being led into a small side room, only to experience another lengthy wait before he actually appeared.

In the loneliness of the small room a number of thoughts were resonating through Martin's mind, the majority of which were negative and began with; "What happens if..." He was glad when eventually the door opened and the man himself appeared. Mr Mahmood was a small, slim man, around five feet five inches in height and of Indian origin. Dressed in a grey suit and tie with a crisp white shirt, he put out his hand to greet Martin. Martin looked at him, his face was thin, craggy and lined, and he looked weary, bearing all the hallmarks of a long stressful career in the medical profession. Martin wondered how much bad news the man had had to dispense during his long tenure and supposed that each time he did, it merely added another micron of depth to one of the many lines already deeply engrained in his face. He hoped news of his own predicament wouldn't be adding to them! "Mr Price?". He enquired, tilting his head and squinting slightly at Martin. "I'm Mr Mahmood". He sat down opposite to Martin in the small room and explained the purpose of the scan and the procedure that was about to follow. He explained that 'PET' stood for 'Positron Emission Tomography.' 'Easy for you to say!' Thought Martin. And that the scan not only showed what body tissues looked like and whether there were any abnormalities, but also how well they were working. It was all just noise however to Martin and he was more focused on Mr Mahmood's large bushy unkempt eyebrows and the vast amount of hair that appeared to be growing out of his ears. 'How is that even possible?' He thought to himself as he stared at them with a lingering gaze that was probably somewhat rude. It was the little things about people though that fascinated Martin, the little idiosyncrasies that made them different and stand out from the crowd, and if he found Mr Mahmood interesting, unknown to him at that moment, his cup was soon about to runneth over! The whole experience took no more than five minutes and it wasn't long before Martin was sat back next to his daughter in the waiting room and the next patient had been led into the side room to await their appointment. "What did he say then Dad?". His daughter asked. "Not a lot really, he just explained what would happen during the scan and that we'd have to come back up again in a week or so to get the results". Abi nodded and patted her dad reassuringly on the knee.

After what seemed like another eternity, a nurse came to lead Martin down to the room where the scanner was situated. It was some distance away from where they were seated so she gestured to Abi to come with them and she would show her to a different waiting area. They made their way along a number of long corridors heading this way and that before reaching their ultimate destination. "If you'd like to take a seat here please". The nurse gestured to Abi and I'll take Mr Price in for his appointment. It could be anywhere between thirty minutes and an hour though so if you want to go off and get a drink or anything there's a vending machine at the end of the corridor or there's the shop by the main entrance". "See you later Abi". Said Martin. "Good luck Dad". Abi shouted behind him as the nurse led him through to the room where the scan was to take place.

Once inside the room Martin was introduced to the radiographer, Tony Hilling. He was a bit of a strange looking individual, particularly tall with long curly dark hair tied back in a pony tail, with a black beard to match, around eight inches or so long. On the right side of his neck there was a distinguishing tattoo of a swallow in flight. Martin had seen the like of it before and knew that they were usually associated with sailors who historically had them on their neck, hands or chest as a mark of their sailing experience. Martin felt uneasy in the man's presence and had he seen him outside the confines of the hospital he would probably have crossed the road to avoid him and would never have put him down as a member of the medical profession. Tony could see that Martin was looking at him rather strangely. It was something that he had become accustom to though and had seen the look a thousand times before. In fact he had seen a number of looks many times before! Every time a new patient ventured through his door and set eyes on him their range of expressions showed everything from shock and horror through to amusement and even pity. As such he had decided a long time ago to bring up the elephant in the room and get it out of the way as soon as possible to put his patients minds at ease. "Hi Martin, I'm Tony and I'll be carrying out your scan today. Now before we go any further I know exactly what you're thinking; 'What the hell does this guy look like and am I in safe hands here!". It was indeed a good icebreaker that took Martin by surprise but at least he could see that the guy did have a sense of humour if nothing else. Martin's face cracked a smile. "Truth is I play in a ZZ Top tribute band; 'ZZ Stop', not sure if you've ever heard of us but we're quite big in the area?". Martin looked Tony up and down. 'Looks like you're quite big in every area!' He thought to himself. Martin had never heard of 'ZZ Stop' and reiterated as much to Tony. "No, I come from North Devon so probably a bit far away from your patch". "We did a gig down at Tavistock Wharf once if I recall correctly but no nothing in North Devon specifically, probably not much point in giving you one of my flyers then is there?". Tony asked, pointing to a pile on his desk. "I'll take one if you like". Replied Martin. "You never know when you'll be in the mood for a bit of 'ZZ Stop' do you!". The two had a chat about rock bands in general and realised that they had similar musical tastes, both having being brought up in the same era and preferring the heavy rock genre. Once Tony had put Martin at ease he moved on to the main purpose of the afternoon. "Right let's get down to business then shall we?". Tony stated. "I suppose so". Martin replied. "You've probably noticed this beast by now!". Stated Tony, gesturing to the huge machine that took up virtually the whole of the room, save for the small area that contained Tony's desk and his precious supply of 'ZZ Stop' flyers. "Hard not too!". Replied Martin, as he cast his eye over the massive white and stainless-steel machine that consisted of a long platform encased in what looked like a large white doughnut. The only other distinguishing feature of the nondescript whitewashed room was a window of about three feet square along one wall. Martin was instructed to remove his clothes and to place on a pale blue hospital gown that Tony handed to him. Martin picked it up noting that it was about the size of a small tent. "One size fits all!". Tony beamed. Once Martin had donned the gown, Tony lowered the bed and instructed Martin to lie down on it on his back. "OK that's good". Advised Tony, when Martin was in position. I'm going to give you an injection now and insert this tube into your arm. The fluid will spread through your body which helps the scanner to create the images. It shows up places in your body where glucose congregates so it's particularly good for images of the brain".

The injection itself actually contained radioactive material but Tony had learned over the years not to dwell too much on this fact! It didn't tend to go down too well when mentioned to his patients and they tended to start asking awkward questions like; 'Is having radioactive material pumped into my body actually any good for my health?". It was of course the lesser of two evils as without it the scan wouldn't show up potential problems and as such there would be no treatment. The radioactive material did have its downside however and as well as the health implications there were other practical drawbacks. In some cases, patients that had been flying within a few days of their scan had experienced trouble passing through the airport scanners due to the amount of radioactivity still in their system! Tony was hoping that Martin wouldn't be asking too many questions about the injection and as Martin had an inherent fear of injections anyway all he wanted to do was to get it over with as quickly as possible and try not focus in any great detail as to what was being pumped in to his body. Tony raised the bed to its required height and once he was sure Martin was comfortable he exited the room to the cover of an adjacent one where the control panel of the machine was situated, stating to Martin that the two would be able to communicate via the intercom between the adjacent rooms.

"Can you hear me Martin?". Tony asked, checking that the lines of communication were in working order. "Yes". "We'll need to wait a while for the injection to start to work before we begin so just lie there and relax for a while and I'll give you a shout when were ready to start". "OK". Martin replied. Martin lay there; in a whitewashed room no more that twelve feet square on what was effectively a large tin tray staring up at a big white doughnut talking to one of the weirdest looking people he had ever met, through an intercom. 'Yes, just relax, that's easy!' He thought to himself. 'I can't think of any more a relaxing situation than this!' Tony started fiddling with some dials and buttons in the control room and realised that it may be a while before the scan could start. "Would you like a bit of music whilst you're waiting?". Tony enquired. "Go on then". Martin replied. Tony turned on the radio and piped the music into the room. His preferred station of choice was Radio Two and as it was just after three o'clock in the afternoon it was 'non-stop oldies' time. The song playing was 'Forever Young' by Alphaville and Martin recognised it immediately as he tuned in to the chorus.' 'Hmm Very appropriate!' Martin thought to himself! As his mind again began to wonder prompted by the words. Did he really want to live forever? Did anybody for that matter? Well maybe not forever but he certainly wanted to live to a ripe old age as long as his mind and body were intact.

"OK Martin we're good to go!". His thoughts were broken by the sound of Tony's voice over the intercom as the dulcet tones of Alphaville's lead singer faded to a close. "That's a shame, I was just going to put in a request for a bit of ZZ Stop!". Martin exclaimed. Tony laughed. "Hang on a minute and I'll get my guitar out!... Now for this bit I need you to keep very still please". He instructed. "Once I set the machine in motion you'll feel the bed start to move and it'll pass slowly through the doughnut and back again taking pictures as it goes. Its painless but you may start to feel uncomfortable after a while as you have to remain perfectly still. Let me know if you start getting stiff and need to move and I'll pause the machine. OK are you ready?". Martin replied that he was and gave Tony the thumbs up before adjusting himself into the final position he felt relatively comfortable in. Tony had turned the radio off so that the two could communicate if necessary and Martin could now hear the dull hum of the machine as he felt the bed slowly start to move. He hadn't noticed it before but looked up to see a video camera high on the wall, its gaze firmly fixed on the machine and he supposed that Tony could not only see him through the window but through this as well. Ten minutes or so had passed before Martin did indeed start to feel uncomfortable. The machine hadn't yet completed half of its cycle and he was beginning to realise how slowly time actually passed when you were wishing just the opposite. Time was time though wasn't it! He concluded, it always passed at the same speed, a second was a second and a minute was a minute whatever you were doing within that time. There were no bricks to count today. He looked around at the bare walls as best he could, moving his eyes only and trying to keep his head still in an attempt to find some distraction to the tedium. There was nothing though. He closed his eyes and tried to relax, hoping that he might nod off but had no such luck. All the time the bed edged its way slowly through the doughnut building up a picture of Martin's internal workings so that the experts could analyse them and advise him of his fate. He thought of the Roman Colosseum and the emperor standing there with the gladiator in the pit awaiting their fate; was it to be the thumbs up or the thumbs down, life or death! He felt the bed judder to a halt. Half the cycle was complete. If he was on a run, he would be on the homeward stretch now and tried to imagine him and Chris in Gran Canaria with the warm sun on their backs, heading back to the crater after Alberto had dropped them off just outside El Palmital. On the GC-80 for the run back to the Caldera de Bandama after a morning session at the sand dunes in Maspalomas. The thought of the two brought him some solace and he hoped he would be back with them soon having received the good news that all was well and that he could continue with his training. His thoughts then turned to the darker alternative. What if it was the thumbs down rather than the thumbs up; death instead of life. Surely it wasn't black or white though was it? It wasn't life or death, it was merely life or treatment and then life. He opened his eyes to see the white rim of the doughnut directly over his head. He knew that this was the important bit, the scan of his brain and where the problem appeared to be. At that moment he had never felt so alone or so small and insignificant. He wished there was someone in the room that he could have reached out to and held their hand for comfort, but there was no one. He remained as still as he could for the remaining few minutes of the cycle and was relieved when he felt the bed finally come to rest and heard Tony's voice over the intercom. "Well done Martin, that was excellent, you can get yourself dressed now". The radio came back on as Martin took off his gown and put his clothes back on. If asked, he wouldn't have been able to recall what the first song was that he heard, however there was a hint of irony that the second was Billy Joel's 'Piano Man', and he had a wry smile to himself as his favourite verse was playing as he exited the room. He was pleased to see his daughter waiting for him and gave her a large hug before the two made their way back home.

Chapter 26

Back in Gran Canaria things weren't quite the same without Martin there. Nearly two weeks had passed now and although Alberto and Chris were getting along well there was something missing. The final cog in the wheel that made everything run smoothly wasn't there and both Alberto and Chris knew it. "Another Honey Rum Chris?". Alberto asked his young protégé as the two of them sat out under the stars after their evening meal. "No, I'm OK Alberto thanks". Chris remarked, somewhat forlornly. He looked at the old guitar propped up against the wall. Alberto saw him stare at it and knew exactly what he was thinking. "You missing him then?". The old man enquired. "It's not the same without him is it, when do you reckon he'll be back?". "No idea unfortunately Chris. It was his scan today though wasn't it, so hopefully he'll get the results of that in a week or so and be back out after that if its good news". Neither of them wanted to think about the alternative, but both knew that Chris was struggling without his training partner. His times had started to drop off significantly and on his own it was unlikely that he would make the grade to be able to compete seriously in the marathon. Alberto had spoken to Mike and the two had shared their concerns. It was a toss-up as to whether or not they were going to call the whole thing off and send Chris back home. After all he had done his community service. The London marathon was edging ever closer and each day that passed without any news was a wasted opportunity in the training programme and was putting them further and further behind.

Back home though Martin was keeping up his training as best he was able. He was trying to mirror the distances and times that Chris was doing out on the island and was managing his pain levels with the prescribed tablets.

It was just after mid-day, four days after the scan, when the postman pushed a letter through the door of the Price household. No one was home, and the postman came and went as he had done so on many a day before. Martin was out for a run at the time and as he came home and unlocked the front door he was greeted by the solitary letter resting on the hall floor, beckoning him to pick it up. He stooped down to grasp it and could see immediately that it was from the hospital. He weighed it up in his hand, pondering for a while whether to open it up immediately or to have a shower and sit down and read it with a cup of tea. Curiosity soon got the better of him though and it wasn't long before he was sliding his thumb in along the top of the envelope to open it up. He breathed deeply as he pulled the letter from the envelope and opened it up. Its contents though, far from being informative, were meagre and the letter merely contained a time and date to return to the hospital to see Mr Mahmood to discuss the results of the scan. There was a phone number included which he should ring if he couldn't make the allotted time. The appointment was for two days hence at 9 am. 'Bit early!' He thought, but rather than ring and change it to a more appropriate time which may have incurred further delay he decided that he would set off for an early start that day to meet his allocated slot. That evening over dinner he informed Abi and Max that he had to return to see the consultant. "Do you want a lift up?". Max enquired. "I can probably arrange to take a day off if you want". "No don't worry Max". His dad responded. "It's not like last time and there's no reason that I can't drive up and back myself so thanks for the offer, but I'll be OK". Martin's daughter looked at her father. She wanted to say the words "what if its bad news Dad, you'll need someone there with you won't you?". But she couldn't bring herself to say them. She didn't even want to consider the worst and felt that just by uttering the words themselves, that could inexplicably have some effect on the actual outcome. She was a rational person and knew that it couldn't. Whatever it was that was going on inside her dad's head was already there and probably had been for some time and nothing she or anyone else did or said was going to change that. She still however, even after rationalising the situation, couldn't bring herself to utter the words.

The day of the appointment came, and Martin rose early, had his breakfast and headed out the door before his offspring were even awake. The journey up to the hospital was relatively quiet and uneventful that morning and it wasn't long before he was pulling into the second of the three car parks. 'Still busy even at this time of the morning'. Martin thought to himself as he drove around looking for a space. Within ten minutes though he had parked up and was sat in the same waiting room as he had done previously. The very same seat in fact. This time however the seat next to him was empty and he was on his own. He looked around at the other patients all sat in silence, some engrossed in books or magazines, some fiddling with their phones and some like him engrossed solely in their own thoughts, wondering what their fate was to be, pondering the greater question of what life was all about, what the purpose of it all was and why indeed we were all even here in the first place.

"The Emperor will see you now!". Martin looked up to see a young blonde-haired nurse stood in front of him. "Sorry I was miles away!". Martin replied. "What was that you said?". "Mr Mahmood will see you now Mr Price, if you'd like to follow me please". Martin stood up and followed the young nurse. They went past the room that Martin was shown into the week previously and headed further along the corridor to the last door on the right. As they stood outside Martin noticed the white plastic plaque on the door inscribed with the words 'Mr J Mahmood, Consulting Surgeon'. Martin had no idea what the J stood for but supposed it may have been 'Julius!' The nurse knocked three times on the door and waited a few seconds before opening it and peering in, making sure it was OK to enter. Mr Mahmood was sat directly in front of the door at his desk. It wasn't a grand desk by any stretch of the imagination and certainly nothing befitting of an emperor. The kind of thing that one could purchase at Ikea or B and Q, made from chipboard, veneered with a light woodgrain effect laminate. Mr Mahmood nodded, and the nurse showed Martin in to the room and shut the door behind him. He and the emperor were now alone. "Take a seat please Mr Price". Mr Mahmood gestured to Martin as he made the short trip across the small room. Opposite Mr Mahmood's desk there were two brown chairs; the kind with four metal legs that were designed to stack upon one another if the need arose. Martin supposed there were two chairs there because most people getting their results would want someone with them, either to share their relief when given good news, or to console them and take in what the consultant was saying if it was bad news. Martin's heart started to beat faster as he heard Mr Mahmood utter the words; "Are you on your own Mr Price?". Why was he asking that? Of what consequence was it that he was on his own? After all, all the emperor had to do was to give him a quick thumbs up and he would be on his way and back down the motorway quicker than you could say Jack Robinson. "Yes, I'm on my own". Martin replied politely, hoping that there wouldn't be the need for a few microns of depth to be added to the lines in that already well furrowed brow.

Mr Mahmood waited until Martin was settled comfortably before he began. "OK, we've got the results of your scan back Mr Price". Martin looked directly at him in anticipation. 'Come on get that thumb up'! Martin thought to himself, his breathing getting deeper and his palms starting to sweat. He thought that it was only women of a certain age that experienced hot flushes but right now he was giving off enough heat to power up a small country. "Yes?". Martin replied in anticipation. "Well" …Mr Mahmood paused, scratched his head and started to rub his chin. Martin could see the expression on his face changing. He knew what was coming. "I'm afraid that it isn't very good news as we've found a rather large lump!". "KAPOW!" There it was; the shot through the heart; bullet through the brain, the old thumbs down! Martin remained silent. The only thing that came into his mind was an image of the grim reaper standing over him; black hooded cloak covering his grinning skeletal head and his skeletal hand poking out of his black oversized sleeve with the bony fingers wrapped tightly around the handle of his glinting scythe, sharpened to within an inch of its life, ready and waiting to cut him down and extinguish his very existence. All of a sudden his head was spinning, it was filled with music; the Blue Oyster Cult classic song;' 'Don't Fear the Reaper'. He sang the words to himself in his head.

"Mr. Price?". "Yes sorry". Martin replied, snapping himself back to the reality of the situation. "As I said". Mr. Mahmood continued. "We've found a rather large lump". Martin placed his hands over his face and rubbed them vigorously up and down, as if doing so would somehow wipe away all traces of the news he had just been given but didn't want to hear. He composed himself and took a deep breath. "OK go on, what exactly is it then?". "Well it's a grade four primary tumor". Mr. Mahmood explained. "That means that it hasn't spread to your brain from anywhere else in your body so in that respect it is at least contained in one place which is relatively good news". "And the bad news?". Martin enquired. "Well yes there is some bad news unfortunately, as being a grade four means that it's quite an aggressive tumor, so it's been growing quite fast and will probably continue to do so without treatment". "So, does that mean that its cancerous then?". Martin asked. He hadn't heard the magic word 'benign' so supposed that it must have been. "Yes, I'm afraid it is cancerous. The correct term for it is a glioma". "So that's what's causing the pain in my face then?". "It is yes, the lump is pushing down on the trigeminal nerve and triggering the pain in your face. The brain itself can't actually feel pain so you won't be able to feel anything in your head and in your case the pain is being transmitted to your face". 'Great!' Thought Martin. A million things were going around in his head but now he was confused, and he wasn't sure what he should actually be asking. Mr. Mahmood had seen the look of panic on patients faces a thousand times before. He didn't relish imparting bad news and every time he did so, it did indeed feel like another small line was being etched into his own already well beaten features. He could ill afford any more. There was a moments silence whilst both gathered their thoughts.

Mr. Mahmood put his hands up in a gesture to Martin. "Let me explain a bit more about the situation we have here and the options that are open to us Mr. Price. If there's anything you are unclear of after that feel free to ask. I'll also give you some leaflets you can have a look at in your own time and give you the details of some organizations that may be able to assist". Martin nodded in agreement. Mr. Mahmood went on to explain about the tumor and how it had probably been growing for around six months or so. He told Martin that it was inoperable due to its location but that a six-week intensive course of radiotherapy would have a good chance of shrinking it. He also told Martin that it couldn't be cured altogether and that the best they could hope for was an extension in time. The image of the scythe wielding grim reaper popped into Martin's head again. "So how long have I got then?". He enquired. The grim reaper started to smile; a sweet sickly smile and he started to rub his skeletal hands together as if to say 'you'll soon be mine!'. It was the question that Mr. Mahmood hated answering; too long gave false hope, but too short caused undue despair so he always plumped for longer rather than shorter no matter what the statistics bore out. "Well it depends if you have the treatment or not". "Go on." Martin replied. "Well with the treatment I would say probably between six and twelve months". The grim reaper started to laugh loudly. "And without it?". Martin asked. "Probably between three and six months". The grim reaper laughed so hard that Martin could hear his skeletal teeth chattering together like a pneumatic drill going off inside his head. Martin metaphorically ripped the scythe from the grim reapers hand and struck a blow across his head, severing it so that it fell to the ground. It lay there, teeth still chattering away, its hollow eye sockets peering up at him. Martin kicked the skull away as the rest of the skeleton collapsed into a heap on the ground. "So, if I have the treatment, would that mean I have to come here every day?". Mr. Mahmood explained that it would and that he would either have to stay locally or make the journey every day for six weeks solid. He also explained that the treatment itself would probably make him feel extremely sick. He would feel weak and there would be a good chance that he would lose his appetite thus making him even thinner than he already was. On the plus side however all the steroids he would have to take would make his face and body swell up like a balloon, so any weight loss wouldn't be noticeable! And finally, to put the icing on the cake he would also lose all his hair. "You aren't selling this very well Mr. Mahmood!". Martin declared, trying to raise a small smile as the consultant finished dispensing the bad news.

Mr. Mahmood gave Martin a number of leaflets containing various phone numbers and contact details of different organizations who would be able to assist should he feel the need. He then asked Martin to think carefully about his situation and discuss it with his loved ones before deciding on his preferred course of action. "Whatever you choose to do Mr. Price, you won't be alone, there will always be someone available to help you, either in person or on the end of the telephone". Mr. Mahmood advised. "Let my receptionist know when you've made your decision but try and make contact in the next few days as it's important that we get started as soon as possible if you do decide to go ahead with the treatment". Once he had finished Mr. Mahmood stood up and shook Martin's hand. "I'm really sorry". He apologised, "But you have my best wishes whatever you decide to do". Martin went to leave the room but turned back just before doing so. "Sorry, I've got one more question for you before I go; is there any problem with me carrying on with my running?". "My advice to you Mr. Price is to continue to do whatever it is that makes you happy and if that's running then you go right ahead and run as far and as fast as you can!". With that he put his thumb up in the air. It meant nothing to Mr. Mahmood but to Martin that thumbs up meant the world; old Emperor Julius Caesar himself had given him the thumbs up, the gift of life; or at least the gift to go and live the rest of his life as he pleased!

On the way out of the hospital Martin grabbed a cup of coffee from the vending machine and upon looking for somewhere to sit and drink it found himself in the hospitals memorial garden. He wandered around between the various coloured rose bushes and shrubs, weeping as he read some of the dedications on the various plaques. One particular one however made him stop and think. It wasn't sad like most of the rest and in fact it was quite simple. It read; 'Harry Walker, played a mean game of poker'. Martin sat down on the somewhat battered mahogany bench that was strategically placed to look out over the garden, itself a memorial to one 'Sally Hartridge', who apparently 'loved to sit here and reflect following her treatment'. Martin thought a bit more about Harry and his games of poker and imagined the old man sat around a table of card sharps contemplating his next move. 'Life is like a game of cards Martin'. His mum had once told him. 'You're dealt your hand when you're born and all you can do is play it out to the best of your ability'. Martin now knew the hand he had been dealt! There was no folding and no re dealing, he had had his one chance to play his best game and it was winner take all. Martin thought about the hand he had been dealt in the game of life and the cards he had laid down so far. Had he played all his aces or was there still one left up his sleeve? He thought deeply. 'The Ace of Clubs', he thought to himself; 'That's an easy one, it was my time at Exeter City'. 'Ace of Hearts', again another easy one, when I met and fell in love with Jane'. 'Ace of Diamonds', again another easy one, a pair of little gems when the kids came along'. 'Ace of Spades'......he paused and thought long and hard about when he played that card, thinking of and then dismissing the various significant times that had passed in his life. None of them seemed to fit however, and it was slowly dawning on him that he hadn't actually played it yet. Then the reality hit him square in the face, he wiped the tears from his eyes and picked himself up off the bench...he hadn't played it yet, it was the one card he still had up his sleeve and his one last throw of the dice. The last spin of the wheel and the last toss of the coin all rolled into one. 'The Ace of Spades', he thought to himself,' The Ace of Spades'. He kept repeating the words over and over again in his head and then started to repeat them out loud 'The Ace of Spades, The Ace of Spades' He eventually shouted out at the top of his voice 'THE ACE OF SPADES'! Luckily for him there was no one else around. He thought of the song of the same name by the group Motorhead, remembering the words of one of the verses; 'Did he want to live for ever?' The theme was recurring, he had supposed he did, but he now knew that the inevitable was upon him and it was all about how and when he played his last card!

"How did you get on then Dad?". Abi asked her father, the second that Martin got into the house. Abi had come out from her room having heard her dad's return and Max also came out to greet him, eagerly anticipating the news. Martin had done a lot of reflecting on the journey home. He had also done a lot of crying; not at his own expense though, he was comfortable with his own mortality and after all he knew that we all had to go sometime, and he had had a good if perhaps somewhat short innings. When it was time to meet his maker, to be reunited with his wife, his parents and his grandparents in whatever format that was waiting on the other side, he was ready for it. No, he didn't feel sorry for himself, but he felt sad for his children and the inevitable pain they would have to go through upon his ultimate demise and during the time leading up to it. The same pain they had felt upon losing their mother and he wouldn't have wished that on them again for the world. He had thought long and hard about whether to tell them about his condition and whilst he didn't want to lie to them he wondered what good it would do them to actually know. He didn't want anyone feeling sorry for him or for them to have the pain of simply waiting for him to die, wondering if the next day would be his last. Then there was the caring that would ultimately have to be done and he certainly didn't want to be a burden. He was torn between the devil and the deep blue sea but had decided on the journey home not to tell anyone of his fate. His mind was set and what people didn't know couldn't hurt them and he certainly didn't want to hurt his children or disrupt their lives in any way. He supposed too that they would have wished him to have the treatment on offer if they knew the truth, but he knew that wasn't for him and that wasn't the path he wanted to take. It was his journey and he wanted to be in charge of his own destiny for as long as he possibly could.

Martin held out his arms and embraced his children, he smiled a broad smile. It felt good to be hugged by those who genuinely cared about him. "It's all fine". He promised as enthusiastically as he was able. "It's nothing to worry about. There's a bit of a lump there that's all and they want to keep an eye on it but it's nothing to worry about and nothing that's going to stop me getting on with what I want to do". "So, are you going back to your training then Dad?". Max asked. "Yep, sure am, I'll see if I can book a flight back out in the next week or so. I think it's usually Thursdays from Exeter to Gran Canaria, so I'll have a look and see what I can sort out". Martin put the kettle on and the three of them sat down to tea and biscuits and chatted about the events of the day; well the events that Martin wanted them to hear anyway! That night upon retiring to bed he felt a tinge of sadness at his dishonesty but ultimately knew it was the right decision.

The next day Alberto's phone rang and he picked it up to be greeted by an upbeat Martin who relayed the same story to him as he had done to his children the night before. Alberto in turn relayed it to Chris who was both pleased at the outcome for Martin as well as at the prospect of getting his training partner back again. Alberto in turn contacted Mike and the two of them made plans for the final weeks of training for the marathon, unbeknownst of Martin's condition.

Martin spent as much time as possible with his children as he could in the week preceding his flight, running with his daughter and weight training with his son as often as he was able and talking and reminiscing with them at every opportunity he could muster. He looked at them both intently, taking in every individual line and freckle on their faces, building a picture of them both in minute detail that he could lock into his brain lest he forgot. They both accompanied him on his trip to the airport and Martin shed rather more tears than were appropriate upon being dropped off. "Dad seemed a bit upset didn't he Max?". Abi enquired of her brother as the two exited the airport terminal to return to the car after bidding him goodbye. "Did he?". Max responded. He was less in tune to others emotional feelings than his sister, but she could feel that something wasn't quite right. She wasn't sure however what it was, but she knew there was something. It played on her mind all the way home but on waking the next morning and heading back in to work and the inevitable stresses and strains that brought with it, normal service was resumed. Life had taken over again and her thoughts were distracted towards other things.

Before heading back, Martin had prepared himself for the forthcoming weeks by stocking up on copious quantities of painkillers. His GP had spoken to Mr Mahmood after Martin had declined the treatment and the two had agreed that the condition could be managed with codeine tablets at regular intervals as Martin deemed necessary. Any side effects they may have brought about were irrelevant now given the prognosis and pain management was the main objective. Martin was worried however that they may have been a banned substance thus preventing him from entering the forthcoming race. As a precaution he had typed the question; 'Is codeine a banned substance in athletics?' into a search engine on his computer and hit the return button. The results had flashed up onto the screen and Martin had eagerly clicked onto the first one that came up. Upon reading through it attentively he concluded that it didn't contain the information he was after, so he closed the page down and clicked on the next, again scanning it attentively. He eventually came across the wording; 'This product does not contain any banned substances according to the IOC, therefore this product can be taken in accordance with the manufacturers guidelines'. He breathed a sigh of relief; at least he would be able to run relatively pain free, which at this stage was probably as much as he could have hoped for.

Chapter 27

"It's really good to have you back again Martin". Chris confided in his partner as the two had once again been dropped off outside the village of El Palmital on a Friday afternoon and were heading back to the base. "Yes, it's good to be back mate". Martin smiled. "Truth be known Martin, my times have been tailing off a bit without you here and it's been a job to get motivated, it's surprising how difficult it is to run on your own with no one pushing you on!". Martin too knew the feeling well. "Never mind Chris, I'm back now so let's try and concentrate on getting as fit as we can for the race." "I think Alberto's been missing you too, he hasn't picked the guitar up since you left and even his wine and Honey Rum hasn't been going down quite the same". Chris added. "We'll have to see if we can put that right tonight then won't we!". Martin laughed as he picked up the pace a little. Since arriving back on the island though Martin was having mixed feelings and much as he would have liked to share them with his colleague he knew he couldn't. On the one hand he was pleased to be back again and working towards his goal but on the other he still had an underlying feeling of guilt at not telling his children the truth. He knew that he couldn't let it eat him up though and vowed to make a concerted effort to phone them every evening to keep in touch, which at least gave him some consolation.

That evening Alberto had pushed the boat out and prepared them a roast chicken dinner with all the trimmings for their evening meal, washed down with copious quantities of Testamento Malvasia dry white wine. For afters there were bananas and ice cream followed by a newly opened bottle of Honey Rum. After they had all finished their hearty fare and tidied up, Martin and Chris made their way outside to the makeshift patio area; the weeds poking their way intermittently through the cracked and broken pointing between the stone crazy paving. Alberto followed them, guitar in hand. He sat down in his preferred position but rather than play his usual

'Cavatina', Martin was surprised to see him strike up the chords to 'Where do you go to my lovely', in honour of his return. There was an even greater surprise to follow as little known to either him or Alberto, Chris had been secretly practising Billy Joel's 'Piano Man', and he took charge of the instrument and gave his two avid listeners a not entirely flawless rendition of the song. They didn't mind though, the more they had to drink the better it sounded and they all went to bed that evening somewhat the worse for wear. As he retired to bed Martin pondered whether his evening dose of painkillers would be a good idea given the amount of alcohol he had consumed. He decided to take them anyway and hit the pillow with the heady mix of alcohol and prescription drugs temporarily numbing any traces of pain he may have otherwise been feeling that night.

The training regime progressed in earnest and it wasn't long before the three of them were back in sync again and doing what they did best. Martin kept in regular touch with his children over the following weeks and had almost managed to put thoughts of his illness firmly out of his head. That was until the early hours of one Tuesday morning when he woke up feeling like he was being stabbed in the face with a pitchfork. He took some painkillers and tried to get back to sleep but it was no use. After an hour or so tossing and turning he got up and got himself a glass of water and took a couple more tablets before retiring again. Still unable to sleep though he got up and quietly put on his vest and shorts, laced up his trainers and exited the farmhouse. Outside the air was still, cool and crisp but not cold by any stretch of the imagination, the kind of evening that if he were at home he may have considered putting a light jumper on just to take the edge off. That night there was a full moon and in the cloudless sky it lit the crater perfectly. He had never seen it look so beautiful and indeed his current condition had heightened his senses and allowed him to appreciate the beauty in everyday things, things that before he had taken for granted. Now however he took in every bit of detail he could, not knowing when the day may come that he couldn't experience it again. He started to jog and made his way along the track and up to the rim of the crater. He decided that he would head out on the road to Las Goteras until he had had enough and then turn back again. As he ran the pain began to subside, he felt good running by the light of the moon with not a soul around or a sound to distract him. He increased his pace and the faster he ran the better he felt; the stabbing pain in his face began to subside and it wasn't long before he felt back to his old self again. He ran downhill through the village, increasing his speed as he did so before turning and doing some hill repeats. Once sufficiently tired he returned and headed for base mixing up some steady jogging with some sprint sessions to defining points ahead on the road. He returned to base at around 5.30 am and slipped back into bed. The next thing he knew he was awoken by the distinctive smell of cooked bacon wafting in through his door.

"Morning Martin". Said Chris as Martin joined the couple already seated at the breakfast table. Alberto had Martin's breakfast already prepared and was keeping it warm under the grill. He got up and took it out and placed it on the table in front of Martin who poured himself an orange juice from the jug on the table. Alberto had some news for them regarding the final leg of their training; "So we're a month off the race now and Mike and I have made some preparations for the last section of your training; you've both been coming on well so now the three of us will be heading back to England for the final part". Chris had been enjoying his time on the island so much that he hadn't yet even contemplated going back to England but like Martin was looking forward to the race. "When are we going back then Alberto?". He enquired. "Next week". Alberto stated. "Mike has booked us into a hotel in London for the final three weeks leading up to the race, it's the Travelodge in Kings Cross, Mike says it'll suit our requirements. I'm sure it'll be comfortable enough for what we want, and it'll give you both enough time to get used to the British climate again! We'll continue the training in London and we can try and get out on some of the routes that will be used for the marathon". "Wont they be a bit busy for running on?". Martin enquired. "They will in the daytime". Alberto advised him. "But we'll try and do a bit in the evenings when its quieter just to get you used to the route. Where we're staying is about half way between Regent's Park and Victoria Park, so we can mix things up a bit between those two in the day time. There are also a lot of other green spaces not too far away if we need them. You'll find that things will change a bit in the last three weeks as you'll be tapering back and not doing as many miles as you've done up to now. We'll carry on this week as we have been and then fly back and get settled in. I'll explain a bit more about the actual details then". Martin and Chris took in what Alberto had said, both somewhat sad that their time on the island was coming to an end. For Martin however it was more than that, it was a reminder that another phase of his life was coming to an end and that he was edging ever closer to the inevitable. "So what day are we actually flying back then Alberto?". Martin enquired, trying to put things into perspective. Wednesday the first of April which will give us nearly three and a half weeks before the marathon on the 26th. "If were tapering back does that mean there will be some days off then?". Martin continued with his questioning. He was thinking about whether he would be able to fit some time in visiting his children. Alberto knew that he was missing them but equally didn't want to throw a spanner in the works at this late stage by interrupting the routine. "I'm sure we will be able to sort something out Martin!". He replied. "Oh, and Mike is picking us up at the airport and will be spending a couple of days with us when we get there. He's then got to go up to Newcastle for another project he's working on but will be back with us again for a couple of days before the race".

Chapter 28

The next Wednesday Mike was indeed waiting for them in the arrivals lounge at Gatwick airport as flight TOM 4126 from Las Palmas de Gran Canaria touched down safely on the runway at 08:45 hrs. The three had run the gauntlet of the stampede at the baggage carousel and emerged at the other end relatively unscathed to be greeted by Mike's beaming smile. He gave each one of them a hug in turn before leading them to his awaiting Mercedes 'C' class in the car park.

Mike wasn't particularly familiar with the streets of the capital and after taking the bull by the horns and fighting with the London traffic for what seemed like an eternity, was wishing that the others had taken a cab and left him to put his feet up back at the hotel. "Come on, get out of the bloody way!". He shouted out of his wound down window at an inappropriately situated articulated lorry; its driver looking as frustrated as Mike was as he tried desperately to park the leviathan as close to his delivery destination as possible. "Chill out Mike, you'll burst a blood vessel at this rate!". Alberto grinned. Chris and Martin merely sat giggling on the back seat; they had never heard Mike lose it before and it wasn't long before he was at it again much to the three passengers' amusement. Mike's sat nav eventually led them to their destination where he stopped ready to set his passengers down. The three exited the car and collected their belongings before entering the hotel. "Mike not coming in with us then?". Chris asked Alberto. "Mike's not really your Travelodge sort of person!". Alberto laughed. "He'll probably be staying somewhere a bit posher than this, but he'll be paying for it himself of course, not on account like ours is!".

After booking in at reception, Martin and Chris were somewhat disappointed to find out that the 'account' only allowed for one room between the three of them, so they soon began to understand why Mike had made his own arrangements. Given that their contribution to the whole venture to date had amounted to a big fat zero though, neither of them were about to complain. It was however a 'family sized' room so both supposed that it would be of a significant size. Alberto had the key and opened the door to room 510 as the three had exited the lift and eventually found the room in question after a bit of toing and froing. He pushed open the door and the three went in. Chris was immediately behind Alberto and as he manoeuvred his suitcase along the tight entrance the first thing that sprang to his attention was that the room, although not of a bad size, only contained one double bed and no other obvious sleeping arrangements. "Is this the right room?". Chris asked. "Well it says room 510 on the door and our key opened it so I suppose it must be!". Alberto assured him. "I know we all get on quite well but there's no way that I'm sharing a bed with you two!". Chris exclaimed. Martin by now had made his way into the room and also noted the obvious. "Relax". Alberto assured them. "The bed is for me; your sleeping arrangements are in there". He pointed to the recesses in the adjacent walls and the two fold down beds that were hinged upright. Chris went over to the one nearest the window and unlatched it and pulled it down. "I'll call shotgun on this one then". He proposed, looking out of the high-level window in an attempt to admire the view. Unfortunately, there wasn't one! The hotel appeared to have been built in a triangular shape and the only view the window afforded was of the two other external brick clad walls of the hotel. He looked down to the small triangular courtyard below to see the copious quantities of rubbish that previous occupants had inexplicably decided to discard out of their windows rather than simply put in the bins provided. "I guess that means that this one is mine then". Mused Martin, pulling down the remaining sleeping portal in the room.

The three familiarised themselves with the remainder of the room and a quick look around gave rise to a meagre inventory as there wasn't a lot to write home about; one double bed, two pull down singles, a couple of wardrobes, a dressing table with a light above, a hairdryer, a couple of bedside tables, a phone adjacent to the bed and a small flat screen tv fixed to the wall. Blue carpets and the standard Travelodge curtains and bed throw made up the décor of the room. There was also a small en suite bathroom containing the shortest bath Martin had ever seen, with something that resembled a shower head hanging off the wall above it. Still it was clean enough though and the three would have to make the best of it for the coming weeks. They quickly decided whose things would go where before unpacking and arranging them in their allotted spaces as best they were able. Upon finishing they placed the empty suitcases under Alberto's bed and retired to the restaurant for their evening meal. "Hawaiian pizza, my favourite!". Martin declared, upon examining the menu at the restaurant. "I'm having some of that!". "I'm quite partial to the old ham and pineapple myself". Chris added. "So I think I may join you old man". "Woah not so fast you two, I'm afraid that you don't get a choice, I'll be picking the meals for the duration we're here as we still need to stick to the eating plan". Alberto interjected. "As it's our first night here though I'm going to let you have what you like, but from tomorrow onwards we're back to the high carb and protein diet. As it happens pizza probably isn't that bad for you, so you'll be OK with that. And whilst we're on the subject of eating and drinking there's to be no more alcohol either from now on in; strictly soft drinks, preferably water, or tea and coffee without any sugar". Martin's face dropped as Alberto went on to point out the items on the menu that they were able to eat in the forthcoming days. He and Mike had also taken the liberty of prearranging some special meals with the kitchen that weren't on the menu for a small extra charge. He got out a hand printed sheet and showed the two what they would be eating on each given day and when they would have free reign to choose their own selection, again within his predetermined range of course! When he had finished explaining he went on to order himself a nice fillet of steak and a bottle of Cabernet Sauvignon to wash it down with. Martin and Chris watched in envy as Alberto drained the last drops from the bottle as they sat sipping their water. Alberto licked his lips and wiped his mouth with his napkin before the three of them headed back up to the room.

"So, how's it going then Dad?". Abi enquired, "Not long to go now, is everything alright as you seem a bit quiet?". It was Saturday Morning, 8:45 am, the week before the London Marathon and Martin and Abi were stood patiently awaiting the announcements. Martin had arranged for Abi and Max to come up and join him for a couple of days before the big event and had booked them both into the Travelodge for a couple of nights. He was missing them both terribly and wanted to spend some time with them before the race. They had taken the train up to London on the Friday night and were heading back on the Sunday afternoon, so it was a whistle-stop tour. It was a long time since Martin had run with his daughter and as the two of them were together again they seized upon the opportunity to do something that they had wanted to do for some time; something that any other parkrunner worth their salt would have done whilst in the capital, and that was to attend the Bushy Park parkrun. Both Martin and Abi had had it on their bucket list for some time and were now looking forward to finally taking part. Outwardly, if anyone had looked at Martin that morning he would have appeared to be a picture of health; his body was lean and tanned from his time in Gran Canaria and the muscles in his arms and legs showed probably the finest definition that they had in all of his life; he had a stomach like a washboard and the overall appearance stature and presence of a finely tuned athlete. Even his running attire and shoes were in pristine condition. Inside his body however things were a lot different and it was all starting to go horribly wrong; the tumour was growing with avengeance and Martin had noticed that as well as the pain in his face, there were now headaches and balance issues. When questioned by the others he had tried to brush it off or make a joke about it, stating that it must have been all that Honey Rum back on the island, but he believed that the others could detect that something was wrong having spent so much time with him. As a result, he was often quiet and reflective for long periods of time which wasn't in his usual nature. He told the others that it was merely pre-race nerves and that he wanted to concentrate on his final preparations for the race in a calm and collected fashion.

Bushy Park was indeed the home of the parkrun and the Holy Grail of parkrun courses as far as many a parkrunner was concerned. It was where parkrunning began back in 2004 and the concept had grown from its humble origins back in the day to become the global phenomenon it is now, enjoyed by millions worldwide who take part not only for the running but for the friendly welcome and camaraderie that exists between those kindred spirits that religiously don their attire on a Saturday morning to take part.

Martin never did get to answer his daughters' question and as the two stood there amongst the other thousand plus runners that were there that morning, both stood in silence with their own thoughts as the race director gave out the announcements for the mornings run. Martin held out his hand and took hold of his daughters in his. He gave it a squeeze as she turned to greet him with her loving smile. He reflected on how lucky he was to have such a beautiful, loving and caring daughter and he held back a tear knowing that their time together was limited. Today for Martin wasn't about getting a personal best or achieving a quick time, if anything he wanted to run as slowly as possible, to savour the experience, making it last as long as possible so that he could cherish every moment. Every step, every pace, every breath he took he wanted to last for ever, he just wanted to be part of something and feel part of the global parkrun family, right at the heart of where it all began, and he wanted to share that experience with one of the people in his life that meant more to him than anything; his beautiful daughter.

"I'm going to run with you today Abi if that's OK?" Abi stared at her father for a moment. She had automatically supposed that he would have wanted to start at the front of the pack and go hell for leather and try for both a personal best and to try and win the coveted number one spot at the place where it all started. "Yes of course Dad". She smiled, somewhat shocked by her father's statement. "I'd love to run with you, are you sure though?". Martin was never surer about anything in his life; winning today wasn't important for him, and had he been back on home turf he still wouldn't have felt any different, he just wanted to savour the moment and hoped in his own mind that the race would never end and that the two of them would simply be running together in perpetuity.

The runners lined up on the start line; father and daughter way back in the crowd; so far back in fact that neither could hear the starters instructions and they were only aware that the race had started when the crowd in front of them started to slowly edge towards the start line. After what seemed like an age they finally crossed it, breaking out into a slow jog, unable to go any quicker due to the wall of runners both in front and to each side. They turned to each other and laughed at their meagre progress, tip toeing through the sea of bodies being careful not to invade anyone's space. As they made headway, the crowds started to thin a little and they picked their way past a few of the slower runners eventually getting up to somewhere near Abi's natural five-kilometre pace. They ran side by side around the course, taking in the stunning scenery and flora and fauna of the park as they ran from the start near the Princess Diana fountain through the figure of eight course past Hampton Wick Cricket Club and on to Sandy Lane Gate. Here the two turned left and headed towards the Teddington gate before following the course to its culmination near Heron pond. All too soon they had crossed a small bridge and headed around the south of the pond where they could see the finish line in sight. The two held hands and upped the pace for a sprint finish to the line, giving each other a hug before collecting their finish tokens. "Well we can tick that one off the list then Dad, I wonder if we'll get the chance to run it again sometime?". Abi shrieked gleefully. Martin looked at his daughter and a tear started to form in his eye. He tried to stifle it as best he could but failed and as it started to trickle down his cheek he quickly wiped it away with a flick of his finger. He looked lovingly at his daughter and he knew that whilst she would have many such opportunities, this would unfortunately be his one and only time. "You never know Abi, let's hope so!".


It was the Wednesday morning prior to the marathon and Mike was awoken shortly before 8 am by a phone call. "Hello?". He answered blearily, after realising it was the phone that had woken him and not the alarm clock that he had repeatedly been trying to silence unsuccessfully. "Hello, is that Mike?". Enquired the voice on the other end. "It is". Mike confirmed. "Morning Mike, its Brian Cawsey". Mike was still half asleep and was trying to think who Brian Cawsey actually was, his brain hadn't registered it yet, but he went along with the conversation as it was obvious that Brian was someone who knew him well. "Oh, Hello Brian". "Yes, morning Mike, look I hope that I didn't wake you and I'm sorry to ring so early, but I've got a bit of a dilemma that I'm hoping you can help me with?". "Yes, go on". Mike replied, still trying to register who Brian was. "Well its regarding the race on Sunday". Bingo; Mike's brain suddenly clicked into gear; Brian was the race director for this year's London Marathon and one-time nemesis of Mike back in the day. The two now however had a mutual respect for each other's work. Mike sat up in bed, suddenly wide awake. "What's the problem Brian?". "Well I've got a couple of no shows from two of the elites for Sundays race". Brian explained. "Right, how can I help?". Mike enquired. "Well we don't want the elite bunch to be too light, so we need a couple of capable athletes to step in. I've been looking through the championship places for some possible candidates and I saw a couple of athletes registered with you as their agent; Martin Price and Chris Clarke? I thought if you had any involvement that they must have something about them so was wondering if you thought they would be capable of stepping up. I did see that Martin is in his fifties though, is that right?" Mike's ears pricked up, his eyes widened in anticipation and suddenly all his senses and faculties were wide awake. He didn't know where to start but didn't want to blow the guilt edged opportunity that had presented itself. Equally he didn't want to make a fool of himself or his two athletes if they weren't up to the challenge. "Well the truth is that they've both been out in Gran Canaria training with Alberto Romero and have been working solely towards this race". The mention of Alberto's name meant a lot in the business and Brian knew that if they had been working with him for any length of time and he hadn't kicked them out they must have been of a reasonable standard. "In reality what sort of position were they hoping for?" Brian asked. "Top one hundred". Mike replied. "I was hoping for top fifty for the elites really but given that you and Alberto are involved I think I can take a punt on them. Are you really sure that the old guy is up to it though, that's pushing it a bit on the age front to be keeping up with the elites?". "Many a thing improves with age Brian, as you know!". Brian was dubious, but he needed to fill the places as quick as he could and at that point in time these two seemed as good a bet as any. "OK, time is against me really so I'm willing to give them a shot if you want. If you're in agreement and if you can give me the nod now, I'll make the arrangements?". Mike thought about running it past Alberto first and speaking to Martin and Chris, but time wasn't on his side and he couldn't imagine that after all this hard work they wouldn't relish the opportunity that had now presented itself. As such he did indeed give Brian the nod and went on to satisfy his own curiosity by enquiring who it was out of the elites that had dropped out. He was surprised to learn that one of them was the race favourite; the Kenyan, Akayo Jaramogi, who Brian informed him had sustained an injury during training. The other was the hotly fancied Ethiopian; Ezana Tasifa, who had pulled out without giving a reason. "It's thrown the race wide open really". Brian explained. "I would say that the favourites now are probably Bworo Deresse and Hakim Bayu from Ethiopia and possibly the Kenyan, Gitonga Chibuzo, but as I say none of them have been that consistent of late so it's anybody's race really, it just depends on who's got the will on the day! Should be an interesting race though and certainly no foregone conclusion!". Brian gave Mike the instructions that he would need for the race and stated that he would confirm them by e mail, and that if there were any problems Mike could always contact him on his mobile. Mike got up and prepared some breakfast before ringing Alberto and delivering the news.

Later that morning back at the Travelodge the three were indeed pleased to receive the news and Chris and Martin headed out on their training run with renewed vigour. Things were starting to get real now and the big event was only days away. For Martin it couldn't come quick enough as he realised that he probably only had a couple more weeks before things really started to deteriorate, and he wasn't sure that he could hold it all together much longer. The final week brought about the end to the carefully planned tapering programme. Martin's 5k parkrun wasn't part of it but Alberto had conceded that five kilometres at a relatively steady pace wasn't going to make a lot of difference either way. It would also be of benefit for him mentally to spend some rare time with his family. Chris however was concerned about the lack of training in the final weeks and was worried that cutting back on the mileage would hamper his performance on the big day. Both Mike and Alberto however had stressed its importance, both to allow the body to recover and to enable it to reach its peak performance on the day. "You won't lose any fitness in a three-week taper". Alberto had assured them, and Mike had stressed that; "In the last few weeks it's the rest that will make you stronger, not more work!". As such Martin and Chris had put their faith in them and did exactly what the pair instructed them to, after all they had got them this far and there was no reason to change things now. On that mornings run, the two reflected on just how far they had both come in the space of a year; Martin from a casual parkrunner and Chris from the brink of a prison sentence to an elite entry to the London marathon. "Could you ever have imagined you would be here doing this twelve months ago?". Chris enquired of Martin as the two of them completed their second lap of the park. "I still can't really imagine I'm doing it now!". Martin replied. "I can remember watching the race on TV last year and wouldn't have imagined in a million years that I'd be running in it this year, not in any capacity, let alone as one of the elite entrants!". "Where do you think we'll finish then?". Chris enquired, knowing that Mike and Alberto's plan was for the two of them to run together to achieve their best possible chance of a decent finish. "No idea; Mike and Alberto seem to think we can make the top one hundred, so I suppose anything in that region would be good". Chris had been studying the times of the other athletes however, and the fact that two of the best had dropped out gave him some renewed hope that they both may do better than they had first imagined. Whilst Martin had been concentrating on his training, managing his pain levels and trying to put some semblance of normality together from all the different emotions that were whirling around inside his head, Chris had been prompted by Alberto to study the form of the other athletes. He knew how they raced, what their tactics were and how fast they were capable of running. He also knew that their own starting position meant that they would be lining up with forty of the world's best long-distance runners and if they were able to maintain anything like the pace they had in training there was every chance they could come in at the tail end of that pack. In short, however optimistic he may have been, he was aiming for a top forty place.

# Chapter 29

After what felt like an eternity in the Travelodge, the day of the race had finally arrived, and it was Chris who woke first. At least he thought he had woken first; pulling himself out of bed at 6 am and heading to the bathroom as quietly as he was able, he noticed that the other two were sleeping soundly. The truth was though that Martin had hardly slept a wink all night; he had been dreaming of his wife, the same recurring dream he had had twice before over the last couple of weeks and he was struggling to work out its significance as the images were confused and muddled in his mind. That, coupled with Alberto's snoring, his own headache and the anticipation of the big day had led to him tossing and turning for the past eight hours and getting more and more frustrated at his inability to get to sleep on the very night that he had needed it most. The training and the healthy eating regime had been tailored to perfection and the tapering during the last few weeks had led the two athletes to feel strong and refreshed ready for the race. All Martin had needed was one last decent night's sleep to finish things off, but unfortunately it wasn't to be. "Morning Chris, how did you sleep?". Martin enquired of his colleague as he returned from the bathroom. Chris came over and perched himself at the bottom of Martin's bed. "Morning Martin". He whispered so as not to wake Alberto. "I thought you were still asleep, sorry if I woke you". "No, you haven't woken me Chris, to tell you the truth I've hardly slept all night". "You OK?". Chris enquired. "Yes, fine mate, just pre-race nerves that's all". Martin was far from OK but didn't want to burden Chris with anything at this late stage. "I'm nervous as hell!". Chris confided in his colleague. "Me too!". Martin admitted. "Come here!". Martin gave Chris a reassuring hug. "Don't worry, we've come this far together haven't we, this is what we've been working for all this time so let's get out there and do it, let's show them what we're made of". Their embrace was broken by the sound of Alberto snoring and they both had a chuckle to each other. "I'm going to try and get an hours sleep in before I get up". Martin proffered. Chris nodded and indicated that he would do likewise. Martin's head hit the pillow and this time he must have dropped off straight away as the next thing he knew was that he was being awoken by the sound of Alberto singing to himself during his morning shower.

It wasn't long after when Martin's phone rang. He answered it to the sound of his daughter's voice at the other end. "Morning Dad how are things this morning then?". "Not bad thanks Abi, I didn't have the best night's sleep but we're all awake now and just getting ready to go down for breakfast before we head over to the start". "London is absolutely manic this morning Dad so don't leave it too late. Max and I are at Paddington and were trying to get over to the finish but the queues for the tube are just ridiculous, we may just walk over as it's only a couple of miles so will probably be quicker anyway". Max and Abi had travelled up for the race and through Martin's elite entry had tickets for the VIP area at the finish so would be well catered for once they arrived. "What's the weather looking like?". Martin enquired, not having ventured outside yet. "It's not a bad day, looks like it's going to stay dry, warm but not too hot so shouldn't be too bad for running in". "OK thanks Abi, I'll see you at the finish line then…. if I make it that is!". "Don't be stupid Dad of course you'll make it; look Dad the two most important days in your life are the day you are born and the day you find out why; the first has long gone but the second has now arrived so get out there and show the world why and go and smash it!". "Thanks Abi I'll do my best!". "Max wants a quick word as well". Abi handed the phone over to her brother who reiterated her sentiments and wished his dad all the best for the race before the two headed off across London and through Hyde Park to make their way to the finish.

Rather than run the gauntlet of the London underground with the forty thousand other runners and many hundreds of thousands more spectators, Alberto had booked them a taxi to get to the start of the race. There were three separate starting positions; red, blue and green and they had been instructed to report to the blue start near Blackheath no later than 9 am for a 10 am start. Upon finishing their preparations and donning their running attire and tracksuits, the three headed out of the hotel towards the awaiting taxi. Martin had taken his painkillers and made sure there were more in is kit bag for good measure should he need them before the start of the race. The weather was indeed as Abi had stated; warm but not too hot, and it was dry, a good day both for running and spectating and that certainly proved to be the case as the taxi slowly made its way from the hotel towards the start. "You guys running in the marathon then?". The taxi driver enquired, stating the obvious. Alberto barely had chance to explain that they were, before the driver began to dish out copious quantities of advice on how to run the race based on his own experience some years previous. Chris had heard that London cabbies were invariably experts in most things but was having a chuckle to himself at hearing the driver's tales first hand. Still it whiled away the time stuck in the traffic and it wasn't long before the cab stopped, and the driver announced; "This is as far as I can get". Before advising the three how to complete the short remainder of the journey on foot. Martin however was sat with his eyes closed, deep in thought and unaware even that the taxi had stopped. Chris gave him a nudge; "Come on Martin, we've arrived!".

The first thing that was apparent as they exited the cab was the sheer number of people that were around that morning; all heading in the same direction towards the start of the marathon. It wasn't long before the three got swallowed up by the tide of bodies, ebbing and flowing in waves, all swarming towards the start; they couldn't have turned to go elsewhere even if they had wanted to. Martin noted various athletes clad in fancy dress costumes; one as Spiderman, one as Snow White, two who were the respective halves of a pantomime horse and one wearing some form of large globe, although he couldn't work out exactly what it was supposed to be. All of whom were running for their own personal reasons but generally to raise much needed funds for the respective charities they were involved in. The two men in their halves of the horse costume were laughing and joking as they made their way along the road and Martin contrasted their demeanour with that of his own that morning. On the one hand he should have been happy that all his hard work had led him to where he was today and the chance to compete against some of the world's best, but on the other his morning was tinged with sadness and the intermittent thumping in his head and pain in his cheek acted as a constant reminder that the race for him was probably going to be his last. He had to put these thoughts to one side though for one final day and concentrate on the task in hand. Chris in comparison was in a buoyant mood and on a natural high at being part of the occasion and as they reached the elite athletes checking in point Mike was there waiting for them. He greeted each in turn with a hug and a firm pat on the back before finding a bit of spare space in the compound where they could go through a few things. All Martin and Chris had on their minds though was where the nearest toilets were as nerves were starting to get the better of them and they both had an urgent desire to go to the loo. Mike pointed out the bank of portaloos inside the compound and the two queued patiently before doing the necessary and returning to their trainer and mentor. Mike was showing Alberto two running vests as the two returned. "You'll need to wear these during the race if that's OK?". Mike informed the two, handing them each a red, white and blue Great Britain team vest with their name emblazoned on the front. "I ordered you both a medium and there are a couple of spares in the bag for good measure. There are some shorts as well if you want them, but the important thing is the vests as they like all the elites to wear the relevant vest of their country if possible". Martin and Chris felt an immense sense of pride overwhelm them as both took off their club vests and donned the new attire. Martin tried on the shorts as well and did some light jogging around the compound to ensure the new gear was a comfortable fit; it was obviously of a good quality and upon seeing how smart Martin looked in the full regalia Chris quickly followed suit, handing Alberto his phone and asking him to take some photos of the two of them for posterity. After they had done so Mike called them over for a bit of a pep talk before the race. "OK the first thing I'd like to say to you both is well done for getting this far, you've both put in an enormous amount of effort and Alberto tells me you've been a couple of model professionals so on behalf of us both we thank you for that". Alberto nodded in agreement and couldn't have wished for a couple of more willing charges, he was going to miss the two of them as much as they were him and he had no idea at the moment what the future held for any of them and whether he would still be working with them after the race. "Now you're aware that there are a couple who have dropped out, and Chris I know that you in particular have been studying some of the other athletes' form haven't you?". Chris nodded. "So, what have you noticed then Chris...if you were the trainer what would you be telling me?" "I'd be telling you to go out there and get stuck in that's what!" Mike smiled. "Would you indeed young man, and why is that then Chris?". "Well because when it comes to the crunch, a lot of these guys haven't actually run that much faster than us, that's why, even Bworo Deresse and Hakim Bayu, who are two of the quickest here have only ever run nine minutes quicker than we have!". "To be fair though, nine minutes is a hell of a lot quicker!". Martin interjected, "You can run a long way in nine minutes". "You can!". Stated Alberto. "But these guys have been running for years and those are their 'best' times not their average times. All these guys need is a bad day at the office and anything can happen". "That's right". Mike continued. "And the advantage you have over them is that you've got each other; you know off by heart what each of you is capable of and if you work together and take it in turns sharing the load and pulling and pushing each other around there's no reason why you shouldn't do well. No one else is running with someone they've trained regularly with so try and work with that". Martin and Chris were suitably enthused and with that carried out their pre-race warm up before Martin queued for the toilet again. He managed to fit in a further two visits before the athletes were called for the start of the men's race such were his nerves and even on the start line he felt like he wanted to go again!

Martin and Chris stood there patiently at the start with the rest of the elite bunch, each consumed with their own varying emotions as the clock ticked down. Immediately behind them were the championship athletes and in turn behind them in Zone 1 were the first wave of general runners. Thousands upon thousands of them stretched back as far as the eye could see. Chris looked around, breathing deeply to calm his nerves and to take in the atmosphere of the day. To each side of him was a solid wall of spectators at least twenty deep for as far ahead as he could see. The road ahead of him was divided for the first 100 metres or so by cones, indicating the place where the athletes from the wider start point would converge into one. Overhead there was bunting and flags and numerous different advertising banners giving the whole event a carnival atmosphere. Police and marshals clad in hi viz jackets lined the inside of the crowd barriers on the edge of the road, ensuring that the masses remained firmly behind them and that everything ran smoothly. The noise from the crowd was more than Chris could take in and as the overhead electronic clock gradually ticked down towards the start time of 10 am the crowd began to fall silent. Not more than twenty feet away from him stood the Queen on the starting podium, dressed in a flattering duck egg blue two piece ensemble, poised and ready to start the race. The whole experience was surreal.

Martin too was struggling to take it all in; he gazed intently at some of the other runners in the group, some of the best the world had to offer; Bworo Deresse and Hakim Bayu, the Ethiopians clad in their traditional green and yellow tops, athletes from Kenya in the black, red and green colours of their national flag, depicting the African people, their struggle for independence and the countries agricultural resources. The black vest of New Zealand, the red of Spain, the green of Ireland, the red green and yellow of Portugal; all were duly represented along with the colours of many other nations. Each athlete wearing their colours with national pride and wanting to do well, not only for themselves but also for their nation. Martin looked down at his own attire and at Chris stood proudly next to him clad in his. Did the nations hopes really fall on the two of them? He certainly couldn't see any other British athletes in the initial line up, so he supposed that they did. It gave him a renewed sense of pride that for today at least he and his companion were the best the country had to offer and that it was their duty to do justice to the colours they were wearing. The final countdown began, a mere sixty seconds left on the clock until the start and the moment that the two had been working towards for so long. Martin and Chris turned to each other and offered some final words of encouragement, taking in some deep breaths of the capitals air to steady the nerves. Neither had ever experienced anything like it before and Martin's body began to shake with nerves. Ten, nine, eight…the final countdown began, all Martin could hear now was the sound of the crowd counting down the numbers; seven, six, five, four; he took one last long deep breath and looked towards his colleague, giving him a knowing and determined nod; three, two, one; BANG, the race was on!

Chapter 30

Martin's legs immediately sprung into life; his brain sending signals through the body's neurones to his muscles, working in pairs to pull his joints in opposite directions to form the smooth rhythmic running action that could be observed by the crowd. These were the same muscles that had been honed to perfection during the previous months of meticulous training, all tailored so that they could be at their peak of readiness at just this precise moment. Despite what was going on inside his head, his legs and his body were certainly stronger than they had ever been before and certainly than they ever would be again. He knew that this was his moment. He glanced beside him to see his partner right by his side and they both felt the enormous roar of the crowd lift them as they set of on their 26 mile and 385 yard journey. The cones in the road soon disappeared behind them in the stampede as the athletes merged to form one solid mass; the championship athletes sprinting flat out to get as far into the elite pack as they were able, as if to prove they were also some of the world's best despite having to suffer the indignity of wearing a number instead of their name on their vest. Before long, it was impossible to distinguish between the two groups.

It was certainly a manic start and Martin was surprised at how quickly so many runners appeared to be in front of him. He knew though that for the next two hours and however many minutes that passed after that, this was to be his job; putting one foot in front of the other as fast and economically as he was able, whilst trying to keep pace with the world's best and still have something in reserve for the end. 'For the next two hours.' He thought to himself; in that time he could have taken a plane and flown down to the south of France or driven from London to Birmingham; indeed there were any number of things he could have done in a two hour window, but instead he was here doing the one thing in the world he loved to do more than anything else; running!

Martin and Chris tucked in to the pack and it was Chris who took the first stint in front. He supposed there were somewhere between fifty and sixty runners in front of them and upon glancing over his shoulder estimated a similar amount in fairly close proximity behind, although it was difficult to tell exactly. He decided to concentrate on who was ahead rather than who was coming up behind him and for the first mile condensed his efforts on building up a rhythmic pattern of breathing and stride length. He knew it was important not to go out too fast, however strong his body felt at this early stage as he only had finite reserves that would have to be allocated out proportionately during the race; too much too soon meant too little for the final sections and hitting that wall with nothing in reserve really hurt!

As they neared the first mile marker and merged into Old Dover Road, Martin pushed up on to the shoulder of his companion. The two had decided not to expend too much energy by talking during the race but through their time together had built up an almost telepathic understanding, instinctively being able to read each other's thoughts and movements when it came to running. Chris knew that Martin was trying to nudge him on a bit as he could see the group in front of them start to string out rather than to run in a bunch and he knew that they couldn't let them get too far ahead.

Up at the front, some one hundred metres, and around sixty athletes ahead of Martin and Chris it was indeed the expected athletes Bworo Deresse and Hakim Bayu from Ethiopia that were setting the pace, closely followed by the Kenyan, Gitonga Chibuzo. The motorcycle cameras ahead of them were tracking their every move in close up detail with the overhead helicopters focusing in intently on them, monitoring their every move. Behind these three were Sabio Himinez of Portugal, Juan Ramirez of Spain and Scott Netherton the New Zealander. Behind them were the main body of runners.

By the end of mile two Martin and Chris had managed to edge past a couple more runners and the two were cruising along at a fast and constant pace. At mile three they reached the transition section where the red start athletes would eventually merge with the blue group in the main body of runners behind them. For now though the road at Artillery Place lay empty, merely waiting in anticipation for the hoarding masses to arrive and wear down its tarmac surface underfoot. The entrance to the main thoroughfare was currently blocked by a line of marshals and a solitary police car, ensuring for the moment that no runner inadvertently took a wrong turn. The crowds waiting patiently at the barriers began to crane their necks and turn their heads to try and get a first glimpse of the lead runners going past, knowing too that it wouldn't be long before many thousands of others would be passing where they stood, albeit at a somewhat gentler pace.

"I can't see Dad anywhere Max, can you?". Abi and her brother were sat waiting in the VIP area adjacent to the race finish line watching events unfold on the large screen that had been set up specially for that purpose. "No, I can't see him!" Max reiterated. "I don't think the camera has come off those two in front yet has it?". "I guess that people aren't really interested in the also rans are they, I mean can you remember who came fiftieth in the London Marathon last year?". Abi enquired of her brother. "I don't even know who came first!". Max exclaimed. "That's because you're a philistine!". "If I actually knew what that meant, I may be offended!". Max laughed. "What I do know though, is that there's more than two people in this race, so it would be good to see a few more of them wouldn't it". "Give them a chance, I'm sure we will in a bit".

Miles four and five passed and the runners made the long drag along Woolwich Road. By now the pack was stretched and athletes were mainly running in single file or in small groups where two or three athletes of a similar pace were having their own personal battles. Martin and Chris were running side by side, Martin in his preferred position on the left with Chris on his right shoulder. The two had got into a pattern and were breathing and striding at an identical pace. If there were such a sport as synchronised running this would be It; two athletes of similar stature wearing the same attire running side by side, step by step. It wasn't long before a motorbike pulled up alongside them and the pillion passenger focused his camera firmly on the pair. It had been too dangerous to do so before hand but now the athletes were spread out a bit and there was more available road space to work with, the cameras had started to spread out a bit and focus on some of the different individual athletes.

"There's Dad and Chris!". Abi stated enthusiastically as the image of her father and his running partner flashed up onto the giant screen. "Bloody hell, Dad looks a bit old with the camera that close in his face doesn't he!". Max exclaimed. "And here we have the first British pairing of Martin Price and Chris Clarke". Stated the on screen commentator as the images were beamed globally for all to see. "I would say they are probably back in about fiftieth place and a significant way behind the leaders". The cameras quickly panned back to the lead pair; Bworo Deresse and Hakim Bayu in their familiar yellow vests. The two race commentators could be heard describing their careers in minute detail, lauding praise upon praise on them regarding past race successes and career achievements. "They didn't do that for Dad did they?". Max complained. "That's because Dad has never won anything has he!". Abi stated, emphatically. "He's won quite a few parkruns hasn't he!". Max protested. "Yes, that would sound good on international TV wouldn't it! "Here's Bworo Deresse, winner of the Boston and Madrid Marathons in a record time, and here's Martin Price; he's won a few parkruns!". The two had a good laugh to themselves and conceded that perhaps their fathers' achievements to date weren't a lot to write home about! They refocused on the monitor, agreeing to high five each other every time their dad's image came on to the screen. They had to wait quite a while though before it did again and that was only via a long distance shot from the overhead helicopter, where two athletes in British attire could just about be seen running in tandem.

Approaching the seven-mile marker the athletes took a sharp left at the end of Trafalgar Road and headed out towards the River Thames and the famous Cutty Sark; the only surviving tea clipper in the world. Her build came at the end of a long period of improving design for the clippers and as such she was one of the last and fastest ever to be built. Their eventual demise however came about soon after with the introduction of steam powered ships meaning there was no longer the dependency on the trade winds to propel them back and forth across the Atlantic. Martin gazed in awe at her majesty as the athletes made a U turn back on themselves heading towards Greenwich. As they did so and came off the bend, Chris could see the distinctive yellow vests of the front runners making the right turn into Creek Road towards Maritime Greenwich. Those front runners were still the two Ethiopians; Bworo Deresse and Hakim Bayu with the Kenyan, Gitonga Chibuzo tucked in just behind them, trying to get a tow in their slip stream. A few yards behind them were a group of three runners; Ramirez, Netherton, and Himinez and following those was a strung out line of around fifty runners containing a combination of elites and championship runners all out to try and make a name for themselves.

Water was available at each mile marker station but at mile seven the stakes were upped with sports energy drinks being provided. Martin and Chris took the opportunity to avail themselves of a bottle each, doing their best to sip what they could whilst not losing rhythm or momentum.

It was evident that the two yellow vested Ethiopians were also working in tandem and sharing the load, much like the British pairing. Unlike the British pairing however they weren't quite the close comrades that Messrs Price and Clarke were and certainly wouldn't have dreamed of training together, such was their dissension for one another. Both had been in the shadow of their great rival and fellow countryman Ezana Tasifa for a number of years and neither had yet managed to beat him in a race they had competed in together. Both saw today as a prime opportunity to reverse the balance and have their own share of fortune and glory. Although they were fierce rivals both knew that, much as it pained them, the best opportunity either of them had of winning the race was to work together as a team for as long as they were able, and then it was every man for himself as they headed for the line. Each was also conscious that the Kenyan, currently getting a free ride at their expense, was also thinking the same thing and that today too was his best opportunity in a long while of clinching the coveted gold medal. They knew too that his quick finish was legendary, so if he was sticking with them now they would have to try and keep something in reserve to combat that.

Someone who was struggling to keep anything in reserve at the moment though was Martin, who broke the silence; "I'm not sure that I'm going to be able to keep this pace up for the whole race Chris". He confided to his colleague, breathing heavily as he struggled to get the words out and conserve enough air in his lungs to maintain his pace at the same time. "Come on Martin you'll be OK, look the eleven-mile marker is just up ahead so we're nearly half way around". The two of them ran side by side along Brunel Road adjacent to the River Thames and Martin could indeed see the eleven-mile marker edging ever closer in the distance. There had been little change in position for the past few miles; each athlete had by now found their natural pace. About ten yards ahead of Martin and Chris were a group of four championship runners; in front of them several smaller groups running together behind the first two packs of three runners. All those ahead were still within sight, which at this stage of the race was no mean feat. Chris glanced across at his partner who he could see was visibly struggling, teeth gritted and lolling from side to side with a look of pain on his face he was certainly not looking his fluent best. Chris knew that he had it in him though; he had run with him for mile upon mile and had himself often struggled to meet the elder man's speed and endurance. He thought of the many times that Martin had picked him up when he had been down, both physically and mentally and had always somehow managed to find the right words to spur him on. 'What would Martin say to me right now if the roles were reversed?'. He wondered. Then it came to him and he did his level best to get the words out in short sharp bursts between breaths;

"Imagine your back, in Gran Canaria Martin, Alberto's dropped us off, on the road back to base, sun's on our backs, we're running back to camp, through Las Goteras, we're hitting that incline, no one else there, just you and me, and the open road, no crowds, no competitors, no race to be run, and no medals to be won, just the two of us, running as hard, and as fast, as we can, in the sun, just because we want to, and just because we can!". It took a while, but Chris got the words out. Martin could easily imagine the scenario in his head as it was one that had played out in real life many times, in an instant he was back there doing exactly what Chris had described, running for fun and for the love of running.

Martin went one step further and imagined what would be waiting for them at the end of the run and could picture Alberto stood outside the farmhouse; a chilled glass of Malvasia waiting with a large glass of Honey Rum thrown in just for good measure. He pictured Alberto getting out his Gibson and the three proceeding to have a good old sing along!" "What song do we sing then Chris?". Martin enquired out loud to his partner, picturing the scenario in his head. Chris was taken aback but he instinctively knew where Martin was, almost telepathically beaming himself back to the farmhouse as well and picturing the three of them back there. He smiled to himself and the feeling gave him a warm glow, as if he had eaten a bowl of ready brek on a cold winter's morning. "Well the song I'm thinking of right now Martin is......". "Yes, go on Chris what is it?". Chris knew that Martin loved his music and he thought for a moment about what song would inspire Martin at this current time; he knew he liked to sing the words inside his head and take inspiration, but what would give him a lift at this particular moment, a song from his era that would mean something and give him a much needed kick up the backside to get him reengaged. He pondered further before smiling and nodding his head; he had it…. "We'd be singing 'BAT OUT OF HELL' of course!". Martin liked the sound of that and immediately began to sing the words to himself in his head; "Yes nice one Chris, that'll do for me!". He smiled. He was back in the game!

"High five Max, there's Dad and Chris again!". Abi observed as the two of them made another all too brief appearance on the screen. No words were forthcoming from the commentators this time but an overhead shot from the helicopter showed that the status quo was being maintained. They were holding their own amongst the race leaders as they headed along Jamaica Road and past Bermondsey tube station towards the twelve-mile marker. The next iconic landmark they would be passing, and indeed crossing, would be Tower Bridge and the magnificent structure and marvel of Victorian engineering was looming ever closer. The first to set foot on it was the Kenyan who had decided that it was time to try and test the two Ethiopians to see what they were made of. By the time his trailing foot had taken its last step on the structure, a gap of a few metres had opened up. As they turned right and headed for the thirteen-mile marker it was the first time in the race that pole position had been occupied by someone wearing other than a yellow vest. Martin emptied a cup full of water over his head after grabbing it from the drinks station and it wasn't long before the two had passed the half way marker. "All downhill from here on in mate!". Chris pronounced.

# Chapter 31

Buoyed by his partners words and refreshed by the cooling liquid, Martin's temporary blip in fatigue had passed and the two by now were veritably flying. Martin removed an energy gel from his pocked and squeezed it into his mouth, wiping the sticky residue from his hands onto his running vest. "How are you feeling Chris?". Martin asked, focusing intently on the road ahead. "Yes good, and you?". "Yes, not bad, do you think there's any way we can move up the positions a bit or are you happy where we are?". Martin panted. He found it a lot more difficult to speak when running than his younger companion and often wondered how Chris managed to run for mile upon mile without Martin even hearing him breath. By contrast, someone could have heard Martin creeping up on them from at least ten metres away such was his clamour for air. Martin supposed that thirty years ago his own respiratory system may have been a bit quieter and likened the scenario to the difference between the engine noise of a new car and one that had been around the clock a few times. "Never happy when there are runners in front of me!". Chris stated. "Come on, let's do it if you are up for it". Martin was indeed up for it and gave his colleague the thumbs up rather than waste more precious air. With so far to go in the race both knew that any change in pace would have to be subtle, an increase of a few seconds per mile to try and eat away at some of the runners in front of them. Chris mentally set a target of passing the two runners immediately in front of them by mile fourteen and then would reset the bar at every mile thereafter depending upon progress. Chris pointed to the two runners in front and whispered the words; "By mile fourteen!". Martin knew what he meant and nodded in agreement.

By the time the two had picked up their water at mile fourteen the first goal had been achieved and they continued the same process for the next four miles, gauging their progress through the water stations at miles fifteen, sixteen and seventeen and gradually easing their way through the pack. Various runners had tried to tag on to them and stick with the dynamic duo as they eased their way through. One French athlete had succeeded to stay with them for a two mile stretch, much to their annoyance as he deliberately ran between the two of them, interrupting their momentum. The two British athletes however were determined to shake him off as there was no way they were letting him spoil their party and by mile eighteen he had dropped back and become a distant memory. The two were now getting more time on the big screen, the motorcycle camera man focusing in on them as they gradually made their way up through the pack, edging ever closer to the race leaders. As the two British frontrunners there was inevitably going to be some national interest in them, but the commentators had little to go on in relation to their backgrounds or achievements and were merely resigned to stating their names as the camera panned in on them. The race director was in the commentary box and knew that the two athletes had been trained by Mike and Alberto so desperately looked around the VIP area to try and find one or other of them to glean some information that may be of interest. Mike was watching the race unfold on the big screen but was too excited to sit down, jumping up and down like a cat on a hot tin roof, his body bobbing and weaving every time his athletes appeared on the screen. He was metaphorically running the race with them, urging them to do certain things at specific times and then getting frustrated when they weren't doing them, willing them to overtake certain athletes, imploring one or other of them to take the initiative and pick up the pace when he thought they should have done so; he knew he was powerless though and that his actions were fruitless as all that jumping around, shouting encouragement and running on the spot wouldn't make a blind bit of difference, he had to put his trust in the fact that he and Alberto had done a good job in getting them this far and that their bodies were fit enough and that they had the mental ability to run an intelligent race. Martin had indeed remembered what he had been taught, on occasion word for word, he also remembered the words that his friend James had told him; 'run the race with your head as well as your legs' and 'put yourself in the right position at the right time', today the two were certainly utilising that advice and running intelligently as well as efficiently. In contrast to Mike's demeanour on the day, Alberto was taking a more chilled out approach and took some time out to visit the VIP bar. "I don't suppose you have any Honey Rum, do you?". He enquired hopefully of the bartender. The question was met with a puzzled expression on the bartender's face; "Sorry, never heard of it sir!" He replied, as he shook his head.

The next landmark the runners passed on the route was Canary Wharf, one of the United Kingdom's main financial centres, notably containing some of the country's tallest buildings. Martin was by now too focused on the race to take them in and was happier to see the energy drinks station at the nineteen mile marker than the landmark buildings around him. He grabbed out at a bottle held aloft by a marshal as he ran past, and his colleague followed suit, also availing himself of a bottle of the precious liquid. Martin sipped at his before its weight in his hand became tiresome and he eventually discarded the vast majority of the liquid by the roadside. Martin hated to waste things and felt a tinge of guilt as he threw his three quarter full bottle onto the floor, closely followed by Chris. He wondered by the end of the day just how much valuable liquid would have been wasted in a similar fashion and how much plastic was utilised in the making of all the bottles that would be consumed today. The fact that recyclable cups were also on offer at certain stations and that the likelihood was that their use would increase in subsequent years gave him some small consolation, as he watched the bottle bounce uncontrollably along the road before ultimately coming to rest at its destination. He had heard that spectators sometimes liked to keep the bottles discarded by famous runners as a souvenir but supposed there wouldn't be much of a clamour to claim any of his particular bottles today. He was to be proved wrong though as soon after a young lad of no more than five or six years old placed his hand underneath the barrier and picked it up, holding it aloft and smiling proudly as he showed his souvenir to his parents.

Mile nineteen came and went and Mike was summoned up to the commentary box to give some background on his athletes. They were gradually moving up the field and it was becoming impossible for the commentators not to mention anything other than their names every time the camera panned in for a close up on the pair. Mike quickly grabbed Alberto from the bar and the two headed up the makeshift flight of stairs to the overhead gantry that was the commentary position for the days race. They were met by two television presenters; one a professional broadcaster and the other a former professional athlete whose task for the day was to provide expert analysis on the athletes' performance during the race. A researcher was also on the gantry armed with various background information on each of the top runners, except in Martin and Chris's case he wasn't, as he hadn't actually heard of either of them and upon fervently searching the internet for information, it was as if they had both just been transported on to the planet from outer space, and he had drawn a blank. Brendan, who was the athlete doing the analysis immediately recognised both Mike and Alberto from times past and after introducing them to the others the five quickly got down to business. "Right!". Exclaimed the researcher. "We need as much information about these two as you can give us as this is all getting a bit embarrassing; all we have is their names and ages and the fact that they're British, but that isn't really making for very interesting viewing!".

By the time the front runners were passing the twenty-mile mark and heading along the West India Dock Road, the race commentator had a bit more information on Messrs Price and Clarke that he could impart to the watching public as the cameras panned in. "Here we see the British pairing again of Martin Price and Chris Clarke. The couple qualified for the London Marathon via the great South West Run in Exeter and we understand that they've been training together for the last twelve months in Gran Canaria, what do you think of their chances today Brendan?". The BBC sports correspondent, Paul Jones, enquired of his commentary box colleague. "Well they certainly make an unusual couple don't they Paul, I mean Martin is in his early fifties and for someone of that age to be competing at this pace and distance is generally unheard of. And as for Chris, well eighteen is young for a marathon runner but the two seem to be going fairly well so if they can keep this up they could be in with a shout of a top twenty place, which would be quite remarkable". "I understand that they've been training together in Gran Canaria?". Paul enquired of Brendan; already knowing the answer as they had both been briefed not five minutes earlier by Mike and Alberto who were still sat with them in the box. "Yes, that's correct Paul, they've been trained by Alberto Romero who was an Olympic champion marathon runner back in the seventies". A warm smile crossed Alberto's face as he fondly remembered the race in question.

The on-screen picture flashed back to the front runners and the angle from the motorbike camera ahead of them clearly showed that in the background Martin and Chris could be seen running along the same section of Commercial Road as they reached the twenty-one-mile marker at Limehouse station. "Five miles to go Martin!". Chris observed. Martin was by now getting too tired to speak and knew that every drop of energy expended in doing so would detract from that he had left to drag his ageing body through the final five miles of the race. Again he merely nodded and gave Chris the thumbs up. They weren't making a lot of progress on the group in front of them and if anything, the gap appeared to be getting greater rather than smaller. That however wasn't because they were slowing but because the chasing pack in front were also redoubling their efforts to get closer to the athletes heading the race, working together to try and push each other on as Martin and Chris themselves had been doing. By mile twenty-two however the two had once again dug deep and somehow summoned the energy to latch on to the pack in front. It consisted of twelve other runners in addition to themselves and all were now condensed and running in a tight unit jostling for position. The two felt hemmed in and decided to go wide to steer clear of the crowd and run on the outside of the pack. Every now and then, through the loud and enthusiastic general cheering of the crowd, an individual shout along the lines of "Come on Price!" or "Come on Clarke!" could be heard by a crowd member who had read the name on the front of their vests and spotted the Great Britain colours they were so proudly wearing, which served to spur them on to greater things.

Max and Abi were starting to get excited now and particularly so as the cameras panned to a helicopter shot as the leading athletes passed the Tower of London. After focusing initially on the front three the shot switched to a wider angle, showing that there were now three distinct groups of three athletes at the front of the race followed now by a larger group of runners. This larger group was the one that their father was firmly entrenched in. Upon zooming out further the various groups of runners, some individual, some in twos and threes and some in small groups could be seen, like a colony of ants darting in a line back to their nest after an expedition foraging for food. Further back the road was a sea of runners, heads bobbing up and down as they all made their way along the route, each aiming to achieve their own personal targets. Back with the front runners it was evident that Martin and Chris, along with a French athlete, Justin Lacroix, had now managed to push away from the larger group and were now a few metres clear of the chasing pack. Neither Martin or Chris were keen on running with another athlete, but it was an inevitability under the circumstances, so they had to get used to it and try to blank it out and run their own race. It was difficult though as Lacroix, like the previous Frenchman before him earlier in the race, had decided to position himself right between the two of them, and try as they may they were unable to manoeuvre him out of his position. Lacroix was like Martin, somewhat of a heavy breather and running alongside him his deep breaths were all that Martin could focus on. Martin made another attempt to try and get in front of him, but Lacroix came with him and was still firmly wedged between him and Chris. Martin dropped back a little and let Lacroix go on in front of him, giving him the opportunity to move across him from behind and once again retain his position alongside Chris, but on the outside line of Lacroix. He was now on Martin's left shoulder though which was a position that Martin never liked to be in. "I thought I'd lost you for a minute there!". Chris observed. "Still here mate!". Martin replied. "You OK?" Chris asked "No!" Martin replied. "Are you?" "No!" Chris replied emphatically, shaking his head.

Both athletes were by now experiencing the metaphorical 'Wall'; the period in any distance race when things go from being extremely hard to impossibly hard; the point at where all plans go out of the window and the main focus is just on survival. Both were hurting, and both their brains were now on auto pilot with the body's internal systems concentrating on sending vital nutrients and oxygen rich blood to the muscles to keep them functioning, rather than to the brain. In training the two hadn't really experienced the wall to the extent they were now; there wasn't the pressure there was today to do well and however hard they may have felt they trained in the run up, today was different; neither realised that they were running significantly faster today than they had ever run over this distance before and their respective brains and bodies weren't thanking them for it. In particular Martin's cocktail of painkillers seemed to be having an adverse effect and he was starting to feel light headed and dizzy, making it extremely difficult to concentrate. Lacroix seemed to be coping OK though, at least from the outside, and by the time they hit the twenty-four-mile mark at Blackfriars Bridge he had started to pull away from them.

The Landmarks were starting to get iconic now; London Bridge, Millennium Bridge, Blackfriars, Victoria Embankment; all places Martin and Chris had heard of and seen on the screen during previous races. They knew now that there wasn't far to go but also knew that it was hurting so much that both were doubting their ability to maintain their progress. Martin summoned the energy to speak; "Two miles left Chris". He drew in some precious air before uttering his next words "One steady mile." He drew in some more oxygen. "Last one we go for it!" Chris nodded in agreement. He could see that the older man was struggling more than he was, so gestured for Martin to tuck in behind him.

At Waterloo Bridge, Lacroix had moved further ahead of them and was easing himself towards the three runners in front, themselves not more than twenty metres ahead. He was desperate himself for a podium finish and knew that his best chance to achieve one would be to latch on to the group in front of him and work with them to try and reign in the distance between them and the top three. Chris was getting concerned that he and Martin wouldn't have enough left at the finish to make up the distance so gestured to Martin that they too should up the pace and try and go with him now. Martin's energy levels were depleted though, and he was struggling even to maintain his current pace let alone step things up. "You go mate!". He managed to splutter to Chris as the pain of every step was now starting to show. Chris didn't want to leave his partner but knew that this close to the finish it was every man for himself and that he and Martin now had to plan out their own strategy for the remainder of the race. They had come this far together and worked well as a partnership to give themselves a fighting chance but now they had to go their separate ways. Chris knew that he did so with Martin's blessing, as he too would have given the same blessing if the roles were reversed. Chris briefly took his partners hand, giving it a squeeze as he prepared himself to leave his side for the first time in the race. Martin looked at him and nodded in resigned acknowledgement as he let it go and felt a tinge of sadness as he watched Chris up his pace and pull away from him, soon latching back on to Lacroix. Martin was now alone. As they hit Hungerford Bridge and the twenty-five-mile mark, he watched helplessly as Chris and Lacroix joined the three runners directly in front, swelling the group number to five.

"Looks like Dad is dropping back a bit!". Max groaned to his sister, somewhat forlornly as the overhead shot now showed him as a solitary runner behind the group of five in question. They themselves were now only about twenty or so metres behind the front three athletes and each felt that the possibility of a podium finish was within their grasp. Any such thoughts now though had been firmly erased from Martin's mind as he was cast adrift in no man's land, his body and head hurting and the runners behind him rapidly closing him down. The motorcycle camera focused back on the leaders again; they seemed to be flowing effortlessly, long smooth strides, chest upright, head firm and eyes fixed rigidly on the road ahead without so much as a sideways glance to those running immediately next to them; they were certainly in the zone. "Just over a mile to go now Brendan!". Paul stated excitedly, as Bworo Deresse, Hakim Bayu, and Gitonga Chibuzo passed Hungerford Bridge and hit the twenty-five-mile mark. "What are your thoughts?". "Well someone's really going to have to pull something out of the bag if they're to challenge these three". Brendan stated. "They've led from the front since the start and I don't think there's anyone who will be able to touch them. They've worked together and ran a good race and it's definitely going to be one of these three who wins it, which one of the three that will be though is anybody's guess!".

Chris and Lacroix had now not only latched on to the second group but were firmly ensconced in it. Martin could see from behind that there was a lot of jostling and elbowing going on between the runners of different nationalities therein. Ramirez, the Spaniard, was well known for liking a bit of a tussle and getting physical with his competitors and he was now running alongside his arch rival; Himinez of Portugal, which in itself was a recipe for disaster. Also in the group was Scott Netherton, the New Zealander, clad in the all black attire so much associated with the country. Martin watched on from behind trying his hardest not to let the gap between them open up too much. He fetched into his pocket searching out another energy gel to give him one final bit of sustenance for the closing push, his pocket was empty. He knew however that he always kept one in reserve for emergencies tucked inside his shorts and this was certainly an emergency. He pulled it out and ripped it open, gulping the thick sticky liquid down and squeezing out the last drops before discarding the sachet. "Come on Martin!". He heard a voice in the crowd shout. Then another came, and another, giving him renewed momentum. The crowds seemed even thicker now as the end approached and the noise levels were increasing; the British vest he was so proudly wearing giving rise to patriotic encouragement from the watching throngs.

Martin noticed something catch his eye in the group in front and suddenly three runners were sprawling in a heap on the floor. Martin wasn't sure initially who it was but as he got closer and ran past the fallen comrades he could see that Chris was one of them and he now lay prostrate on the floor. He had got caught between Ramirez and Himanez and as the two tried to pass him on either side their legs had become entwined and the three hit the deck like a stone. "You OK Chris?". Martin shouted as he passed his colleague, who along with the other two was trying to get back up and re-join the race. All three however had lost precious ground and were visibly rocked by the encounter. "Go on Martin, you can do it!". Chris shouted to his colleague at the top of his voice as he picked himself up from the ground. He held his arm aloft with his thumb in the air, acknowledging his partner and Martin knew that Chris would live to fight another day. As for himself however, he knew he wouldn't be afforded that luxury. He had to do it now, not only for himself and his country but for Chris as well. He knew the effort the two of them had put in couldn't be wasted and had to count for something. He knew too that he also had to do it for all the other underdogs who had ever entered anything in their lives, the ones who weren't given a realistic chance, but who had overcome adversity and hardships to truly make their mark. Today he knew that this was his one and only opportunity and he had to do what he had to do, and he had to do it now! 'Put yourself in the right position at the right time'. 'Run the race with your head as well as your legs'. He focused on his running mantra.

The incident played out on screen much to the presenter's surprise and Martin now found himself in fifth place as the athletes hit the turn at Westminster Bridge and started down the straight towards Buckingham Palace. Five metres ahead of Martin was the New Zealander and twenty metres in front of him the race leaders. A trigger suddenly switched on in Martin's head; all that stood between him and the finish line now were four athletes; four athletes who stood between him and glory; they were only four human beings the same as he was, and this was his opportunity, it was his day, his time, his first and last chance all rolled in to one. Suddenly he was alert, his senses heightened, and he was more focused than he had ever been on anything in his life before, as if everything that had taken place in his life to date was merely a preparation for this moment. The sight of Buckingham Palace looming ever closer meant only one thing; that the final straight along the Mall would soon be in sight. He focused his thoughts, he had to put himself in the right place at the right time. Where was that right place though? Well the first place he wanted to be was in front of the New Zealander and then he wanted to be on the two Ethiopians and Kenyans shoulder going in to the final straight to at least give himself half a chance. He knew he was too far back at the moment for his final attack. It was time to fire the synapses into life, time to activate the fast twitch muscle fibres that had lain dormant in his legs for the best part of the last 26 miles eagerly awaiting to be called into action to perform their duty. It was time to flick the switch! Martin hit down hard onto the ground with his right foot powering his body forward as he did so, consciously making the effort to ensure his muscles eeked out every last drop of propulsion left in them, he did the same with his left leg, then right, then left, then right again, ensuring that the legs worked ever harder and ever faster, his body upright, his chest out, his head still, his mind focused, focused on the one job in hand; to win this race.

Martin was unsure how fast he was running but the noise of the crowd and the grandeur of the occasion spurred him on to run quicker than he had ever ran before. He knew there was no point leaving anything on the track, he had to give it his all, every last drop of blood sweat and tears that oozed from his pores had to be put in to the remaining distance. He passed the New Zealander bang on the 26-mile mark and by the time he rounded Buckingham Palace and hit the Mall he was level with the somewhat taken aback Kenyan who had dropped back from the Ethiopians and had at least thought that third place was a certainty. He soon realised that wasn't to be though as Martin passed him and focused the crosshairs of his sights firmly on the front two. Bworo Deresse and Hakim Bayu were now sprinting for the finish line for all they were worth, wondering which was to take the coveted gold medal and which the consolation of silver. It was now afterburner time for Martin and he flicked the last switch available to him, there was no turning back now, every last ounce of life left in his body had to be expended over the last two hundred metres. He screamed out in pain with one last battle cry as the fuel in his engine ignited; The air drawn into his lungs and into the fan of the engine, into the compressor to increase the energy potential, through the combustor to be mixed with the fuel and ignited; into the turbine causing the blades to rotate and out through the nozzle, in this case his legs producing the untold amount of thrust that was propelling him ever quicker towards the finish.

"It's anybody's race now, it just depends on who wants it more!". Peter bellowed in excitement. "Come on Dad!". Max and Abi screamed from the viewing platform they were now stood on. "Come on Martin, you can do it!". Mike roared. Alberto stood there watching, eyes agog, unable to take in the spectacle he was witnessing. "Martin, Martin, Martin!". The sound of the crowd was deafening as the three sped towards the line, neck and neck at thirty metres, neck and neck at twenty, neck and neck at ten! nine, eight, seven, six, the finish line was nearly within grasp and Martin could taste it. Five, four, three, two; Martin launched himself at the line with everything he had in one final lung busting lunge. Peter stood up and shouted; "And the winner of the London Marathon is.............".

# Chapter 32

Martin wasn't sure where he was when he opened his eyes. He did however feel warm and safe like he was enveloped in a cocoon and as he lay there and looked around in the gloom he could just make out his daughters outline beside him. He briefly felt the warm touch of her hand grasping his before he fell back to sleep again. It was to be two more days before he next opened his eyes and once again in the dimly lit room the one thing he could make out was his daughters' silhouette by his side. "Abi, is that you?". He whispered. She woke from the half sleep she had been in at the sound of his voice and leaned forward from her chair to where her dad could see her better. "Yes Dad it's me, are you OK?". "I'm not really sure, where am I?". Martin enquired. "You're in hospital Dad; you probably don't remember but you collapsed at the end of the race and they couldn't bring you round so they brought you in by ambulance, everyone is really worried about you, we thought we had lost you there for a minute!". "Don't worry, I'm still here, you can't get rid of me that easily!". He whispered. His mouth and lips were dry, and he was struggling to speak. "Is there any water here?". He asked, trying to raise himself up. His daughter set out his pillows so that he could sit upright and helped him up before handing him a glass of water. Martin took a small sip, and then another, swilling it around his mouth to lubricate the inside. "Where's Max?". He enquired. "He's asleep in the waiting room just around the corner, we've been taking it in turns to sit with you". "Remind me how I got here again?". Martin asked his daughter. "It was after the marathon, you collapsed, you've been out for three days now!". Martin cast his mind back but had no recollection of the race, his condition had now deteriorated to the point that it had affected his memory and the physical exertion of the race had taken an untold toll on his body. "How did I get on then, did I do OK?". Martin enquired. "Did you do OK? Dad you only won the bloody thing!". "That was good then". Martin replied nonchalantly, totally oblivious to the importance or significance of the fact. "I think I'm going to go back to sleep for a bit now, I'm feeling a bit tired". With that he drifted off again.

The next time Martin awoke he was very weak but still coherent. His son had just left and once again it was his daughter by his bedside. Martin had begun to recall bits of the race and the events leading up to it, but it was all very sketchy. Abi fetched out her phone and showed him a video she had taken of the race ending so that he could reflect on his achievement and a small smile crossed his face as he saw the three athletes crossing the line. "They couldn't separate the three of you initially Dad, it was a photo finish, but you got it based on that last-minute dive for the line". The video then focused on Martin's body, lied prostrate on the floor, apparently lifeless, before cutting out when Abi had turned it off and rushed down to her dad's side, along with Max, Mike and Alberto. "Chris, Mike and Alberto have all been in to see you Dad, but you haven't really been awake until now; there was a brief spell a couple of days ago, but you drifted off again." He knew the time had now come to tell both her and Max the truth; he had run his last race, he had seen the results and things couldn't have gone any better for him. His legacy was there for all to see; Martin Price, winner of the London Marathon 2020, the oldest ever winner by some margin and something that was unlikely ever to be repeated. He knew it was time to go. "Abi I've got something to tell you my love". He had trouble even saying the words. "What is it Dad?" "Abi, I don't think I'm going to be around much longer darling I'm afraid. I'm sorry that I didn't tell you everything before, but I didn't want to burden you with it but it's a lot worse than I said. There's nothing more that they can do for me unfortunately and it's only a matter of time". The tears started to roll down Martin's face as he tried to get the words out; it was the day that everyone dreaded would ever happen but for him it had finally come. All those years of feeling invincible and immortal, of always being the strong one that people turned to in times of trouble when they needed help and support and now the tables had turned, and he felt weak and insignificant. Abi put her arms around him and started to cry, she held him as tightly as she could, and Martin responded in similar fashion. "Have you told Max yet?". She enquired, trying to stop the flow of tears streaming down her face by wiping them away with her sleeve. "No, not yet". Martin replied forlornly. "I've no idea how he will take it, he's not as strong as you are, and I think it will just about finish him". "Do you want me to tell him Dad?". Martin thought about it for a while. "No that's not fair on you is it, or Max really, I need to tell him myself. Oh, and Abi, before I go, you do know that you're the best daughter anyone could have ever wished for, don't you?". "Well I had a good role model didn't I Dad!". She responded, trying to smile through the ongoing stream of tears rolling down her face. The pain inside however was burning her up. It wasn't fair that someone had decided to take her precious father away from her, someone so full of life and who had so much to live for, someone who had always done his best and never hurt or had a cross word to say about anyone, someone who always saw the best in and brought the best out of others. "It's just not fair though Dad is it, why is this happening, why you?". "I know Abi, no one said that life was fair though unfortunately darling!". He stated philosophically before giving her another comforting hug.

"There's something I need to tell you Dad". Abi informed him. "And it's in relation to what started all this off". Martin looked at her somewhat confused. "The reason I got you the race entry for Christmas Dad was because of a dream I had. In it Mum and I were at home talking, and she was asking me how everything was going. I explained to her how you were feeling, and she told me to get the entry for you to cheer you up and give you something to focus on. I dismissed it at first as I thought it was a bit bizarre but after a few weeks I had the same dream again and it seemed so real that I thought I'd better do it.

Martin sat in stunned silence.

"Mum always did believe in you Dad and you know how much she liked to look after you and guide you when she was alive, and I think she's still with us now. I think she knew you could achieve this, and it just goes to show how powerful love really is and that it has no boundaries". She paused for thought for a moment. "Of course, it could all just be a coincidence couldn't it, as dreams are just…. well they're just dreams aren't they, everyone knows that dreams don't come true!".

Martin closed his eyes for a moment and lay back on his pillow. He focused his mind on the dream he himself had been having. Suddenly it was all there in front of him; the scene that had previously been so hazy was now available to him in vivid high definition technicolour, the tuning knob, like that on his broken Roberts radio, having been tweaked slightly allowing it to finally manifest itself with lucid clarity. He smiled to himself, grateful that at last he fully understood its significance and opened his eyes and raised himself up to share his thoughts with his daughter.

"Well there could be something in it Abi!" He stated, his voice now soft and weak. She leaned in closer. "I've been having dreams as well, but I couldn't make them out. I thought it was your mum stood under a bridge calling to me, but it was always a bit fuzzy. Now I realise though that what I thought was a bridge was actually the arch of an underpass, and the underpass in question is the one that goes underneath the road to that little cove in Lanzarote; you know, the one that me and mum loved spending time together at, just lying in the sun or paddling in the water. I think she's calling me home to our special place Abi!". Abi smiled, and put her arm around her father; it gave her some comfort to know that there may actually be a chance of her parents being reunited after all these years and although she had no idea of where or even if this Elysian Plain of perfect happiness at the end of the mortal realm actually existed, she hoped for the sake of them all that it did and that one day all four of them would be together again.

She wanted to fetch her brother, sensing that the end was near, but her dad held her tightly, fearful of being alone in his last moments and not wishing yet to let go. He spoke again, the words even softer now than before and it was evident he was struggling to get them out. "It's OK Dad, I'm here, take your time".

"When I go Abi I don't want you or Max to be sad, your Mum and I will be back together again, like we should have been all along. You and Max have to live your lives now and go and achieve your dreams, as I have mine. Unfortunately, your mum never got the opportunity to see you both grow up as her life was cut cruelly short, but this has shown how strong her love for us all really was. Now you know that I'll be looking down on you both as well as mum, so you'll have two guardian angels watching over you!". He squeezed her as hard as he was able with what little remaining strength he had left in his body and looked her directly in the eyes, a weak half smile on his face knowing that the inevitable wasn't far off. A tear rolled down his cheek, but he didn't have the energy or will anymore to wipe it away, another followed and dropped onto his pillow, the final mark he would make in the earthly world. He had often wondered what this moment would feel like when it finally came, he didn't want to go of course but he knew he was powerless to stop it, he felt no pain though, only tiredness and an overwhelming urge to close his eyes and go to sleep. He knew if he did though that it would be for the final time and he still had a few things to relay to his daughter. He fought against the beckoning Sandman, darting around, sprinkling his magic dust and trying to entice him into a world of eternal dreams. He fought hard to keep his eyelids at least half open despite the fact that their weight felt immense.

"Look after your brother for me Abi as I know how devastated he will be when I go. He always acts the tough guy but underneath he's soft and vulnerable and he'll need your support. Stick together though and whatever you do always hold the thoughts of the times we spent together dear to your heart. I know that I always will. And remember I'll always love you both". Martin smiled and gripped his daughters' hand tightly. The words had drained every last drop of energy from his body. He had however managed to get them out and relay them to his beloved daughter for which he would be eternally grateful.

Martin never got the opportunity to tell his son of his fate or say a last goodbye, his eyelids slowly closed and his door to the mortal world was sealed shut. His time on earth had come to an end and he never woke again. It was a little after two am when Abi watched the colour finally drain from her dad's face and felt his hand fall limp in hers.

The silence was broken as the door burst open and Max entered the room to the sight of his sister sat at their dad's bedside, holding his hand tightly, floods of tears streaming down from her face and dripping on to her dad's. Max looked towards her in anticipation and she reciprocated simply by shaking her head from side to side slowly, the intensity of her tears increasing.

Max fell to his knees at the bedside.

"It will be alright Max… Dad told me it would be!" His sister said softly as she took his hand and smiled gently in his direction. "Dad's on his way now to run one last parkrun; the great parkrun in the sky. I just hope God's up for the challenge!"

Printed in Great Britain
by Amazon